WHERE I'M CRAWLING FROM

WHERE I'M CRAWLING FROM

and other stories

WAYNE K. GREENWELL

ISBN-13: 9780692911242
ISBN-10: 0692911243
Library of Congress Control Number: 2017910032
HorseLight, West Tisbury, MA

To those who helped me make words ring true.

Contents

Been Lāden with Terrorette's Syndrome

I t was *"the times."* Any parsing—best, worst, incredulous—was laughable, like there was perhaps an escape clause.

This place was crowded (chained fire exit) considering it was well past lunch, but a packed convention center with an appliance show a half block away skewed things like that, like arguing over a taxi (Mace; knife) or even if an elevator door were held for you (dodging flung acid).

Perry was shown the only free deuce, a tippy café table in front of the big sidewalk window (flying glass; being "seen"). He took off his suit jacket, put it on the other chair, faced the gray buildings outside (falling body coming into view—wait, that *did* happen, and a exculpatory wave of relief went through him). He remembered the Life magazine photo of the suicidal jumper, blurred speed in focus, taken from a coffee shop's opposite sidewalk. She's just about to enter the street level view of the sole diner inside, his cup poised, him for one more split-second oblivious, looking at gray buildings; her skirt a-billow showing the tops of her gartered stockings (dying of embarrassment?—quaint these days). Black-and-white it was, from the 40's, back when falling bodies were not the chance of rain they are now.

He had carried in his drink from the bar when the hostess said a table was ready. He thought about a refill but he had two more demonstrations of "The Succor"—the higher-ups had used his suggested name with its soothing overtones for their latest vacuum cleaner—scheduled this afternoon. He rubbed his knees; standing all day on the center's cement floors, even with his patch of shag carpet to clean, was a young man's game, never mind trying to make the back and forth of that beast seem dainty. Besides, the first martini was doing its job, easing the ache from his legs, the muscles in his face from "rictus confident smiling" all day. He had thought his body language matched the company's "results do result" paradigm but an aisle-stroller with his competitor's brochure in her hand told him this morning to "cheer up, it's not that bad." He had frozen his mien and taken it immediately to the men's room mirror and could see nothing amiss. But something had tipped the lost potential customer off—

My god, he hadn't even caught her reflection in the window to warn him and his auto-rictus-shield started to flare into place but the drink had its hooks into him and he calmed. She was attractive and his thought now was how to play his lolling, evaluative move that would re-gain the upper hand. He pocketed his glasses.

"My name is Cass and I'll be your waitress this afternoon."

He tilted his chair onto two legs and went with Ricardo Montalban: "Me llamo Roderigo de los Sueños, 'Roderigo of the Dreams,' and I'll be your dark, doe-eyed stallion of las pampas."

"'Pompous' indeed. The badge on your jacket says Perry Thornton."

"Ah, forgot to take it off," dropping his clunky Spanish accent. He let the chair settle. He combined the unpinning of the badge with the loll-move-plus-visualization (her mouthing "lubricious"): "You know, I never could figure out if Cass was short for Cassie or long for ass."

She looked at her watch as though maybe her shift was near enough over and the union would back her leaving this guy in the lurch. "You 'long for ass.' I get it. Sir, you're not my first conventioneer this month. This week. This day."

"Okay okay." He stuck his pricked thumb into his alcohol (sidewalk syringe stabbings with AIDS…then he remembered these were called safety pins for a reason).

"This meal."

"Yep. Well, 'yo' tried." He started to hand the paper menu on the table to her.

"Our special tonight is—"

"No specials. I know what I want. Steak tartare and Caesar salad."

"Hmm, my my, can I heat that up for you? It's a long shot," she said with a sympathetic shrug.

"The steak?"

"Certainly not the salad. Our chef would never compromise."

"But he'll heat up steak tartare?!" he said.

"I know what you're thinking."

"I'm thinking that in every restaurant from the Mumbai Marriott to the Kuala Lumpur Hilton, steak tartare is raw. Red, cold, raw."

"But probably not British," she said.

"You get your beef from England?"

"This particular shipment. This rather attractively priced shipment."

"Wait, you expect me to be worried about the mad cow disease they've had? Now *that's* ridiculous, we have to draw the line somewhere. I mean, even if I ordered cow brains tartare there's no proof I'd catch it. Now I've been working hard all day and I'd like to just take a load off my feet—"

"Like a downer cow that still ends up in the food chain?"

"No! Like an associate vice president of a Forbes 500 company in 16 countries, most of them in the Third World. And setting up offices and a sales force there means lots of diplomacy first to grease the wheels, which means I've eaten everything on my plate from Phnom Penh bird's nest soup—basically twigs in bird upchuck—to Mongolian live-monkee-in-the-table-hole-collar-with-his-cranium-sawn-off and...you don't want to know." He usually didn't mime the delicate spooning action of the diners but he did now; this woman still had the upper hand. "Anyway, I'm not going to come down with mad cow disease."

"Creutzfeldt-Jakob. It would be the human variant called Creutzfeldt-Jakob Disease."

"Steak *tartare*. With the Caesar salad."

"There's often E. coli in the lettuce and salmonella in the egg."

"Jesus, just the steak!" He thrust the menu to her again. Again she didn't take it.

"Even if I heated the meat to 800 degrees for 20 minutes," she said, "it wouldn't kill the mad cow prions, which are some kind of dead/undead virus, nobody knows. "Look," and using his hand and hers she held the paper menu taut and stabbed a half dozen holes in it with her pencil point. "You know Swiss cheese when you see it, right?" she said, holding it to the window like an X-ray.

"Yes, so." He was feeling an incipient sweaty brow.

"So will whoever does your autopsy when they take slices of your brain." She tapped the paper. "Big synapse gaps. You ever get bored at PowerPoint presentations?"

"Isn't that a given?"

"After mad cow you'll be *fascinated*. Your slurried brain will only be able to latch onto primary colors and movement. Like a pollinating insect without whatever fun an insect has. So. Back to your order."

He licked his lips but his mouth and tongue were dry. He couldn't help visualizing her visualizing him unplugging The Succor in her living room, DEFCON 2 all over her face, telling him to take his demo and get the hell out. "Kind of lost my appetite. Maybe just a cup of tea."

"*Tea?*"

"Yes, uh, I, yes…hot tea. Something soothing."

Her scrunched look of disbelief put him back in grade school for the scolding to come. "*Tea leaves* hand-picked by indigents with no toilet paper? Just *tea leaves?*"

He put his glasses back on for some protection, anything. "Just hot water, then?"

She snapped to approval. "An excellent choice! It's our special tonight. Boiled Icelandic Glacial Runoff. 89 dollars and 95 cents." She took the menu, wheeled, and only then did he notice the paucity of food on tables around him. Several diners glumly lifted their demitasse cups of glacial water to him, the hailing salute of the all too plausible eschatological fraternity: Omega Rue.

———

Traffic was light (ricin on the change back from a toll booth) and Thornton as usual used each speed limit sign to correlate his speedometer. He passed a scruffy, hooded hitchhiker (Ted Kaczynski, released on his own recognizance), sodden from too long in the drizzle, and feeling like doling some out, tapped his brakes to slow and edge into the breakdown lane to give the man hope; he even saw him try a stumbling jog before Thornton accelerated and re-joined the flow of cars.

The tidy lawn looked verdant in the gloaming (lawn service pesticides—thank god we're off the well; can't think of how people presently could use that percolation effect but they will). He unlocked the door.

"How'd the convention go?" his wife asked, taking his coat and checking the pockets before hanging it up. He couldn't get mad at her, this petite thing he'd married a few years after college (one had to go back a bit these days for the nostalgia to be untainted) but he let some pique through: "I *already* checked my pockets for anything the dry cleaner could charge extra for."

"Well, dear, you usually come back with mints or gummy bears (CIA LSD experiments)," she said. He could tell she hadn't substitute taught today; she usually dolled herself up for it, even though it was grade school, since she didn't get out much.

"Same old same old. Are there any leftovers? I didn't really eat anything since breakfast."

"There's some meatloaf I can heat up," she said.

"Meatloaf?! Our oven doesn't go to 800 degrees, does it?"

"Silly goose, no oven does. Why on earth?"

"Kind of off meat right now. Got a bit of a scare."

"Oh, the big wed-bwooded wug got a scawe."

"I'm not in second grade—" There was a loud rap at the door and they both jumped. "Nobody followed me!" he whispered. "Certainly not Ted Kaczynski."

"He's in prison, Perry. Or dead. Either way, we have to draw the line somewhere. No, it's the plumber," she said, patting him. "He said he had to see me about the estimate. I'll scrounge up something for you in a minute."

"Oh. Well, I'll let him in. Then I'm going to get something for my stomach." Over his shoulder from the foyer he said, "I'm off tea, too. Anything with indigents."

Flo could hear the door being unlocked, a brief exchange and then Perry's steps to the upstairs bathroom. She came down the hall and the man removed his ball cap. He was too clean for a real plumber at the end of the day, she thought, which dusted up distrust but that was allayed a bit when she noticed the cigarette pack rolled up in the t-shirt sleeve. His company logo on the front was above a softball with a swarthy turbaned face on it exploding in angry flames off a bat. He wore his tool belt askew and low, like a gunslinger.

"Evenin' missus. You like my shirt, I see. My littlest plays Pee Wee ball and I sponsor the team. Never too early," he said, plucking at it. "Get their minds right and all, know what I mean? Anyway, your husband said just talk to you is okay. He went upstairs holdin' his stomach; I figure it's somethin' came from your pipes."

"No, he's just stressed from a business trip. Anyway, what was it you couldn't tell me on the phone?"

"You have any kids?"

"No."

"Not yet, you mean?"

"I'm not sure what you're getting at."

"I mean, you're of child-bearin' age and your husband is presumed spermed?"

"Now this is none of your concern—"

"Excuse me, but exactly it is my concern." He hitched his heavy tool belt with a swagger. All he was missing was a cheroot and tumbleweed rolling past, she thought.

"What is it? We just need a new hot water heater, I told your son."

"No. When my Tommy Junior goes into a domicile and estimates, he's on the lookout and what he told me, I had to come over personal."

"Because it's a gas heater?" She heard the shower running and wished Perry had waited.

"That's just the tip of it but at least you're comin' around. First let's go over the lead pipe problem."

"But they're all copper," she said.

"There's one section from the well pump."

"We don't use the well anymore; we connected directly to the town's line recently."

"What if the town shuts off your water, bureaucratic snag, not your fault, and your infant needs water for, uh, whatever, *drinkin'*. You're gonna have to run that well water through lead pipes and you know what lead does to kids." His laugh was more a bark. "They try to learn the alphabet but they can't tell a *bowel* from a *continence*. That's some plumbing humor but rest assured, I only joke when it's very serious."

"We don't have any children and the well is not hooked up!"

"Now look Mrs. Thornton…." He yelled up the stairs; the shower had stopped. "Mr. Thornton! You spermed up solid?" He nodded, waiting. "I'll take the household silence to mean 'yes' since most people are too embarrassed to deal with the truth I drop in their lap. Now missus, you are gonna have kids and they'll find that lead. It's just the way human nature is. Now I've got to rip it out and put in copper!"

"But that's expensive, I'm sure."

He tapped his fingertips together and dropped his head a bit for gravity. "When you think of the Roman Empire, do you think… *boy-ying?*"

"What on earth is *boing?*"

"No. Boy-*ying*, boy-*ying?* Rubber checks? No, you don't 'cause the Romans was good for the money, right? Being an empire and all? So they could afford to swap out their lead pipes but they chose not to. And the empire? Poof. If the kids can't learn the letterals and numerals, it's pretty hard to run a buncha foreign countries. So the Huns who stayed away from lead even in their armor, whatever, solderin', come in and Rome becomes their foreign country." He stepped into her, put his arm around her shoulder. "You want that to happen to America, or are you just stubborn?"

She shrugged him off petulantly. "I am not stubborn!"

"*That* kinda talk doesn't help your case. Look at it this way: What's remedial college going to cost you couple decades from now when your baby finally graduates high school after repeatin' three-four grades?"

"Gosh, I just, I mean I never worried—"

"That's *exactly* what I'm here for." He pulled a sheet of paper from the jeans pocket. "Here's the estimate." He crossed his arms, spread his stance, tilted his chin: the plumbers' textbook dare-defiant body language.

"Thirty-two hundred dollars?" she blurted. "For a three-foot section of pipe? This *does* include changing over to electric hot water?"

"Incorrect. I have that estimate." He pulled a sheet from another pocket and she reflexively stopped his arm, then rubbed her hand surreptitiously on her leg (norovirus from where that arm's been snaking).

"We can't afford both of those, I'm sure!" she said.

"Whoa now. Two hundred eighteen houses blew up in this country last year. That's just from gas heaters, not counting the homemade bombs that pre-detonated. So I can also install ammonium nitrate detectors in your kitchen, in your livin'—"

"*I* do not make bombs in my kitchen!"

"A neighbor?"

"My *neighbor?*"

"Not a neighbor. A stranger. Or, could come in the mail, ever thinka that?"

"Stop, stop. How much is the conversion to electric hot water?"

"I won't nickel and dime you," and he pocketed the second estimate. She felt a bit of relief until he said "I didn't tally it all up so just double the $3200," poking the estimate in her hand. "I got you scheduled for later in the week. Night."

"Wait. I should talk all this over. I mean, ammonium—"

"Missus! That ammonium nitrate detector is not a luxury item. You need it ASAP, which is plumber for 'ass speedy, ass protected.' $620. You probly could use three, maybe four with one in the baby room."

"*One* in the kitchen will do."

"It's *your* bundle of joy. Night."

The back of his t-shirt was an extension of the front's exploding face, flames carrying what looked like organs…landing in, were those bleachers, and all blonde girls?…with a sign that read "72 Virgins Section"? She locked the door behind him. Perry saw her shudder as he descended, not fully dried off.

"What on earth is going on? Did I hear talk of bombs in this house?" he said.

"He left. I don't feel so good."

Thornton circled. "That kind of talk affects me adversely as well," he said, louder than necessary. She checked ceiling tiles and he continued, projecting his voice: "I know they tell us terrorists are everywhere who would destroy—"

"Who would destroy—"

"—our very Americanism—"

"—our very Americanism—"

"—and spit on the dust—"

She brushed some cobwebs from high on a wall. "What?"

"And spit on the dust!"

"I was going to add that."

"Well add it!"

"And spit on the dust. I *did* vote for the 1.7 trillion dollar lie detector implant program to move forward."

"Don't look at me like that. I voted for it before you."

"It was the same election day, Perry. You just went in the morning."

"I'm just saying." Now he was talking into the basement, she into the attic. "For the record!"

"But we don't think anybody's listening!"

"I don't need to verify for anybody that I'm not eavesdrop material!"

"Nor do I, Flo Thornton, 367 Hyacinth—"

"Shhh!" And he whispered gibberish to her.

"What are you—"

"Shhh!" and he cocked an ear. "Sometimes if eavesdroppers turn up their recording devices you might hear feedback."

She slapped his arm away hard. *"OF COURSE, THAT'S JUST A THEORY!"*

"OF COURSE! I'M IN AGREEMENT WITH EVERYTHING!" he said, backpedaling.

They looked at each other, let the tension slump from their shoulders. "We're being silly," she said.

"Yes, I suppose so. But there's something in the air. I mean, people were always manipulative, out to get the better of you. But *now*."

"Yes! It's so much worse now. Everyone's acting like...little terrorists! I picked up the dry cleaning and, you know the plastic the clothes come in? Well Mr. La Fong who's usually so nice, he never charged much for your stuck candy in the pockets, and his daughter's just starting grade school—"

"Stay on point! What did he say to you?"

"More like a threat."

"He threatened you?"

"Not in so many words. He said there was now an escort charge."

"What the hell is that?" Perry said.

"Mr. La Fong said his key employee had to come to our house with the cleaning and remove the plastic."

"From your skirts."

"Now that you mention it they were your things, your shirts." Her gaze narrowed. "Why would *your* shirts be escorted—"

"So shirts, so what?"

"He said he would safely transport and decommission the plastic."

"Transport and decommission? You mean like spent nuclear fuel?"

"I don't know. He said transporting was key to keeping them..."

"From what? From *what?*"

"From your airway is my guess! He doesn't speak English very well but he was gesturing a lot like a man choking."

"So what happened?"

"It was only $25 plus mileage so I paid it and his man drove the shirts here, put them in the closet and took the plastic away in an orange can with hazardous warning stickers on it. Then he seemed to want a tip."

"I hope you didn't."

"Well he also took a lot of wire hangers with him. He showed me how one can slip over your head and snap a windpipe."

Thornton's hand flew to his neck. "Jesus! Of course, now that I think about it. Did he get them all?"

"He's coming back for the rest. I never knew we had so many. Look, though," and she reached into the hall closet and pulled out with both hands a nest of wire. "I started glueing them together as he suggested, until he could come back for them. It would be very hard for these to get over your head but I guess they could if..."

"Don't even *play* with those," and he took them from her as she struggled to enmesh her neck to make the point.

She saw his watch. "Oh, what time is it?"

"Eight ten."

"Oh my, we're supposed to be next door for Livio's poetry night."

"That's tonight?"

"He got something published so...."

"I don't think I'm up for more 'doe-eyed pony' sonnets. I'll fall asleep."

"Stay home. I'll make up something."

"While you still can," he said, hanging the wire mass back in the closet and checking that the door stayed latched.

"What do you mean?"

"Before the lie-detector implants—" and with a tremor to convey sincerity "—*I voted for!*"

"*You in the morning, me later that very same day!*"

———

Flo slipped sideways through the one gap in the thick hedge separating her neighbor's house and wondered if Perry should do something about that to seal it off—"Electric fences *are* your neighbors" she parroted from somewhere. She quietly opened the screen to the sun room where several other women nodded as she took a seat. The only man there, Livio, was the barnyard chanticleer with his puffed chest, red turtleneck not covering his wattle, and bouffant silver hair as he intoned from memory, gazing into the distance: "...Stygian... Phrygian...doe-eyed ponies."

Livio lowered his head and the polite applause was met by him with an almost imperceptible startle, as if he had been brought back from a reverie in a Greek fig orchard. He met their gaze and blinked away his "amazement." Flo wondered why she kept expecting any variation in these recitals. Him being a widower from a plane crash ("the penis bomber"; airport screening worldwide now slapstick mirth for Al-Qaeda, ISIS, etc.) gave him carte blanche to strut his poems. These suburban matrons certainly weren't going to rein in this handsome, albeit aging, Mediterranean.

"Thank you. A few of you here tonight know I've just had a book of poems accepted by Oxford University Press called 'Pony Dunes'— thank you—and while it's a feather in the cap, university press pay is insulting to start and when it's poetry, well, they don't even apologize. And every day the bills—my daughter has chosen Bryn Mawr—well, 'the bills roll in as on a Thessalonikian tide.' So I hope you don't mind but I've written something a little different for tonight and it's called 'Frisky Awakening,' about a young girl's dark, nay Plutonian childhood, raised by a backsliding minister"—he thrust his pelvis a few times, the poem in his hand flapping like a loose codpiece—"if you get what I mean, Flo, when I say *back-sliding*."

Her yawn was cut short. "My father?"

"Now poetry can be a language that defies translation, so it's hard to pinpoint exactly what's being said sometimes: father fodder, further fondle."

She went to the front of the room and turned him aside to whisper. "Stop right there; I told your wife—*dead* wife—about that in confidence."

"This is only poetry; nothing to worry about," he said. "When I false rhyme 'poppa' and 'trauma,' only you will take it past the simile stage."

"Everyone here, all my neighbors will know! That was a secret I thought the penis bomber had her take to the grave."

"You're mixing something there but…."

There was restless rustling from the group: "C'mon, read us your new work," one interrupted as she re-filled her white wine glass to the rim and said "bouquet be damned!"

"They want to hear it, and, well if I'm to curtail my artistry," Livio said, nuzzling her ear, "I guess it should be the same as getting a grant to express my artistry."

"You want…to be paid not to read it."

"I do have a substitute ready."

Flo sighed, went for her purse, and offered him $40. "It's all I have with me." Livio pocketed the money, pulled out another poem as Flo sat down.

"You're all in for a treat. We will have a mixed media event called 'Un Frisson de Uh Oh.' Note that the poem is accompanied by strobe lights."

Flo rushed him again, now beyond whispering. "I *know* you are aware I have epilepsy and strobes can start a seizure."

"Once again my art should suffer?"

Her purse was still on her shoulder. "Will you take a check?"

Now it was…the times. No escape clause. No way around it. Through and through. Across-the-waterboard.

The man and woman stand in the middle of the closed off kitchen in a motionless hug, sweating terror; their empty oven—door open—on its highest temperature (rogue mad cow prions).

"I have an itch," he says.

"I can't help you."

"It's just below your hand. Your right hand just has to slide down an inch."

She tilts her head to the ceiling "I don't know what you're after or what your game is, mister!"

"*Mister?* I'm your husband! I'd reach it myself if I could."

"There's no itch of yours I want any part of."

"Just leave your hand there, then. Maybe I can scrunch down—"

His movement makes her cinch the hug. "No! First it's a scrunch, and then, then, you, you've made my hand do something illegal! Which I've never done! I voted for the lie detectors, my hand voted for the lie detectors, *my hand voted*—"

"Stop stop, you're out of control."

"Am I? When our dry cleaner charges 1680 dollars to make our house perchloroethylene free, when it was Mr. La Fong's chemicals in the clothes in the first place! His chemicals. We didn't put them there! *I wouldn't know where to put a fuse*—"

"Shh, shh. You're right, dear." He squirms; the itch now has breached the perimeter.

"Stay still! Stock-still," she implores.

He steals a slight wriggle to no effect. "Maybe when they show up, they'll put the implant there."

The Separation Tango

The room in the downtown community center is unadorned but for mostly expired postings on the bulletin board and a washed-out color photo of the center's ribbon-cutting on the porch years back, the civic leaders squinting against the fading to come. Mismatched, battle-scarred metal folding chairs are a necklace of discomfort around the perimeter, baring the Wednesday night dance floor.

Laura and Preston come in, vaguely measure their late-20's against the older set. They sit with an empty chair between them, then self-consciously put their jackets there, her bag. He points to a sign and starts unlacing.

"Got to take your shoes off now. Floor's been refinished since...."

She follows.

"A lot more women than men. I guess that's standard for dancing lessons," he says.

She doesn't follow. "That's good for you, right? Maybe you'll meet somebody."

"I wasn't saying that."

"Comparing bells and whistles—. I'm sorry. I didn't mean that." She had made an effort, as had he, to treat this as an occasion; even gel south-of-the-border style in their short hair.

"A fact can be just a fact," he says.

"I know. It's not you. I mean, it *is* you. Let's just get through this." More to herself: "I'm frazzled; I have so much stuff, packing to do."

"Hey," he says gently. "All this? It's not just about you. For better or for worse, we still have feelings."

"We didn't get to 'for better or for worse.'"

"Okay, right. But I don't think you've thought this through. Forget about us, you're uprooting Taffy. What if she—"

"Preston, there is no more 'what if.' Three weeks tomorrow I'll be a thousand miles from here."

"The Badger State Department of Corrections, Fine Arts Department."

"Make fun. 'English for Inmates' is what some of them need to function on the outside."

"So they can say 'stick *them* up' instead of 'stick 'em up.'"

"Look. Things are raw now between us; fine. But there's business at hand. You've got to get your stuff out by Thursday."

"Thursday? I thought you said I had the weekend?"

"The movers called today and said they'd like to start earlier. Juggling trucks or something."

Aggie, the instructor, backs herself from a couple and says, "Good evening. Nice to see so many of you here on this beautiful night." Her fluidity softens her angularity; she wears a black skirt, sensible heels, red blouse and too much black and red make-up to match. "This is beginner's tango, lesson one, square one: a no recrimination zone. Now which couple won the free lesson raffle on our website?"

Preston and Laura look at each other, raise hands.

"Great," Aggie says, "so you're Preston and Laura. Ever tried tango before?"

"Not really."/"We haven't."

"Well once," Preston offers, "we were under the covers and this bouncy Latin number came on the radio—"

"The short answer is no," Laura says.

Aggie turns to the group. "You're in a whole new world, all of you, of sensuality, mystery, and seduction."

Preston whispers to Laura. "She got the mystery part right 'cause I don't know why the hell we're here."

This sets Laura off, a rich laugh from the past. "Right, I mean—"

"No, right. Just because we won this thing."

"We won—"

"We entered months ago—"

"Back when we—." Her laugh trails to a flat, "were."

"We promised to do this sometime."

"We promised a lot of things."

"And maybe that means something, honoring—"

"'Honoring'? Like you sort of 'honored' your marriage to Amy *after* the divorce?" Their sizzling whispers draw glances. Aggie walks around, doing her get-to-knows.

"Oh Jesus. I told her no. Over and over."

"And why couldn't you make 'once' stick?" she says.

"I stayed with you."/"You had one foot out the door—"

"I stayed with you."/"—before I took this job."

"I stayed with you," he insists and it's left there.

"We've been through this," she says. "I want to clear my head, leave the stomping grounds. You do know you made me ache so much I went back to writing songs, which I swore I wouldn't do."

"Sing it."

"Here? Oh no."

"The first line. Just to me; look, they're still doing intros, they won't hear you."

She yields, sings softly. *"You had shoes in my closet lookin' for a shine—"*

He adds, *"Remember when all we did was pine—"*

"Okay stop, bad idea."

"Everyone's been introduced," Aggie says, "so let's gather in the center. Now the tango is about the unexpected. Of course it has proscribed steps but there's a lot of latitude within the structure. So the first thing we do is get you out of your comfort zone. Pick a partner, but someone you don't know. And don't try to fool me; I know who you walked in with."

Preston moves away but quickly circles to Laura.

"What are you doing?"

"Trying to be a stranger," he says.

"A what?"

"To start over."

"That's not how reality works."

Laura goes to the other side of the room, shakes hands with someone. Preston picks an older woman who is pleased and pockets the blue sticky badge on her shirt, a male partner designation to help balance the ratio.

"Okay," Aggie says, "now we'll set the dance frame. Men, right hand middle of her back, left hand here. Women, hands like so and stay firm so you instantly feel his 'directional thrusts.' I told you this was sexy." She works the room, making adjustments. "Okay, now cut the space between you in half. That's it, nice and snug. Now just walk around the floor, no music yet, no fancy footwork, just circle, giving your partner what I like to call 'daggers of love.'"

Preston and Laura circle slowly with their partners but all the while stab each other's gaze.

"Great," Aggie said with a bit of applause. "Some of you were casting daggers beyond your partners, but okay," as she wagged a finger at Preston and Laura. "The unexpected; flirting with some unknown mystery you two? Now, my partner Espo and I will demonstrate the basic tango step...." She starts music on her boombox and Espo steps back inside the room from the porch, flicks his cigarette out the door, adjusts his graying pony tail. He is framed-up dancing within his walk to Aggie who oozes toward him but breaks the sensual flow by adjusting a bra strap. The couples lag behind the instructions which seem to be on their shoe tops; bewildered, counting to eight, smiling oopses. Preston and Laura mix, smile benignly. Perhaps there's a glance to the doorway, remembering Espo's glowing cigarette when it arced before into a dousing rain.

———

"So let's get started this stormy summer night," Aggie said. "My partner Espo and I," and he flicked a glowing cigarette into the rain, stepped in from the porch, "will show you the basic fox trot, so look for a partner."

Laura and Preston gravitated into each other's orbit. "Looks like we're the only ones not paired up. My name's Preston."

"Laura."

They shook hands and began a simple box step to Aggie's instructions.

"You're here for ballroom," Laura said, "so do you like it or do you put 'dancing' on your dating profile 'cause your roommate mother said it would help you get a girl and move out?"

"Quite a conversation opener. My roommate *who*? What dating profile?"

"A lot of guys say 'dancing' but they'll vacuum the house in a full body black rubber wet-suit with white apron French maid outfit with photos being taken before they'll step on a dance floor. I know for a fact."

"I haven't done a dating profile in a while, but everybody tells those little white lies on the Internet."

"How tall do you think I am?" She straightened.

"Five seven."

"That's what my profile says. Everything up front."

"*Height's* pretty basic."

"When I say I like mountains, I don't mean on postcards from inside the tour bus. I go up them, and if it's a first date I carry a backpack with foods I said I liked, the book I said I was reading, and Taffy. My one-year old daughter."

"That's a helluva first date." He offered his frame and she stepped into it.

"I have herpes. So it doesn't matter if you have it. Or catch it," she said.

He leaned back, flustered. "*Catch* it?"

"I'm just saying I don't care if you've caught it."

"I would only catch it from *you.*"

"If that's an endearment, have a chat with your mother when you get home."

"I don't live with my mother."

"What little white lies?"

"That come to mind? I really, I…." He rubbed his head with his left hand, which she scrutinized.

"Ah, Freud at work," she said pulling them together and trying to lead until he subtly wrested it back.

"What are you talking about?"

"I'll help you out. The tan line."

"What tan line?"

She thrust her upraised ring finger at him accusingly, tongue in cheek.

"Oh, that's there because, uh, this is happening as we speak."

"I'll bet it is. Did you take your ring off in the parking lot?"

"Well, I just—. I mean, I haven't told her yet."

"Because…?"

"Since, well, it's recent, I mean, still fresh, as an idea, you know, you were married, or are married—"

She shook him gently, to unstick him. *"Because…?"*

"I don't know. Time to heal a wound?"

"The wound of telling her?"

"Uh, yeah. Can we change the subject?"

"Which hasn't happened yet—"

"Well—"

"—because you're doing your healing ahead of time, holding your pitty-pat kersplat broken heart out there for someone new to mend first."

"God, why do you have to make it so complicated?"

"Me? I'm not the married one. All it took was Vic's first raised hand to me."

He faux meekly raised his hand: "Was he asking to leave the room?"

———

Preston ducked into a coffee shop and closed the door quickly against winter on his heels. He took off gloves, blew on his hands, saw Laura at the first table snugging her jacket reflexively from the draft or her snuck glance.

"Oh, it's you! You remember me?" he said. "Last time I saw you was the fox trot thing at the community center, in the summer. Did you ever go back for lesson two?"

"So I gather you didn't," she said holding her cruller in abeyance.

"How's your daughter…can I join you?"

She hesitated; he showed her his empty ring finger. "Been to the tanning salon, have you?"

"Funny how there's always one next to a divorce lawyer's office."

She moved her things aside and he sat. "Just out of curiosity, would you have invited me to sit if I wasn't divorced, well, getting divorced?"

"*'Getting'* divorced? Waiter, separate checks," she said flatly. "That was a joke. That I would be serious. Enough to care. If you were married. That kind of joke." It was a rare glimpse of awkwardness.

"Explaining jokes is for couples on the rocks. Okay. A British couple getting a divorce walk into a bar...*rister*...."

She put her cruller down, dusted her fingertips. "Why do people say 'just out of curiosity' when they're really demanding to know something? Just demand it. Or they say, 'speaking honestly now,' so you can presume everything up to then was a lie, right?"

"Can I ask you—"

"There's another one. You're going to ask me whether I allow it or not."

"And why wouldn't—"

"'Candidly,' that's another one," she said.

"Why wouldn't you allow me to ask it if you don't know what it is?"

"Why would you need permission?"

Preston took out a notebook, wrote a bit, pocketed it in his shirt.

"Okay. What was that?"

He stood. "My work here is done."

"What 'work'? What was that you wrote?" She grabbed for it.

"Nuh uh. You have failed. You are not cult material." He "read" from the notebook: "Unresponsive to outside influences. Recruiting attempt off The Chart of Futility."

"What's The Chart of Futility? How far off was I?"

"Beyond our inculcatory reach—"

"Aha. 'Inculcatory'?! There's no such word. I know my Scrabble."

"—beyond the reach of the inculcatudinal—"

"Aha."

"—powers of even a born-again Christian Scientologist."

"Beyond *what*?"

"—yes, *and* he excels at multi-level marketing!"

She smiled and he looked hard at her, then excitedly crossed out his entry, and as he re-wrote said, "A smile! Possible hint of a glimmer of a wisp of a snippet of receptivity from subject. However, complete mind meld with plunder of her life savings for cult's metaphysical sky hook junk is unlikely."

Now she laughed as she would in the future.

"How's Taffy? What, freshman now in college?"

"It's only been six months, Preston. It is Preston?"

"And you're Laura. Anyway, I heard kids grow fast—"

"Let's stick with you. Still living with…?"

"Amy. Yes...but no."

"But yes."

"I'm moving into a friend's apartment."

"Guy's?"

"No, not a guy's."

The cruller became her dull interest, then the keyboard the table over, then the waitress wiping yesterday's colorful chalk items to black on the sandwich board. "Why are we pretending there's some fate here?"

He held her arm before she bit, locked her gaze. "You know, you're not exactly the freewheeling hitchhiker hippie-type bouncing from California ashram to New Mexico sweat lodge, and I'm not exactly Mr. Manacled Business Suit holding us back."

"Do those freewheeling hippie-types even still exist?"

"Sure! I mean," he hedged, "she's iconic."

"Hmm."

"What."

"Nothing. But not a guy's apartment."

"No, it's a chick's."

"Well. There you go. I figure I can take a bite now," she said. "Ruminate while you…ruminate?"

"But at the risk of 'speaking honestly,' it's an ex-girlfriend I knew before I got married. She left me for a lesbian so no old flame."

"Hmm."

"Yes, really. And I should have guessed her preference early on. Our third real date, we pull into her garage and get high. Then after the first two-three minutes ever of me giving her head she pulls my ears, lifts me out, and says 'now do something for me.'"

"Oh my. And?"

"Not bad enough, right? But then she had me hold the trouble light while she changed her car's oil filter."

She laughed and took the notebook and pencil from his shirt to write. He tried to read it but she playfully put it in her bra. He reached for it and she turned away, plumping her breasts.

"Nuh uh. *These* are what we lesbians use to keep our secrets from men."

Preston cocked an ear for something above the cafe's chatter. He stood, extended a hand.

"They're playing our song," he said.

"What?!"

"C'mon. The fox trot. Lesson one."

"Oh no."

"That couple over there will probably join us. Then others, even strangers out on the sidewalk; then other sidewalks across town, other towns, across the ocean. Laura, maybe this is the one. The Buddha says one single act can bring peace to the planet."

"Wait, is that the same Buddha who said peace would only happen when all the garage sale items in the world attain their ultimate *shelf*?"

"Oh that's good. Now, c'mon, dance with me. You don't want to owe me a Nobel peace prize."

She shook her head. He lifted a chair as partner. "Don't make it look like I picked 'her' over you. She does have better posture."

"It was barely a lesson; the thunderstorm cut the power, remember? We ran to the cars in the rain and said 'see you next week.'"

"I was sent on a business trip for a couple of weeks."

"My mom got sick, I had to fly back. I guess we fell through the cracks."

"Yeh, but now, here, instead of dancing, you'd—what—rather vacuum the house in a full body black rubber wet-suit with white apron French maid outfit?"

"Did I mention Vic had me shave his body first?"

"Really?"

"'Really?' is another thing you don't need with me."

"Uh, truly?"

"Well. There's always room for 'truly.'" She stood to dance and he put the chair down, smiling back at the elderly couple he thought might join in.

The windows were all open in the apartment but there was no exchange of air: August was everywhere. Preston sat heavily at the kitchen table and idly sorted through the mail as Laura said goodnight to the babysitter.

"Thanks again, Tish," she said. "We may need you next weekend; I'll let you know." The door closed and Preston paid more attention to the mail.

"What a nice girl," she said as she got the water pitcher from the fridge and filled two glasses. "Guess what Taffy calls her."

"Tish."

"Yeh, what Taffy calls Tish. Guess."

"I'm saying 'Tish.'"

"That wouldn't make my story very 'dramatic' would it, to use your word of the evening? To say, what does Taffy call Tish if what Taffy calls Tish *is* Tish?"

"I didn't *say* the film wasn't dramatic; Japanese movies often aren't. I just felt manipulated by it."

"Well it was your choice."

"I know."

"So the next one's mine." She razzed her tongue with a spray he shied from. "Na na, you wasted your choice. God, the last Japanese movie I saw was probably Smog Monster Marries, or Eats—or both—Godzilla. I remember nearly every subtitle had an exclamation point."

Preston opened a few envelopes.

"I was gaga," she said, "for British sitting-room dramas, where how your pinky looked sipping afternoon tea mattered. Of course they'd all be primly discussing some woman's egregious village indignity, some moral code shattered, but as outcast as that person was in their midst, she could always fight back and reclaim her social standing with proper tea pinky placement. And now you've got me watching some poor disgraced samurai commit hara-kiri, when all he had to do was adjust his tea pinky—. What are you doing?"

Preston had gone to the drawer and sat back down. "Balancing the two checkbooks. We got the monthly statements."

"Now? It's nearly 11." She rubbed his shoulders. "C'mon, I'll do your neck. Tough day slingin' computer pixels?"

"Just going to do this."

"You're a real pu-pu platter tonight."

"Won't take long," and he shrugged off her massage. She let his action be the impetus to put the water pitcher back.

"You know, it's been four months since you moved in, maybe we should think about merging bank accounts. Instead of column A column B, you know?"

"Yeh, could." he said. "What's Nocturne Boutique, $79? That specialty food place? So both of ours?"

She laughed. "Give me that one, put it in my column. Although you did nibble on the last intimates I bought there. C'mon, Godzilla says 'Bedtime for the cranky smog monster' exclamation point."

"I'm not two."

"You know, when Taffy starts her terrible twos, saying 'no' to everything, do you think double negatives would work? 'Taffy, do you not want to take a bath?' 'No.' 'Gotcha. You said you did not *not* want to bathe. So you want to bathe.' 'No!' Well, we can try it on her but probably won't work."

Preston looked up, holding another check, wanting to say something.

"Give it to me," she said, taking the check. "If you don't know whose it is," she slowed, "just give it to me. Sunny's Coffee House. Why so high last month?"

"She called."

"$136. Who called?"

"Amy. Called. Been calling."

"Been having coffee."

"Ran a tab. Planned to tell you. Obviously."

She matter-of-factly slid the check across the table. "This would be in your column. No confusion there. Or *not* no confusion?"

He talked to the table, made it listen with a finger to its chest. "Maybe this is just how the world has gotten: too complicated for clear choices. We're besieged, it's like catapults keep lobbing options over the walls. I mean, I keep trying for—forget enlightenment—just some plain answers that hold up. I work the Buddhism, the eight 'rights.' Right action, right meditation, right intention, right livelihood, all of them—but it's not enough. I want 'right now,' dammit! The universe came from somewhere, and is going somewhere. Why aren't I swept up in that?" he asked her, feeling unencumbered enough to lift his head and meet her gaze, surprisingly soft. So he finished. "I'm unsure how to move forward—with you—and unsure whether to go backwards. Back. Oh God, maybe I'm just Modern Man."

It was a young sigh, a first anguish. Not, say, from a pet dying but more cerebral in that there had been an element of control. Like accepting a prom date with the wrong twin brother. The slimmest choice. Ignoring a tan line on a finger.

She regained the edge he hadn't seen in a while: "Oh Preston is so evolved, you with your opposable 'numbs.' And I promised myself, after Vic the 'shave my body first' nutter that I wouldn't live in a Greek play where my fate was decided by a chorus of The Ironies. But here I am, having given up my physics for you."

"Physics? I'm not sure—" He cocked an ear for any distraction; ballroom music seeped in from above.

"My physics! It's what kept me sane after kicking out my daughter's father, which was hard despite him. My personal physics. I would scrutinize any electron of emotion being stripped from me, being attracted to a guy. Was any mote of loss worth it? I couldn't just yield. I had equations, and I gave them up to be a free spirit—hah, my version maybe—for you. And you don't want it. It's like the 'Gift of the Magi' with a goddamn return counter!"

"You'll wake Taffy—"

'I won't wake Taffy. She knows my voice.'

"She knows my voice. I love your little girl. And you, I—"

"Stop! This apartment isn't big enough for a full The Ironies chorus, where you love everyone."

"I'm just asking—"

"Ah!" She stood. "How *stupid*. How *stupid* was I. I just put it together. *She* was the hitchhiking hippie. California New Mexico Amy; your icon. The 'original' free spirit. And I was so different from her, you were drawn—opposites—to me. But I started to be more like her, right? Me opening up? 'C'mon, move in, it's okay for Taffy that we're not married.' 'Sure, I'll try some pot.' And you started to compare me."

"That's not what happened."

"Yes, compare me the way you looked at that row of TVs in the appliance store the other weekend. Each TV had a neighbor down the shelf, an extra $50 on the price tag and an extra bell or whistle. You wandered back and forth and finally said, 'let's go, I'm just fried' and I said, 'but we need one for the place.' And we left empty-handed. Choosing one would have left something with an extra bell or whistle behind, right, Modern Man?"

"I'm just asking for some time—"

"Those assholes!"

Laura headed to a closet and clawed out a broom through the shopping bags, aprons, ironing board; thumped the ceiling hard with the handle. "They'll wake Taffy, clomping around."

"Don't. It's just that old couple."

"What the hell are they doing?"

She went to thump again and he held her arm down, the way he had in the cafe when bridges still had shores.

"They're dancing," he said. "It's the Anniversary Waltz."

"...flirting with some unknown mystery you two?" Aggie says. "Now, my partner Espo and I will demonstrate the basic tango step." Espo flicks his cigarette into the dark, adjusts his graying pony tail.

Moments pass; Aggie says "change partners; get uncomfortable again."

Preston and Laura leave who they were with, edge together, square up. "That's it, Preston. Keep that frame firm so she knows your intentions, left right, forward backward."

"'Knows your intentions,'" Laura says. "Sounds like we should have taken this lesson first instead of the fox trot."

"She said 'no recrimination zone.'"/"Never mind. Kind of a joke."

"Mine was a joke too," he says.

"Explaining jokes: only for those couples on the...." and she trails off, watching the others' stuttering shuffling somehow a unison, the accordion music's ebb and flow never rising above a siege of loss.

"Don't forget those daggers of love," Aggie says and Preston catches Laura's misting eyes.

"Yeh, 'explaining.' Hmm. You remember," he says tightening their frame, "when we were in the Chinese restaurant; the waiter—"

"Cheng."/"Cheng."

"He was taking our plates," he says.

"I asked for a doggie bag—"

"Cheng was clueless—"

"Barely spoke English: 'For leftovers,' you say pointing. 'Left-overs.'"

"And he's standing there, dumb—"

"And you try to help him: 'Cheng, tell her,' you say, 'tell her—'"

"No reft-overs; we use whole dog."/"No reft-overs; we use whole dog."

They stop dancing; held hands in front of them making them seem even younger than the others. "Do you really want that job?" he says.

"It's only for a year."

"Oh? I thought the contract was for two."

"Yeh well. Free spirit that I am, I said that was too long."

"So. A year."

"Well, six month probation."

"It is a prison, after all."

They share the smile and re-start the steps but now there is no counting, no hesitation, no separation between the music and the lilt of their bodies as they weave dazzlingly past couples.

"Remember when?" he says.

"Which? What?"

"Just…remember when?"

Her head swings back on the beat, the hair she'll have to cut for prison regs enjoying a last fling of freedom. "That's not a word," she says.

"Sure it is. 82 points. 'Tête-à-tête.'"

"Hyphenated, French, and three accents. Go to Scrabble jail."

"At the zoo, the macaw peeled a Brazil nut with its beak—"

"Lengthwise like a banana—"

"The bouncing lake—"

"You losing both oars—"

"Stuck in the middle; your wet summer dress—"

"No one around, we said 'what would Henry Miller do with all this bouncing?'—"

"Our first—"

"Stillborn—"

"Julie—"

"No, we never named her—"

"Our next, Stevie—"

"*Stef*-an would have been nice—"

"His first day in kindergarten, comes home: 'I know everything except about Africa and horny'—"

"Taffy chooses purple braces—"

"The Victorian museum, high tea—"

"Perfect pinkies and clotted cream mustaches—"

"Our Japanese rock garden made the town's walking tour—"

"Bosco the dog, a blue jay and Boxie the five-and-dime store turtle all buried out there—"

"Boxie's plastic palm tree as headstone—"

"Thunderstorm while we're in the labyrinth hedge in Williamsburg—"

"Getting soaked but 'no cutting through the hedge' we said—"

"You hid the last Easter egg up in the maple's top branches—"

"Stevie and Taffy climbed like monkeys—"

"Taffy says, 'Lazarus rising from the dead, Jesus rising to Heaven, they ought to call it "*Yeaster*"'—"

"The weddings—"

"I can't, I'll cry—"

"Our tango lessons—"

They stop.

"My -oscopies, -ologies," he says.

"My 'et ceterectomies.'"

"I bought a TV."

"Ah, the bedside portable," she says, remembering things in black and white.

We All Turn into Howard Hughes

The dying fly is on its back on the windowsill, still twitching its Kafkaesque (love it; first saw the word in the bathroom at the VA Hospital) dance. I hold the rolled, loaned Fly Fishing Monthly, unread but no longer care if it has the smear of its namesake's ex-sauciness.

I am a billionaire with $2271 in the bank. No other assets greater than a gold Cross pen with Mickey Mouse on the clip, a souvenir I was told at the garage sale of the fudged conflation of the 15th anniversary of Disney World and the 200th of the signing of the Constitution (a year apart but Mickey's fingers are one off as well). Even the trashy RV I live in illegally on a side lawn that neighbors are petitioning against (I had a kid remove the tires and hide them to slow down the take-it-the-county-over sheriff) is borrowed from Corky, a pal and the ex of the neighbor/lawn owner, Belle.

I say billionaire because there's so little time left I can't spend the $2271 I have, even if I had the energy to walk to the bank and fill out a withdrawal slip, receive the bills from the life-affirming young teller who usually pats my palsied hand and steers the cup of Kafkaesque lollipops to it.

I was naked yesterday when Belle tapped on the side wall; she has learned to avoid the picture window. She checks each day to verify life as she doesn't want to fumigate any more than necessary when I go. I knocked back on the plastic wall (ready to spontaneously burst into flame if the class-action lawsuit has any merit, Corky hopes) in a precise echo or else she's a wreck half the day, dropping and picking up a head of lettuce, for example, off her kitchen counter until the OCD gods are appeased.

Yesterday was a completely fair fight; it will be less so today since I'm wearing briefs. I'm scrawny, about 145 pounds now and 6'1" but I was buck naked then in the steamy summer heat so the mosquito had more targets than I did as a napalm bomber in Vietnam (everything!). Its zeroing drone made me spin to cover my back. I got dizzy and had to crane my neck to wedge my head against the low ceiling and keep my hands free. Recovering, I rolled my kid-clay dick in my hands to create a hot zone, opened my hands and the skeeter fat-wafted in like a Huey gunship into a clearing only to hit a land mine.

I picked the bitch off the linoleum and inspected it as Howard Hughes would when one of his Mormon aides would present a fresh bug kill. The ex-flyboy's nails were long by then (I heard a couple of inches), his hair an oily rat's nest, his handsome facial symmetry skewed from ingrained squints of paranoia as he spent his last years as a recluse holed up in the 9th floor penthouse of the Desert Inn casino he owned. I do go outdoors.

Today Belle, headed straight toward my door, wants to talk I see. She crabs over the yard with body-language aversion and shielding her eyes, giving a hailing smoker's-cough yodel in case I'm naked again with my eyes closed standing at the graveyard picture window with bug entrails like scattered tombstones on Boot Hill (I was the "poet napomber" of Nam; somebody else took "poet bomber"). But no need for caution on her part today, especially with my no-fly briefs. I rap the window first and open the door to save her some OCD debit re: echoic tapping and she gives a wide store-bought toothy half-smile (she hasn't done the lowers yet), walks in and stops short.

"Whew. Why don't you run the AC?" she says. I have sealed it with Saran Wrap as part of my obviously defective hermetic quest. She grew up near here in the Florida panhandle and she can handle the bugs, a throwback maybe to when she was a kid developing breasts. Her uncle had cornered her, lifted her shirt and called them mosquito bites and she briefly figured a chest full of them was even sexier. He was castrated in later life with two bricks in the mountains near Bajos del Toro, Costa Rica, by a nun's brothers who took her word of God over his.

"Well you'll die of heat festation," she says leaving the door open. I close it faster than a gook's jungle jig when the F-4 jet's screech was first detected. Didn't matter then or now as I see her wash sweeps in two droners in wingman formation.

"Damn Belle," I say unable to shove them out. "I got no backup Mormons. Never mind," I add when she gets her wrinkles into a confused look.

"Reader's Digest has an article on reincarceration," she says. "Oh it's real. You ought to read it, close as you say you are. It's short, you know, the way they do so it won't take much of the pie chart of your remaining…there I go harpin' again, sorry—oh god, 'harp,' sorry. But you're just a sacka bad karma, I think they called it, so maybe you shouldn't opt in if you got a choice. Anyway, a man in Indiana said he'd been Genghis Khan in another life and it was bore out by DNA on a mongrel's bones. He was buried in common clothes, though, but could have been in disguise, they said, 'cause he was hated by so many."

"But if he was dead already, why would he need a disguise—. Never mind. So this Indiana guy has a 'mon-gol' in his family tree?"

"He *was* the tree, Lar! That's the point." She catches herself, starts rhythmically nodding an OCD mantra: "Mongolwhat'dIsay, mongolwhat'dIsay, mongolwhat—"

"Belle stop."

She sits down on the chartreuse swivel chair at the dinette, the one that's not just a beheaded post. I take the white-and-faded-tan love seat and fold Special Ops deep camo into it with my white briefs and sallow skin. I told you I was a poet.

She takes her pack of cigs out but remembers my lungs, re-pockets. "There's also an article about how to write better fiction, your old haunts. 'Write what you know' was top of the list. Didn't make sense to me. Fiction is what you *know*? That's an exymoron." That's Belle's favorite word ever since her divorce lawyer's typo referencing her ex's desire to maintain conjugal visits.

"Well if I come back it's gotta be as a goddamn woman," I say. "I'll take the raging hormones over war chemicals any day. I'm sure the VA knows napalm and Agent Orange (defoliant on my rainy day runs) are in my immune system. You think I don't like bugs out of spite? I got no resistance to whatever Florida's carrying." But she has heard all this before. Rants about Nam from her ex, Corky, and his PTSD. That's where I met him, at the VA. I stopped him from heaving a typewriter at a bureaucrat. Not one week later there was a fancy laminated sign with code violation number, warnings, etc., for such actual tosses or—subsection—attempteds. That's what they're efficient at: codifying your limbo.

"If you're even half a man, and I'm not labelin'," Belle says, "you already been a g.d. woman. If you figure *reincarnation*—I said 'reincarceration' before and look at me skippin' the OCD." She was nostalgically puzzled and pleased, as if she had finally broken free from the ubiquitous high school yearbook dictum to "never change."

"That's it. Small steps, Belle. Let's you stop short of a gook trip wire on the trail."

She hardened right into her sour apple face default. "I *don't* like that word 'gook.' My ex Corky even stopped using it finally, although he kept 'slipper slappin slopes.' I told him as a tunnel rat, which he was in Cu Chi district—"

"I know. He was nuts."

"—being small for his size he would crawl in after them, I told him he had to *respect* the Cong. These were people could figure the exact crimp in a tunnel bend to wedge a beer-belly American but—his words—let a 'slippery slope past.'" She let out a sad "huh…that's the one bit of table wit in eighteen years of marriage, countin' both husbands."

Corky and I had bonded right away after the typewriter incident: we realized we had been double fucking the enemy, him from under in the tunnels and me on top in the air. We fantasized over beers about my napalm and his flame thrower coming at the same time.

"Anyway," she continues, "if you figure reincarnation is a step up, as a man you been the woman already. If it's a step down, though, when you come back you're gonna get hitched when you're 17 and your eye sockets hadn't lost their flesh color yet. I still got hearing loss from the wedding night. Ruptured my ear and my hymen, blood tricklin'—"

"I get it Belle," I say, checking my droning aura. "What do you want 'cause I hear them circling."

She stands, straightens the magnetized pot holder on the mini fridge. This dinky place came well stocked, no complaints there. Even a grapefruit spoon. There is mostly one of things. Even a one-slice toaster. I eat them, grapefruits. The VA doctor said them and blueberries for immune help. I told him "you be grateful Reagan invaded Grenada so you can line your bird cage with your worthless medical degree you were able to finish up there with."

She looks around, tidies the salt and pepper Bobbsey Twins. Well I always knew it was day-to-day here. And I've been through these dickering minuets enough times.

"Lar, where's the kid got the wheels? You got to put them back on. The small claims court said it's mine and I sold it."

"Ah Belle. *Now*? I don't have much time. You see my skin tone."

"I got bills overdue. This thing is tappin' my electricity with that extension cord."

"I'll use candles for chrissake," and I lunge at a skeeter but crush air. Now with this zika—I heard the word was Nigerian for 'easy birth' what with the micro heads—plus the dengue, malaria, West Nile, chikungunya to name a few things they carry, plus my weather front of vitreous floaters that serve as anti-aircraft flak cover for them, I should go nuclear but I got no tolerance for pesticides; I rash out and god knows what beyond skin deep. Talk about sad sacka karma.

She pulled her face taut in her hands. "I might want to do something about this sun damage." She jabbed toward her lips. "And I wanna get the lower set done."

"You can't really see them unless you try."

"I used to not mind havin' a, well, downtrodden look I could fall back on to show people I didn't care what they thought but—. Jeez, it's hot in here." She flaps the waistband of her clamdiggers.

It hits me. Surprised it took so long. In Nam I was—full title— "*oracle* poet napomber." Guys handed me letters all the time from their girlfriends or fiancées (those were tough) to decipher what the hell was going on back home; to "read between the loins" I called it. They deferred to my two semesters of community college where I took courses in comparative literature and the philosophy of "Peanuts." The hardest part was stating the obvious to a gym-rat grunt who's beered up, neck muscles still twitching from lingering reps, ready for amorphous righteousness. I mean, come on: "Quiet week. My mom and I went shopping for underwear" and I'd just shake my head. Likewise any sentence that started "you never." Just hand it back, force it on them; get their fists to unclench.

They'd grab at straws like "but she says here 'I got my tits done for you.'" Or jab at the page: "But that's a tear drop, no?" I'd say "this is a sad-ass country, soldier. No telling. Could even have snuck out of you." Often I had to clarify "bead of sweat" when I'd obviously crossed a macho line.

So I knew Belle had met a man, probably somebody from Pensacola Lanes who wanted to see her outside the swirling dry ice clouds and strobe lights they use for the AA-sponsored Friday Extreme Bowling nights. Romantic as that darkened, pin-clattering ambience with the Captain and Tenille hurting your ears would be, natural light is the next step for those tentatively mixing sobriety with reality.

Besides, she has a cool 10-year-old (Stu) to consider. He's doing well in school, plays Little League, and is patient about teaching her how to play solitaire on the computer, a Sisyphean nightmare based on my one lesson for her. Of course, I had no patience since as an F4 fighter pilot I played the best video game of all: evading ground-to-air missiles, although they were Chinese firecracker junk. I'd see the blip on the radar, let it close, go into eyeballs-out negative g's and turn it back where it came from, shake it and say "sayonara." Somebody might say wrong war and I'd say they all look alike to me.

Stu and I get along though I've only been here two months. "Stu" is really "Stew," a fact her ex does not know. Belle used to secretly swing a bit (until she got the nickname "clapper") and in the worst of her meth days (that's what got her teeth) one night went along with the parlor game of "who would you fuck to be the father of your kid knowing he would immediately take off?" (The game was started as a way to take the sting out of some real-life soap operas that had hit the group.) Her indecision somehow led to a turkey baster, a Tupperware bowl of semen from four guys, and voilà—as they say on the cooking show. Corky was in the pleasant dark and married her, getting a button-nosed towhead aberration of a son who, with Belle's insistence favored her paternal grandfather in a crinkled sepia photograph.

It's a cookie-cutter cloudless Florida Chamber of Commerce day and when Belle parts the curtains over the sink to answer Stu's "I'm home," the relentless light justifies her cosmetic consideration. This is the time of day when I would pour a stiff one, screw the cap on hard, and "hide" the gin bottle disingenuously on a high shelf in a cupboard. Now of course, with the Orange in me wrecking my liver, I (as did Howard and his Mormon enablers) don't touch the stuff. When the palsy first hit my hands, I used to kid myself I still had it, could still plunk her down on the heaving skillet in the ocean they called an aircraft carrier. All I would have had to do was sync the palsy to the hundred control ticks you needed to square up and hit one of the four arrester cables with your tail hook—timing the full throttle just right in case you missed them. Doing a touch-and-go "bolter" cost you a big round of drinks. Doing a "wingwag"—no touch—was two rounds and the raunchier blow job jokes; "too busy sucking on the joystick" the only one that made any sense without the beer filter. "Arrester cables"; that was the daytime. At night, when you semi-crashed onto a dancing necklace of pinprick landing lights, they were called "garrotes" 'cause your balls were gurgling in your throat and you couldn't breathe.

I was long out of the service by the start of the palsy but an old flyboy—hell, any guy—never wants to lose the skills that make people kowtow burned shit in their pants.

It dawns on me to buy this heap, drive it until the engine seizes which—judging by the puddle of oil in the dirt underneath every time Belle puts in a quart to loosen 'er up, charge the battery, etc.—I wouldn't need a road atlas. I'd pull off the two-lane road when it happens, climb the flimsy back ladder onto the baking roof and let the Orange in me peck my liver like Prometheus's eagle; my version of the Nevada desert Howard nearly died in until found by Melvin Dummar, later an heir in an invalidated will to 1/16th of everything. That reminds me to scribble a will—no witnesses so not legal—and all my lost cousins can hire lawyers and contest the pennies jar and moldy album covers from the 60's I hear go for a few bucks on eBay. I ask her what she wants for it.

"Don't be loony, you can't afford this," Belle says giving the wall a thump that shuts off the mini fridge. She thumps it again and it restarts. I hope it's a loose plug and not the wiring, which is likely the star witness for the spontaneous combustion lawsuit.

Ack-ack pinballs my insides; I jackknife forward from the pain and think of Corky in the Cu Chi tunnels, bending at a right angle, trying to wrestle a flame thrower and fuel tank like a cranky vacuum cleaner to the next level down. Usually giving the unit up, he'd hold his breath and send the flame around the crimp to at least kill some fire ants, scorpions, snakes; then take out his .45 and kaleidoscope-scratched-lens flashlight, proceed.

"You don't understand," I say with a disturbing sudden slur to my words. "I'm a billionaire...I can't spend the money I have.... you'll get there, we all do...even if you don't have two nickels...to rub together."

"What's the matter with your tongue? Now Corky did you a blue sky favor—"

I clap the air but my hands don't jibe; anyway it's a vitreous floater. I slap my ribs with a gunslinger's instinct and feel death's cage being rattled; no skeeter collateral.

"—by Saturday you have to vacate. Don't make me get mean."

"Now Belle I know some things. About Stu," I say rallying, using a hand on her shoulder to stay her, steady me.

She takes her hand off the door knob. "That was a fall-off-the-wagon meth haze when I told you that. Meth courtesy of you know who? My friend Elvin Vincer from high school, ex-president of the Slave Riders bike gang."

"They're gay. They ride lavender Harleys. With daisy flames."

She bristles. "They do *not*. You should—"

"I know, I should never underestimate the ability of a gay to wield a greasy bike chain by his fingertips."

I finished community college on the GI Bill and, after many jumps from dead-end jobs, was fired—this time from my longest stint, a division editor at Hallmark. It was called "egregious insubordination" and cost me my pension, vacation days, blah. I had had production work up anthrax-themed Get Well cards which held sneezing powder. Okay. When opened, the hologram bouquet of flowers wilted, the patient would sneeze and the jingle chip would sing "Anthrax is nothing to sneeze at—which you did—so you're not going to die. Imagine your relief (the sneezing powder is sweet to take that adrenaline taste out of your mouth!)."

I then found some free lance for a weekly suburban shopper, coming up with fillers for a pittance, like how cows sweat through their nose. I ran across a Slave Riders clipping on their scare tactics m.o.: corner some poor-sap bar-hoppers in the parking lot late at night, show them a deck of cards and say "these are going into the air and you five have to stomp one each when they hit the ground. Low card gets a beating; the rest scram." One kid stopped Elvin's hand on its way up and said "is ace high or low?" Elvin laughed so hard he turned them loose which led, however, to his ouster as president when the other gays felt he had been out-nuanced.

Belle must have caught my subconscious flick to the VA wall calendar. "Don't think social services will bail your ass. I'll call Elvin and he'll put a ramp up that step, park his Harley where you're standin' and squat the house, a lease from me in his hands. VA, hell, even the police will say it's a civil matter." She softened. "Please be out by Saturday. You know, Elvin and me were voted senior anti-prom king and queen. He hadn't come out yet but boy could he twirl the baton I loaned him for a scepter." She held her hand up and out as she left as though being royally escorted down the Hall of Mirrors in Versailles, though I recoiled at the image of her broad backside going funhouse.

I help the door close quickly and parse a distant lawnmower, small plane, Belle's AC unit, and a lawn sprinkler to home into a skeeter behind my back, coming in like a Russian MiG out of the sun. I know it's the Orange making me Section 8 to worry about germs at this stage but I spin crazy anyway and the dizziness drops me to my knees and even that's not enough. I go horizontal, blacking out (the take-a-dump muscles I would use pulling g's in the F-4 to avoid this are long gone), and hit the linoleum like so many other splats.

The high-pitched droning nears, the tinnitus of death. I can't even lift my head for the faintness. All I can do is wriggle some, make myself an aircraft carrier on the high seas for it to land on. I limp-wrist fling a hand at it over my shoulder like a lady loading a purse to put a masher in his place from 50 years ago. I feel a tinge gay and call that gang "Salve" Riders to whitewash the action in my mind.

"Your kill ratio is pathetic," my ex-girlfriend Connie said to me half a year ago at what an arcane historian would pinpoint as the beginning of the end for us, rivaled in the timeline only by her first flossing technique complaints. "Pathetic"? To me? To *me*! Who killed yellow Reds with napalm; killed green with Orange…I did everything in Nam but open a Carvel stand and offer Strycchie Puss ice cream cake to the gooklets.

I had just swatted at a ceiling spider in Connie's apartment bedroom—one of those wolf monsters that belongs in a sink when you groggily turn on the light to piss and, fractionally, before jumping into the door jamb you think "how did my hair brush get there?"—and I missed. I readied another go as it rankled defensively into the ceiling/wall joint and, standing on the water bed, lost my balance when Connie stepped up. I fell backwards and her white terry robe parted to her freshly-showered glistening brown bush right above me. It had been a while (more timeline data for the historian) so, call it art appreciation of the Escher repeating, receding image of brown fuzz—hers to the spider's: I steadied her with a hand as monopod to her pussy. Like she was passing some gripped-balls samurai test, she never wavered as she flattened all eight legs with my of-late Kafkaesque pillow.

She whipped her robe closed and stepped down. I rocked baby-like on the undulating water and she said "that may have been your 'howdy' in Vietnam but here it's a lawsuit." Time to pack. I had seen this coming, of course, me the oracle poet and all. So that afternoon I was at her computer figuring the nearest bus stop when she called me into the kitchen, cut me a slice of leftover meatloaf and wrapped it, then threw the rest out, leaned against the counter, waiting for me to hobo walk out; the last tally of her investment in us.

I croak a laugh now, me wriggling like a metamorphosed aircraft carrier, feeling the RV shimmy on the jacks, and a thumping in my chest way beyond the usual lighthouse heartbeats warning "alter course." It's all I can do to reach the door, push it ajar. Stu is between the two homes, throwing a tennis ball first against Belle's, catching the grounder back, pivoting and tapping the Frisbee with his foot and bouncing the ball off my plastic wall. That grounder back becomes the mirrored double play back to Belle's. It is balletically smooth, a shortstop as perpetual motion machine until I call him.

He finally finds my face in the door crack on the floor and runs over, eases in. I crawl aside and close the door as a turtle would cover her eggs on the beach, flipping sand backwards. He wants to call 911 but I assure him it's just a dizzy spell and implore him to hunt the mosquito. Immediately I hear a clap behind me.

"Done," he says.

I can't believe it. I ask to see it and this blond Mormon-like youth presents it to me, bloodless. A fine kill, Howard and I say.

He helps me to the love seat. "Keen," he says looking at my bowl of marbles above my head. After a minute I'm feeling well enough to drink the fiberglass-tasting water from the holding tank and bring the bowl down from the shelf.

"You know how to play?"

"Play?" he says. "I thought they were slingshot ammo."

There used to be many more in the bowl. Connie, in an alpha-female tirade against the quality of my entire breathing life's CV, put in as many marbles as weeks I had left based on actuarial expectancy (not reality; those tables turned on me). Every Monday morning, she'd take one from the bowl, hold it to my face and swallow it: "That's one more week turned to shit."

I never swallowed them but I kept the equation going on Mondays after I moved into this RV. But the equation was an existential black hole: Everything went into it but nothing came out. No raison d'être escaped. Even regret gave up.

When I got the terminal diagnosis and started receiving flyers in the mail for life insurance I couldn't be turned down for ("the hearse doesn't make practice runs"), I subtracted marbles to conform to the new timetable. Now even that marble-bowl ghost town is optimistic.

Stu's second base pivoting has made a circular dirt patch about four feet across. I move the Frisbee, pick out pebbles and a bottle cap, and roll the dozen marbles out. Stu drops to his knees, corrals them with both hands and smushes the mass around like lemmings driving hot revving cars.

"That's not how you play," I say and make a hole as the pot with my heel. I show him how to shoot using his thumb and the crook of his finger; he's a natural in any of the versions of the game.

The sun bakes a throb into my temples and a quarter-size blind spot in an eye has formed. I go into the RV for the one screwdriver and $2270 (Belle had cashed my check to close the account yesterday, subtracting a dollar for gas). I auger in (who cares now that's the worst thing a pilot can hear?) a hole barely more than a marble wide but deep. I tell Stu every shot in from the grass edge is worth $200.

It doesn't take long for the first and the next three come right after, a muffled ominous click from the Cu Chi tunnel as they drop. Stu tucks each $200 under a stone, like a pro shooting craps. Never put money away; a sign of weakness among us flyboys.

Belle comes out with two gnawed plastic tumblers of iced tea. Stu tips the glass to drink and Belle gets nervous: "Use the straw or take it out Stu, takeitout takeitout takeitout—."

"Mom," he says, "c'mon. We all know someone who's lost an eye."

She smiles, unselfconscious enough to show the lowers. She knows she's lucky with him. She watches the transactions, shakes her head and tells me with a parchment wink that's practically audible I'm on a slippery slope, losing my marbles. I am down to one, which I take from Stu before he shoots. I can see the top of the marble column; I fill the last inch with dirt and tamp it.

"I'm reincarnating them," I tell Belle.

Stu looks at his mother, then tries to hand me back the money. An RSVP pain hits my side and I crimp kowtow-esque into a tail hook looking to catch anything on the way out.

"It's yours," I say pushing the bills back. "Besides," breath now just an aspiration as I hold up $70 and one marble, "I'm a trillionaire."

Nearer Vana

They were once misguidedly referred to as "the two gnomes" to make them feel better. Someone had tried "elves"; that misfired as well as it called up a Christmas which was months away and fading for them like the pale dot on one of the test monitors that would get shut off with an indiscrete shake of an aide's head. Pete chafed at the aides but Jimmie raised a gray eyebrow and said "what about the doctor's clucking? You'd think they'd take a course on shutting up. Bad enough they called us gnomes, all cute like. Next they'll start measuring our height with a pencil line, us standing in a doorway."

That was yesterday, almost a week ago for these two. Their visits overlapped on Mondays and Tuesdays at this Cincinnati clinic which had familiarity with progeria—the rarest disease in the world you don't die from, they had been told. Then came the asterisks.

Today was sunny and held the scent of cut grass. Two grounds-keepers blew the blades off the walk and stopped their backpack machines—one even put out his cigarette—for them to shuffle past. It was Jimmie who had developed a painful limp but for Pete, two years younger, the pace was plenty. They were headed to their bench which would catch the shade until lunch. They both disliked wearing baseball caps, even to cover their baldness, since they bunched weirdly when cinched on their narrow heads. "Poodle heads," they shared only with each other.

Pete looked around at nothing as they walked, well used to the view of the overgrown tennis court, the gutter-streaked stucco buildings, the algae-laden large pool in the entrance circle with its hopeless pennies and dimes—the lone green turtle had died from ingesting them.

Jimmie broke the silence. "Yeh, right, if those two groundskeeper guys ever did any real work...."

"*That's* not what I was thinking," Pete said. "I'm waiting; you know the drill."

"I'm remembering!"

"Sure you are."

Jimmie made sucking noises around a tooth and Pete wondered if another one was coming loose. "Point six."

"Nice," said Pete.

"One point nine."

"Nice."

"Check that, two point nine."

"Still good."

"58."

"Good."

"240."

"Nice."

"Not applicable."

"Still? Good."

"160 over 110."

"So-so."

"And 29."

"That's a good number," Pete said. "So, he tell you you're still alive?"

"His little jokes, yeh," said Jimmie and they both added "any day you can walk away from." They always laughed some at that, more out of a vague duty.

Jimmie slowed. "Let's take this bench instead today. Okay with you?"

"You kidding?" said Pete. "You're just a step ahead of me."

The transition to sitting was always more awkward for Jimmie, the benches providing a sort of basket catch for him. Pete felt the back slats hard against his ribs and adjusted himself. "You want to put your leg up?" he offered.

"For old time's sake?" scoffed Jimmie.

"C'mon, none of that."

"Oh now it's Mr. Chippery-Doo. Just don't tell me to 'be positive.' One more person tells me, I swear, I don't care if it's your mother."

Pete patted the bench. "C'mon, here, put your leg up. You're supposed to be, what, limbler."

"You mean 'limber,' jerk? Doesn't your tutor give you any vocabulary?" and Jimmie brought his leg up with his hands.

"I can do the rub thing they do—" Pete said as he went to help.

Jimmie let it fall. "Faggot."

"Oh, you still on that? Because of the male nurse?"

"I did *not* have the gown on backwards. He just wanted me to turn it around, flash him. Faggot."

"Who knows with those gowns anyway."

"Right. Leave'm be."

"Leave'm be."

"Hands off. Front or back."

"Not like you can't go underneath them," said Pete.

"If it's a nurse. I mean a real nurse."

"Then she can go under—"

"She can turn it around—"

"—inside out—"

"—put a knot in it!" said Jimmie and they both groaned and cupped their baggy groins, their clothes never really seeming to fit. Their laughter sent Jimmie out of control, shaking and holding his chest in pain. He fumbled into his pocket, trying to rise from the bench; he opened a pill case but spilled them out. Pete picked one up and put it in Jimmie's mouth. "Swallow it!" he said but it was a struggle so Pete began stroking Jimmie's neck downward. Jimmie wrenched away and stood, red-faced holding the bench as his shaking subsided.

"What the hell was that?" Jimmie said when he caught his breath.

"You tell me! It's your body."

"No, the neck thing! I was *already* choking."

"It's what we did with our dog, for the roundworm pills."

"Faggot," Jimmie said. "Doing fine on my own."

Pete spastically mimicked Jimmie's shaking and pill-spewing, adding "Nurse said that you got to watch for that. That *denial*. That's the worst thing—"

"Don't you play doctor with me. Heard it all before."

"Okay," said Pete, faux recoiling. "You don't want the benefit."

Jimmie started coughing but caught it. "Of your *years*?"

"Yes, of my years."

"Like you know anything. My father would have called you a whelp behind the ears."

"Whatever that means, and yes, I do, have something. A benefit. A something, a hint, an *inkling,* to use *vocabulary*."

"Out with it."

Pete hesitated. "Okay. Meditation."

"Jesus! Hippie crap."

"No it is not crap! It works for me. Makes me feel better."

"Keeps you young, does it?" and Jimmie, back on the bench, folded his good leg so it at least caught on the edge, then tried to bring his other one up into a lotus position with no success at all. Pete noticed the spindly white ankles and winced at the recognition. "It's something with your legs, right?" Jimmie said. "If I can cross these I get a, what, baby bottle?"

"Your attitude sucks."

Jimmie released his legs and rubbed them. "I earned it."

"Well you sound like an old man."

"I *earned* it!"

Pete pushed himself off the bench, headed off. "See if you can spend it," he said.

Jimmie hobbled after him. "Wait, Pete!" he said. He felt light-headed, moving so fast, his heart always seeming to play catch up one way or the other, needing to slow down or speed up. "Wait," he said weakly and Pete stopped. "Hit that next bench."

They sat and pulled out caps from jacket pockets to ward off any sun. The Cincinnati Reds must have bought a boatload of extra caps, the two figured, knowing how far off the charity radar they were even in this sad joint.

"So. What is it? You hold your breath or something?" Jimmie said.

"No. That's just it. You let go of your breath."

"Let go?! Where?"

"Wherever it wants to."

"Like I been keeping it from having a good time."

"Forget this," said Pete. "Let's see if lunch is up."

"No, no," said Jimmie. "Anything but that. The less time I spend under a big banner that says 'use your spoon' the better. So. Give. Let my breath go. Got it."

"You got shit," Pete said. "Not just your breath! Everything. Let go of everything. Every-*thing* though. Every single damn thing! I can't stress it enough."

"Okay I'm with you."

Now Pete was singsong preachy. "No you're not! Every possession, every idea of a possession, every thought, every clue of a thought—"

Jimmie started singing gospel nonsense, clapping his hands. "*Got no clue Jesus, how to get into—*"

"Every song in your head!"

"*—every girl's short skirt—*"

"Every girl, period!" said Pete.

Jimmie stopped short. "What? Let go *girls?*"

"I am telling you: girls, chicks, babes, honeys—"

"Whoa," said Jimmie. "Let's start with breath."

Pete turned excitedly to Jimmie. "Old man Kaporski over in the cancer ward taught me this. Take a deep breath."

Jimmie did, stifled a cough, puffed out his cheeks. "Okay," he was told, "let it out."

And it whooshed out of him.

"No, slow-ly. Ease it out, let it go, not worried about it since another one is coming along," Pete said.

"Okay, I got that. What about possessions?"

"Simple. Let *them* go."

"Another one's coming along?"

"Sort of—"

"Another GTO?"

"You want another muscle car to come along?" Pete said.

"My only possession and I'm chucking it? Not unless another one is coming along. Cherry red."

"You don't even have a car!"

"It's what I was going to buy."

"So, you're holding onto something you don't even own."

"It's called a dream, jerk," Jimmie said.

Pete remembered how he had tested Kaporski's patience to the point of thrown applesauce. He waited and said simply, "let it go."

"Hell with you! My *dream?*" Jimmie said. "And this stuff works for you?"

"I think I'm nearer Vana than I was last week."

"*Where?*"

"Kaporski said I have to get near Vana, if I expect to—. You know, forget it; it was all these exotic, these exercises, brain stuff, the Tibetan Book of the Dead, even."

"With what?"

"With what *what?*"

"'Dead even,' said Jimmie, "with *what*. 'Dead' *is* even with everything."

"Not '*dead even*.' Besides, the idea is death is a phase and you can come back—"

"Ohhh," and Jimmie leaned back in awe, "just a phase. Like the moon."

"I knew I didn't want to get into this."

Jimmie rolled his head in an orbit: "Waxing, waning, *dead*, new."

"You're hopeless."

"And I shouldn't be?" Jimmie said, thumbing back to the buildings. "You think they're going to find a cure in, what, couple months? The only thing's gonna slow down my autopsy is a wheel comes off the gurney."

"Ouch. *There's* something to let go of. The bitterness."

Jimmie pulled his cap down farther and Pete thought he might be crying. "They can use a scalpel on it, along with the rest of me."

Pete went to sneak a look at Jimmie's eyes but let it go. "Breathe with me."

"Why are you so wrapped up with this, all of a sudden?"

"I don't know. Kaporski seems...sounds stupid, but he seems relaxed about...peaceful with—. He's been *working* on his mind."

The tolerance was gone from Jimmie's voice but it still had the tinny raspiness they shared and hated; shades of elves. "Because that's all that's left that *works*. When's the last time you think he got laid? Twenty years? 30?"

"Hey, he's still got a sex drive, he says. Couple months ago he took a taxi, went to the peep show over by the college. Told the taxi to wait. Goes into the booth, puts one quarter in, the shade goes up for 15 seconds, then he left. 'That was enough,' he said. 'I just needed to see a few young girls. Been so long I wanted to make sure evolution hadn't sewn up the pussy from boredom, so many fags out there.'"

"What was his book," Jimmie said, "'Tibetan Book of the Dead *Dick?*'"

"C'mon, don't make fun."

"God, last pussy I saw was my mother taking her underpants out of the dryer. And her robe...the phone rang...never mind."

"*Honolulu?*"

"*And* suburbs."

"Yecch," and Pete grimaced.

"Yeh. Anyway, I call that scene 'Going Home.'"

"Wait, so you are doing the movie-in-your-head thing?"

Jimmie looked off. "One thing my movie could use is a good wedge of hair pie." Pete laughed too hard. "What's your problem?" he snapped.

Pete hedged. "No, just you with your all-white pubic—"

"White *what?* White *what?*"

"Nothing," Pete said. "A wedge. Go for it. But for the movie, Kaporski said to put stuff from *your own* life in it."

"Well I'll put some extra stuff in there."

"But you're supposed to weave your memories together. It gives a purpose to—"

"Hey, it's my movie! If I'm short a few memories, I can pad it out, okay with you?"

"Jeez."

Jimmie exhaled a long frustrated sigh. "That's it!" said Pete.

"That's what."

"Kaporski said meditation is sighing without the 'Hollywood.'" He did a big theatrical sigh with the back of his hand to his forehead and a roll of the eyes. "Like the silent movies, he told me." Jimmie mimicked him. "Yeah," said Pete, "now cut out the Hollywood and you got it. Do ten. I'll do them with you. Close your eyes. C'mon. Ten."

They started but after a few breaths in sync, Jimmie opened his eyes and saw Pete trancelike. He rose quietly but Pete put his hand on his arm.

"I'm levitating," Jimmie said. "Don't hold me back."

Still with eyes closed, Pete lifted his hand; gave a dismissive flick of his fingers.

During their five days at home, Jimmie learned the word "quotidian" and couldn't wait to share the laughs with Pete.

"Everybody else has a word for '24 hours,'" he said on their morning walk at the clinic and laughed hard but barely drew Pete in. "Get it? *Plus* they use the word to *complain* about whatever's coming back tomorrow. Like, quotidian rigors clean your room! Huh," and he shook his head, "what I'd give for a 24-hour day."

They usually got close to the shade bench before getting serious but Pete suddenly blurted out "point 8."

"Oh. Good."

"Two point six."

"Um hum."

"75."

"Um hum."

"165."

"Um hum."

"Not applicable."

"Good."

"110 over 85."

"Um hum."

Pete slowed. "One four six."

"14 point six?"

"No."

"One *hundred* forty six?" Jimmie said.

"That's what it said."

"You got the paper? Let me see it."

Pete unfolded it from his shirt pocket and they sat. "Not like it matters," he said handing it to Jimmie.

"Yeh, well," Jimmie said, "we know nothing matters." He scanned it, gave it back.

They sat. After an uncomfortable minute Pete said "Nature happening." It was their code for how people who met them usually clammed up, looked elsewhere—at Nature—for some words.

"Okay, then." Jimmie blurted. "Big jump in a week."

"You ever have?"

"Hey, listen. There's always variations: Nurse has her period, runs the test half-assed to fuck over some guy's day—"

"You ever have?"

Jimmie shook his head and felt an annoying slip of his baseball cap. He took it off and cinched it tighter.

"So it's accelerating," Pete said. "Instead of one of my days being, like, four of a normal kid's now it's *five*? A year is five years gone, not four?"

"*Maybe*. Even if, so now 73 days equals a year. That's just down from 91.25."

"Same effin diff, Jimmie! I'm tired of playing with your fractions."

Mondays were the toughest, back away from home, the test results from last Tuesday freshly presented. For all the poking and prodding they got, there was no counseling to speak of, no one who could translate this rocket launch compression of life into what a child could grasp. Even their parents (Pete's dad was long AWOL) were at a loss; they wouldn't stoop to blame *their* quotidian rigors but that's where the parental bottom line had settled.

Jimmie played with the peeling green paint on the bench; thought he'd mention the underworked groundskeepers. "You want to breathe or something?" he ended up with.

"Kaporski died over the weekend," Pete said.

"Ah jeez." He threw the paint chips into the grass to kill it. "Did you ever beat him at chess?"

"I dropped a bag of M&Ms once and it knocked his rook off the corner of the board and he didn't notice. Closest I ever got."

"How old was he?"

"78."

"Huh," Jimmie said more to himself, "he made it." Then: "So. Peaceful was it?"

"The big door mirror in his room fell off."

"Hold on," he said through his laugh, "didn't you tell me he said meditate so you become *one* with the mirror?"

"Yeh, no, it didn't *land* on him. It was the noise in the night. Gave him a heart attack."

"Oh. Still. One with."

"He'll be buried tomorrow."

"Our birthday. Well, if I live that long," Jimmie said.

"Let's stop saying that, okay?"

Being cheerleader was usually Pete's role and Jimmie found himself trying to remember any of the poster homilies in the waiting rooms. He could see the colors; memory was starting to play tricks. "Hey, I been doing that heavy breathing," he said. "In, out...I lock onto 'hey there's a chunk of my carbon dioxide, oh there's another.' I really feel I control where it's going, in out, me steering—"

"Steering?"

"Yeh, in the driver's seat. You shift your breath—"

"This is not some muscle car," Pete said.

"Hey, I'm working it, doing fine."

"No you're not. You're holding onto it."

"No I'm not; I let it go," Jimmie said and took a breath, punched it out in spurts as he mimed slamming through the gear box, his good leg working the clutch, punctuating each shift with a higher whoosh.

Pete got upset. "I don't mean you're holding your breath. You're holding—. You have to let go of the letting go!"

"What?!"

"The process! You can't *grasp* it, you gotta not be part of it, monkey fruit trap where the monkey's got his fist in the coconut hole, all he has to do is let go the mango piece and he won't be caught and eaten—." He slumped. "Man, I wish Kaporski was alive."

"Yeh, he could tell me what the hell you're talking about."

"I got 146 Jimmie! So calm when they tell you, then ask if you want a hard copy."

"They see stuff all day—"

"Not me!" Pete said. "They don't see me all day."

"Take it easy, take it easy. Of course you're special, even if only you know it," Jimmie said finally remembering the poster.

Pete looked at him, said falsely upbeat "special 'oh my!' or...," now with a quavering voice of doom, "special: 'Oh...my.'"

"I thought you said she was calm."

"No, she bolted to get the doctor to tell me, who was all calm. By then."

Jimmie took the paper from Pete's shirt pocket. "It's not a death certificate, you know."

"Look who's talking."

"Hey, respect your elders" and he tore up the results.

———

On the shade bench, Jimmie looked up from his big chocolate cupcake with 14 unlighted candles when he heard Pete's scuffling walk, him cradling his cupcake with its candles. Pete sat gingerly, started to lift off with a grunt, then gave up.

"I did wipe the morning dew but I guess I missed some," Jimmie said. "Wet pants. Get used to it; coming soon."

"Why'd you walk out. Nurse Renata really wanted to spank your wrinkly ass."

"I've seen her fluff a pillow. I don't think I can take 14 of those."

"My mom called," Pete said. "She thought after the tests today she'd take us both for an early dinner. Before your mom picks you up."

"Doesn't she have anything better to do than think about me?"

"Okay."

"I don't want to hear 'happy' from the nurses, from the doctors—" Jimmie said.

"*Okay* I said. It's not their fault, you know. It's 47 people in the world have it, so, really, how could it be anybody's fault?"

"And you and I have the same birthday?" Jimmy said. "You don't think God has a sick sense of humor? Like it's a race to the death already but you and I have to have this extra competition."

"I'm two years younger; I'm not competing against you."

"Oh no?" said Jimmie shaking his cupcake at him. "You don't want to outlive 14? I *am* the oldest progeria patient in the world."

Pete picked at Jimmie's body. "Yeh, you're my ideal. Like Superman, faster than a speeding slug, more powerful—"

"Enough."

"—than a slug, able to leap a slug—"

"Cut!"

"Anyway, I think my last chance to catch you was before the 146."

"You know that chart the doctor has?" Jimmie said. "Progeria stages? Ultimate, penultimate, tertiary, all that. Well, I asked him what it meant."

"All mumbo jumbo with him. Calls it 'pro-guh-*rea*' half the time."

"Shush. So in my movie there's these two guys driving, middle of nowhere. Arizona say."

"You don't drive," Pete said. "Kaporski said the movie—"

"Just shut up for a minute. Middle of nowhere, they've seen nothing but dust for hours. Then, the Last Chance Saloon."

"They're in a muscle car?"

"No doubt," Jimmie said. "It's three in the afternoon; inside this dump there's junk all over the walls and ceiling; license plates, hatchets, broken sled, antlers, old football helmet. And there's six old farts inside."

"Watch it."

"Yeh," Jimmie laughed. "Like us. Anyway, they look like they've been there forever, like the barstools followed their ass out when they were born. And they don't like strangers letting in the light of day."

"How about one guy's passed out on the bar, drooling, and some-body puts a coaster—"

"Yeh, good. And the mean-ass bartender—got an eyepatch and it's got that sleep gunk on it just like his other eye—comes over to the two guys, he says, 'what'll you have?' and when he brings the beers back he says 'I haven't seen you guys before. Where do you hang out?' And the one guy, Jock-o, the driver, messes with him, says 'We usually go to the Penultimate Chance Saloon.' The bartender's confused: 'Where the hell's that at? I grew up in these parts,' he says. 'It's right there,' Jock-o says pointing out the window. 'It's *next to the Last Chance Saloon.*'"

"But your movie is supposed to be about your own—. It's supposed to make it all seem fuller—"

"Don't give me any shit," Jimmie said. "Didn't you get caught up?"

"You're supposed to remember your life, he told us."

"This just hasn't happened yet."

"But it doesn't make sense."

Jimmie stood. "You are so fucking dense!"

"I know what you are trying to do. But I got a 146, Jimmie. That's the top of the chart, ultimate stage."

"I am not changing the scene!"

"Fine! It's your damn movie."

Jimmie looked down at Pete's cupcake: "Jesus, you'd think he'd know what he was doing!"

"I'm agreeing with you! Jock-o knows. Don't change it."

"No, the *cook.* Your cake has 13 candles."

Pete counted by twos; left one finger up. "I didn't even notice," he said suddenly near tears. "How hard could it be, he got yours right! Jeez, giving me a year—" He took out one candle and started to fling it away.

Jimmie stopped his arm. "Let it go."

Pete, unsure, tapped the bench with it, anxiously at first, then slower—the waxing of a dull clock. He slid the candle back into the icing hole. Jimmie pulled out a pack of matches and lit one.

Pre-Coitum-Posterous

Sitting on the edge of the attentively-made bed, Burl fiddled with the drawstring of his new silk pajamas; their creases reminded him of every Cary Grant bedroom scene. He patted the sheets gently near his wife Ev, who sighed then slid a few inches closer, pulled her new nightgown back toward her knees. "This isn't transparent, is it, from the lamp? It's so sheer," she had whispered moments earlier.

Despite, for them, their bold fashion statement this evening, Burl thought this was not a manly bedroom, taking in the baby blue sheets, angel-scrolled headboard, and the Hummel figurines placed like emasculating snipers atop the room's high ground.

He was sorry now that he had stuck around that Friday two weeks ago after work on the new strip mall's paving repair. He was there for the town to check that the altered drainage specs in a low corner had been met. The whole thing felt beneath him, the senior engineer covering for an underling, here at yet another build-out for nails, Chinese take-out, pizza, laundromat, and dry cleaner—five prototypical business rationales to hide cash. The last of the paving crew were even more animated than befitted the end of the work week, Burl thought, and indeed one of them bumming a cigarette was near giggling when he told him to "stick around a few minutes; let everybody else leave."

As the late fall darkness settled, Burl was about to yield to the draw of his warm car when he heard the backhoe start up and head for the far corner with seven men in tow acting beer-starved with only six barstools in sight. The backhoe punched easily through the uncured asphalt and started swinging wildly with its loads as the men checked in conspiratorial syncopation around them. There were no cars yet at the unopened mall except for the parked vehicles the men owned, and no other people, but there was the evening's rush hour building past the gap-tooth newly-planted evergreens.

Burl gravitated over, concerned that one of the other storm drains was going to be damaged by this cowboy operator on the machine. One man shouted into the cab and held up his hand, then jumped a few feet into the ragged pit. The operator got out of the cab and joined the peering surge. These were large men using their girth at the trough and the jostling pushed a second man into the pit.

Burl heard plywood splintering and pieces of wood spat out, then a hand lifted above the pit's rim and held, like the Statue of Liberty's torch if it could quiver in excitement: "A Little Boo Boo!" Guillermo, one of the aboveground men, said. "Look at that sad face under the dirt." He grabbed it from the upthrust hand and brushed it with his tarred fingers. "Madre mia, I'm makin' it worse," he said; he rubbed it zealously on a clean spot of his Carhartt khakis.

Now four hands from below began feeding Hummel figurines to those above. Burl saw it as fledglings in an inverted nest, their piping fingers filled and instantly back after stowing an item in their shirt or cradled arm. "Lantern Fun," "Marmalade Lover," "The Goat Herder."

Hardly a moment's hesitation from the men identifying them, despite the near darkness. When one's arms were filled, the man would trundle to his pick-up and hustle back, cursorily examining the cradled items of anyone heading his way.

One of the men nudged Burl closer to the action. "Grab, man, grab. That 'Teeter Totter Time' that Phil got? $670 retail." Burl found himself reaching for a plump pastel girl in lederhosen plucking flower petals. "Fritzi, Ja; Fritzi Nein," Phil said. "The six-incher. My wife has the 4 and 1/2. Nice find."

Big Gus grabbed one with two children in a dainty hug and looked it over in his catcher's-mitt-size hand. "'Friends Forever.' Huh. This cocoa kid's black, right?" and without waiting for an answer, tossed it to Burl. "No race-mixin' collectible is goin' on my mantel," he said.

"What is—" Burl started but suddenly all the activity from below stopped; one pitsider held the sleeve of a neighbor and gasped. Slowly, reverently, up came donkeys, then lambs, then kneeling camels. "Oh my god," Big Gus said, "pay dirt," as he pawed the air dazedly, a bear fending off bees from the honeycomb.

"What is—" Burl started again but Phil shushed him as up came four infant Jesuses and for the first time a pecking order prevailed because a few men held back while others reached first for them. Next came kings, angels, virgin Marys and oxen and as the cornucopia slowed, the trough shuffle was on again as the men tried to complete their Nativity sets. Burl grabbed what turned out to be a Moorish king and was handed a second one by Big Gus, who just shook his head and said, "What idiot crowned the wrong king?"

Burl thrust out his arms, now somehow full. "What am I doing?"

"You don't want those?!" Phil said, reaching immediately for them. "Gotta be two grand."

"I mean," Burl said, raising his voice since the backhoe had started. "What gives?" The two in the pit clambered out awkwardly not using their hands; they had taken their jackets and shirts off and filled them like cat burglars' pillowcases. One laggard at the edge was imploring the two to return: "I see them, the annual plates," he said. The first man into the pit said, "No! Twenty minutes sharp. That was the window, Manny. We're done."

"Yeh, but they're right there, Sal. I see the rims of them stickin' out. My wife broke '83 and '85 in a righteous fit over my h—" but the backhoe was already scraping in dirt sideways and drowned out what Burl figured was "hard drinking," "whoring," or "head."

Phil pulled Burl toward their vehicles, closed into him. "This is strictly, let us say since we're talkin' Hummels, 'verboten.' You got in on this 'cause you didn't bust our balls and you let us rack up some overtime yesterday, but not a word. Savvy?"

Burl said "I do savvy" and felt foolishly proper, like he was conjugating the word for a 19th century pioneer.

"Okay. Last week," Phil continued, "guy from Hummel corporate in White Plains, friend of this here strip mall owner, needs a favor. They're way overrun, figurine prices are tankin' worldwide, glut glut blah blah. So mall guy gets backhoe Bobby to bury boxes of these things; "a time capsule for the future," he told Bobby. But who's foolin' who. Supply and demand, from push-up bras to my wife's goiter pills."

"From what to *what*?" Burl said.

"You never heard of Adam Smith? The market tightens up in a couple years, out come these 'ooh, rare items.' Time capsule, my ass."

Burl suddenly felt the exposure to the crawling rush hour nearby. Surely the drivers were curious, at the very least. Everything ends up on the some website, he thought: "Obese men race while babying porcelain and holding up pants," the new viral video. How stupid was he doing this; I have a state pension—

"C'mon," Phil said, reading his mind. "You can't steal from a thief. Anybody's guilty, it's backhoe Bobby for takin' $500 to shut up about it." Bobby was working the paver now and the burial plot in the corner would soon be seamless. "After Bobby told us what this shi-, uh artwork, was worth," Phil said, "we all studied up like crazy with our wives, girlfriends. Tonight was do or die; in fact over there's the truck pulling in with the hot air balloon for opening day Sunday."

"But there's nothing in these stores to speak of," Burl said.

"You kiddin'?" Phil said. "The chinks rent all these; they'll come in like a human wave attack and in 24 hours they'll have a bayonet up the cash cow drippin' money."

"Jesus Phil, that's harsh."

"I see the Gulf War vet sticker on your car," Phil said. "C'mon. You said worse than that in the desert."

"Yeh, in the heat of things, but—"

"Hey Bobby," Phil interrupted as he walked by, done with his corner work. "Always worth turnin' Judas for the heirlooms, right?"

Phil put his arm around Bobby as Burl opened his car door and slid his items onto the seat. "This guy didn't want to do it," Phil said of Bobby, "after he let it slip at the bar one night but we told him it was like robbin' from Peter to pay Paul. Hey, that could make a good Hummel. Little boy between the two, a hand in each of the saint's pockets."

"I don't think the Catholic Church would go for that," Burl said. "Abuse-in-the- news kind of thing."

"I didn't *mean* they'd have the simperin' faces of joy like all the rest of these," Phil said, annoyed. "Obvious-fuckin'-ly."

Bobby reached into his pocket and pulled out a tattered business card and handed it to Burl. "I can do your drive cheap. I'll use the leftover here, make it sparkle," and stabbed his card which indeed read, "I make macadam sparkle."

"I have crushed oyster shells," Burl said.

Bobby lit up. "Oh they take tar real good, just look at any oil spill. Hey, you was in the Gulf War? So was I, working on runways. I can do 10 percent off for you. Or," off Burl's hesitation, "maybe pave over a goldfish pond that's dead. Either bonus."

"Let me think about it," Burl said.

"You volunteered, right?" Bobby said. "No officer school crap."

"No, yeh, volunteered," Burl said. "Well, my dad pushed me pretty hard. He did three tours in Nam. 'I'll like Iraq,' he said. 'It's a dry heat.'"

"Well," Bobby said. "It's time to blow this bar mitzvah as the priest with no money said to the Jew looking for a hum job." Phil and Bobby laughed hard, Phil adding, "you gotta do some stand-up, Backhoe."

"First things first is gettin' back on my wife's good side with these geegaws," Bobby said, getting serious. "She's been leavin' me dog-eared Cosmos by the commode for two months now on account I ain't twangin' her girl-spot."

Phil said, "My wife's gonna *kill* me for not grabbin' that one 'Follow the Fawn' that came out. Big Gus knew that number; he shoved my hand away. $1250."

Guillermo walking by overheard, adjusted his booty and managed to pluck out a single item. "Grandma's Treasure," he said. "$2395. Look and weep but don't touch."

"Fuck you," said Phil. "No one's payin' that these days."

Guillermo brushed past Bobby into Phil. "Hey! You got the Nativity in your hands? Watch your language."

———

Burl looked at his two cocoa Moorish kings atop the bedroom TV, bracketing infant Jesus sans creche, on his back, short pudgy legs and arms clawing the air like a flipped turtle. Make that a cat with string, he amended, feeling a twinge of religious guilt and then segued into the cat as another possible figurine. Of course, everything these last few days seemed just another in the Hummel near-infinite catalogue of life: "Borrowed Bank Teller's Pen Ruining Grown Child's Shirt," for example. He had thought maybe his wife would laugh these items out the door, a "him-trying-to-bond-with-some-closeted-gay-construction-guys" kind of moment, but she had ensconced them in the bedroom.

Mr. Elkins sitting on the end of the bed tapped his pen metronomically on his clip board. "You did only purchase 12 minutes," he said as he stood to loosen his tie a fraction. "You're cutting well into your foreplay."

Hardly anybody in 2022 wore a tie, Burl thought as he placed his hand on Ev's breast. She shrugged it off, mirroring his interest level.

"Come on, hon," Burl said. "This is costing us a small fortune."

"Mr. Elkins," she said, with a note of desperation, "perhaps if the TV were on? Sotto voce?"

Elkins sorted efficiently through the four remotes on the nightstand, chose one and quickly had a weather report on low volume.

"Oh, you know your way around the buttons," she said.

"You could say that. TVs come up frequently in my line. Got to know which buttons to push," and he tried a laugh.

The three of them watched a reporter striated in a deluge, struggling to keep her balance in flowing thigh deep water at a town's intersection, leaning into her station's ID-labeled microphone, holding her foul-weather hood in place, squinting to amp things up.

"These weather locals all think they're covering a damn war, in the thick of it," Burl said, "standing like jerks out in the hurricane's surf or on a seawall with the waves breaking over them."

From the edge of the TV screen drifted a man from another station, effortlessly reporting lying on his side on an orange air mattress.

He floated in front of her, talking into his mike. The woman, embarrassed, stopped mid-syllable and lugged herself out of frame as the man hooked a stop sign with his foot to stay in place for his cameraman.

Ev stood quickly to shut off the TV. "That's me, that woman!" she said. "I want to walk out of this picture; I just can't do this, not with him here."

"I did say we could request a girl," Burl said.

"And I said I was okay with that until you started acting like a spoiled brat making a Christmas list. What did he check off on the form, Mr. Elkins?"

"I'll have to get it," and Elkins opened his thick briefcase. "It's a little dark in here...." He quickly shielded the contents from Burl who looked over: "Tut tut" he said. "Part of our effectiveness is what we call our *frisson de surprise*."

Ev snapped around and grabbed for the case. "Is there a French tickler in there?! Burl bought one years ago and I topped his pork chop with it that night."

"That's the lusty spirit," Elkins said.

"*No*, sir. I used it as a *garnish* on his dinner. So you can apologize right now, as he did," she said.

"Mea culpa," Elkins said but raised a finger to add, "*perhaps*. Hear me out. Because with our training with all ethnicities, ages, creeds, Mrs. O'Donnelly, we feel agents—"

"You mean field agents," Burl said.

"—*feel* agents," he continued, "are almost never wrong: 'Perspicacity tramples modesty,' our motto." He pointed above the TV. "I couldn't help but notice the two black dildos. Ergo, 'perspicacity tramples—'"

"Those are Moorish kings!" Ev said.

"Oh," said Elkins, peering across the darkened room. "Then is that...*Jesus*? From here I thought it was a genetically-modified turtle on its back playing with string. You know," he laughed, "giving a turtle cat genes might be a good idea so they're more curious, not bored to death in a bowl with a plastic tree—." He stopped short when he saw their reaction. "Sorry about 'genes.' Some office cubicle humor there. Uh, where's his creche?"

"Yes," Ev said to Burl. "Where *is* his creche?"

"I couldn't...there weren't enough. I told you," he whispered to Ev.

"I know. But the bottom line is I end up with a Jesus with black twin daddies and a monk-faced ox with a horn knocked off."

"There's the Teeter Twins," said Burl pointing to another shelf.

"Yeah, but no Nativity *set*," she said. "And those two look fraternal at best. I think it was a bad batch."

"Well," said Elkins. "Kings, dildos, where's the excitement without the surprise?"

When Ev looked away in disgust Elkins gave Burl a silent urging, tapping his watch. Burl cupped Ev's breasts from behind and she lifted off his hands primly, turned to him, and escorted them to his own lap with a parting pat; an adult nursery rhyme gone wrong, Burl thought.

Elkins rattled his paper.

"Yes," Ev said, "back to his wish list."

"There were a lot of preferences," he read. "Nubile—."

"Stop there. Why would she have to be nubile, Burl?"

"The brochure said there was some dexterity involved," he answered.

"'Hands' are not where 'nubile' is! Anyway, I cannot get in the mood with Mr. Company Man here."

Elkins closed his briefcase, pursed his lips. "I am *fully* trained to deal with your discomfort, Mrs. O'Donnelly. Now, have you ever killed anyone?"

Ev recoiled. "How dare you sit on my bed—"

"Excellent!" Elkins said. "Disconnecting from my presence—"

"You're a jerk," she said.

"Well, now you've put me back in the room," he said.

"And you," Ev said, turning to her husband, "you're the jerk who had to have the creamed corn!"

Burl, who had been wondering if there was any rebate possible for unused minutes if this just ended now, snapped to: "Whoa! You scarfed it down too."

"I said, 'I think it's been genetically modified,'" Ev said. "I mean, it was practically glowing yellow."

"There was no label—" Burl said.

"Not required," said Elkins.

"No government warning—" said Burl.

"Not required," said Elkins.

"Glow seeping out from the first turn of the can opener," Ev said.

"No hard proof," Elkins said.

"Shut up!" said Ev. "Why are you here if your company wasn't responsible?"

"There was a nolo...nolo...," Elkins said searching his briefcase. "It was a definite nolo...ah here it is: Nolo contendere stipulation specifically stating—I'm reading the court documents now—stating that while there was the hint, even glimmer, even wisp, and even imputation—boy they do parse things don't they?—imputation of guilt there was no actual basis for tangible wrongful...intent-ums."

"'Intent-ums?' The judge said that?" she said.

"That last bit was mine," Elkins said. "Just trying to lighten the legalese. Keep the lovemaking flowing. We're trained to help foster words like sweet-ums, snook-ums—"

"Bunk-ums," Ev said.

"So, nolo contendere?" said Burl. "That the best defense that you guys, all your Ph.D.s in chemistry and pharmacology and animal husbandry and what all, can offer to the thousands of victims here. You, the 100th something biggest company in the world."

Elkins cleared his throat. "The largest. Market capitalization, anyway."

"You're kidding," said Burl. "Wait a minute. You *grew* after the revelation that your genetically-modified corn—"

"Pest resistant," Elkins said, "highest acre yield, perfect tassel color."

"I'll give you perfect tassel color," said Burl, "I'll give you all of those except that eating one can—"

"Just the creamed corn," Elkins said, "not the niblets."

"He won't *eat* the niblets," Ev leveled. "They stick in his teeth."

Elkins nodded. "We're working on that gene." The couple shot him a look. "Okay okay, noted. But it was just two weeks production that caused the—. Well, more cubicle humor: How are reluctant homosexuals like the tens of thousands who ate those cans of corn? They all have an extra 'why me' chromosome."

Burt stood, adjusted his pajama bottoms, grasping at bolstered dignity. "Look Elkins, I'm sure I don't have to remind you and your fellow cubicle 'laugh-holes'—

"Burl!" Ev said.

"—that your GMO corn—"

"Creamed not niblets—" Elkins started.

"—shut up—"

"*Burl!*" Ev said.

"You too, Ev!" Burl said. "—that your GMO corn caused a loss of all sensation related to the male and female orgasm. Permanently!"

"Not proven beyond a reasonable—" Elkins said tapping the paper.

"Shut the hell up!" Burl said. "So people can *do* it, they just don't feel a goddamn thing! So, naturally enough, they stopped. No more ripples of incipient pleasure, no roiling of loins clamoring for fruition." He stepped around to face Elkins, his words now carrying spittle, his face red. Ev reached for his arm but he slapped it away. "No bullets in the assault rifle chamber, safety off, we're takin' this bitch's fuzzy paddy you slopeheads!" Burl threw a fist at Elkins which he sidestepped, bringing Burl's arm up behind his back before twisting him onto the bed and letting him go.

"We feel agents are trained in the martial arts," Elkins said, "because many buttons get pushed in the bedroom in these times, and not just for the TV."

"Burl," Ev said calmly but with a tremor in her voice. "That language. Is that what you think, deep down? You're…taking my 'fuzzy paddy' with an *assault* rifle?"

"My god," Burl said. "Did I say that? I'd completely forgotten. That was the gist of my dad's one and only sex talk, sperm-as-bullets, et cetera, when I was eleven. He did three tours in Nam," he added to Elkins.

"Well we can chat about the good old days of Vietnam," Elkins said, "or…time's a-wasting."

"Why don't you take that watch Elkins and—. Never mind. Chrissakes, Ev, hoik up that nightgown."

"Burl!" she said.

"What's the MO here, Elkins?" Burl said, unbuttoning his top.

"Did you view the DVD we sent?" Elkins said.

"Defective. Like your corn."

"I saw part of it," Ev said. "It's an intuition thing. When we get to the point where something should be, you know, friction-wise, happening…but it's not happening…. Mr. Elkins?" she added, embarrassed.

"Right," he said. "Simple enough. At that point, friction-wise as she said, I grab the spray cans and spritz both of you on your….?" He waited.

"Petunias," Ev said, drawing a glare from her husband. "Well he's going to see everything, he might as well know what we call them." Elkins pulled out two large spray cans from his briefcase, one with "XX" and one with "XY" in neon colors: "One estrogen-based, one testosterone."

Burl said "Why can't you just give us the cans and leave?"

"Oh no!" said Elkins. "Not only are these highly-proprietary secret formulas from our best chemical minds, with ultra-quick cellular permeating qualities, but they are very difficult to work with." Off the quizzical looks, he added, "they're incendiary."

The couple looked relieved. "Oh well. They are supposed to spark some fireworks," Burl said.

"Uh, yes, that," said Elkins, "but no. I meant they're flammable."

"My god," they answered.

"Or can be," Elkins backpedaled, "if not handled properly. It's too bad you didn't view the DVD because it does mention 'tonsorial precautions.'"

"Shaving our...," Burl said.

"Which we provide at no charge," Elkins said and started to undo his trousers. "I can show you my work to allay any—"

"Hold on there. You are no part of 'allay,'" Ev said.

"Well," Elkins laughed. "Cubicle humor once again, but I am. Part of *a-lay*."

"Whatever," said Ev, giving up.

"Four minutes left in the session," the agent said. "Time, Mr. O'Donnelly, to sashay that big male...petunia down to the hothouse."

The couple looked forlornly at each other, then embraced with ill-fitting arms as though unsure who was leading this dance. Burl lifted the spread and they slid under, covering their heads. The lump shifted as clothes were shucked. Elkins rose off the bed and put on an flame-retardant jump suit from his briefcase. He added the plastic hood, adjusted the visor, and put on rubber gloves. He peeled the protective caps from the spray cans, then started a CD player's tinny "Strangers in the Night."

A muffled, "What is that music?" came from Ev and she peeked out. She shrieked when she saw Elkins hovering in his lumpy orange suit, spray cans drawn. She sat upright and yanked the cover to her neck; Burl had to claw out.

"Burl," she said, "if you think I'm going to open my pearly gates for you with some alien in my bed and Sinatra singing that crap you should have said 'I do' to my loopy half-sister the way you wanted 14 years ago before she joined that dominatrix spin-off of Cirque du Soleil."

"I don't think," her husband said, "this is the time for dirty laundry."

"Oh don't mind me," Elkins said, sounding underwater in his hood. "I did give you a copy of the non-disclosure form I signed. Now, where were we?"

"I was where I would probably be moaning," Burl said.

"I, I don't...," Ev started. "I can't tell."

Elkins shook his head. "I need the coefficient of friction to be four, plus or minus 20 percent."

"*What?*"

"Oh that's right," he continued. "You didn't review the DVD. Never mind. In the interest of moving the ball forward, huh, I like that...I'm going to lift the access blanket enough for my hands. Burl, may I call you that?"

"As good a time as any."

"Burl, start your game day moves. Mrs. O'Donnelly slide down, that's it, on your sides, and...there! A wormy little rumba you've got Ev, excuse the familiarity."

"I do have some friction whatever," Ev said breathlessly.

Elkins shook the cans and lifted the spread slightly. "I've got to aim carefully."

"I told you," Burl said, "there was dexterity."

"Ladies first," Elkins said. "This will sting each of you at first but the benefit will be *very* evident when the two sprays rub together. Don't stop, but give me a peeping Tom sliver of access...yes, lovely petunias." He tensed his left arm and sprayed for several seconds. As he readied his right, first an alarm bell rang in his briefcase which merged with Ev's ear-piercing scream. She rolled apart from Burl and started slapping the bedspread in her lap.

"I'm burning," she yelled. "I'm burning, it's what he said!"

Burl joined in smacking the cover. "It's her paddy! Fire in the hole! Isn't that your incendiary alarm? Do something Elkins!"

The agent put down the cans and turned off the alarm. "It's just my timer." He took off his hood, wiped his face. "Unfortunately, your purchased minutes are up."

Burl, forgetting his nakedness, leapt out of bed. "Gimme that can, dammit, I must be close!"

Elkins unzipped his jump suit. "I would if I could but we have stockholders to answer to. You can buy another visitation; in fact, I have a coupon book—"

"I want that goddamn can, Elkins!" Burl turned to his wife. "Were you close?"

"I don't, I'm not—" she said.

"Chrissakes Ev, plus or minus 20 percent! Zip that suit back up, Elkins."

"I'm done here," he said. "One hundred million sex acts a day out there waiting for us. Or used to be, before...you know; anyway, we'll get that back up. Speaking of 'up,' put a pillow over that, Mr. O'Donnelly."

Burl squared up. "I will not! Dear, take your nightgown off. Yes, off." She did. "We are the face of reality; we are what you created, Mr. Elkins," as he put his arm around Ev's back. "*Wait* a minute," he said and sat heavily on the bed.

Ev grabbed her balled nightgown and partially covered herself. "What is it?"

"Just one sec here Elkins. Your 'creation,' this whole spritzing 'cure' your company came up with as compensation in the class action lawsuit, is actually a huge windfall, isn't it? I mean, now that you covered the government penalty?"

"From death's door to hot stock in five weeks," Elkins said.

"Five weeks?" Burl said. "Then your chemists, et cetera, had a formula ready to go. People were trained, the testing was done."

Elkins stirred uncomfortably. "Uh, we test in Calcutta. Very fast track in Calcutta."

"And everyone's so happy to get a tingle in the groin," Burl said, "that they don't realize they've been kicked in the balls. This was planned! You all must have thought there could be a problem. It's a *conspiracy*, Ev."

"Fed us the corn," she said. "Might as well have made heroin one of the ingredients because we'll all be hooked, right? On your expensive visits we just crave more of once she gets a taste again—. Oh. Excuse my petunia gabbing, dear."

"Oh let her speak!" Burl said. "Got anything to say for yourself, agent?"

"We are not insensitive," Elkins said, "to the costs. In fact, we are testing robots which will—"

"Which will make you *more* profitable. You'll have 100 percent market share of a most basic human urge," Burl said.

"Primal! I mean, I had a fire!" Ev said.

"With no labor costs to speak of," Burl said.

Elkins rose from the bed. "Buy the stock, Mr. O'Donnelly. People want their orgasms. And we're there for them."

Burl snatched the "XY" can from Elkins. "I want to see what these ingredients are."

The agent didn't resist. "You won't find them there. Or anywhere. There are just two people in the world who know that recipe. The inventor in Oeslau, Germany, and the other a high muckety-muck in White Plains."

"Oeslau? White Plains?" Burl said.

"I see where you're going," Elkins said. "Yes, the key ingredient in our sprays for snapping orgasms to life, turns out, also helps make the best glaze for those dil—, those Moorish kings above the TV. We own that company as of couple months ago."

"Couple months ago, huh? You don't know where I'm going," Burl said as he went to the phone on the shelf, turned on a lamp.

"You mind putting on something," Elkins said. "The nose on the 'face of reality' is a bit much, and I'm off the clock here."

Ignoring him Burl pulled a tattered card out of his wallet on the bureau. Ev started to dress: "No, keep that off. This is Mr. Elkins's new Garden of Eden. I'm going to make him bite a GMO apple— ships great, never bruises or rots, but has no taste whatsoever."

Elkins began folding his jump suit, filling his briefcase, fixing his tie. "Dear," Burl said, dialing, "lock the bedroom door and put the key somewhere he can't get it. He stays here."

Ev sauntered naked past Elkins, turned the door key, looked around with it in her hand, then inserted it into her vagina. "Call it a 'paddy-lock,' and you can play all the Sinatra you want," she said to Elkins.

"Backhoe Bobby?" Burl said. "This is the guy from the town, yes, Mr. O'Donnelly, the drain guy. Hey, I need a teeny favor from you. A teeny favor. No, that's not one of the Hummels. I need the name of the guy who gave you the 500 dollars—. No, not to get you in trouble."

Elkins sat on the end of the bed spinning the briefcase combination.

"I swear," Burl said, "you won't lose your job. What, how can you *trust* someone who's not a Mississippi good ol' boy? In mah heart I am," now going Southern. "I was born in Maryland but the eastern shore is pretty white tr—, I mean, did you know 'Dixie' was Lincoln's favorite song?" Burl lost his enthusiasm as he listened. "Alright alright, yeh, 'fuck that yankee and Abe's a Jew name they changed to Honest Abe.'" Then he rallied with an idea. "Wait, dint you say your better half was giving you grief over not gettin' her g-spot twanged? Yeh, *Paulette's* girl spot. For about two months, right? Okay, now this is important: does Paulette eat creamed corn?"

Burl tensed for the answer, then slapped his thigh. "It's the only kind that don't stick in her craw," he directed to his audience. "I'll be hog-swaddled! Oh, *horns*woggled. Now, you say you're all right, hunnert percent, in the uh, twanger department? What, does an owl drool on his ass? Not sure what that—. Oh, that's an affirmative. Now, just as important: Do you eat creamed corn?" Burl did an unselfconsciously-privates-flapping jig on this answer: "Where you come from corn is *pig* food. I'll be! I always wanted to summer in Miss'ssippi and I tell you true, I love chitlins at a picnic—. What? 'Washed or slung?' Oh, two ways clean them…ah, part of your stand-up."

Ev looked at Elkins and they shrugged.

"Now Bobby, I feel like we're on the same page in the hymnal," Burl said. "You heerd of any class action suit on the TV about how corn—. Never watch it? The TV is the devil's codpiece? Yeh, and 'what's a class action suit, what Superman got buried in?'" Burl yucked. "Dang, if there's not more of yur stand-up. Now, what you did miss on the news was that creamed corn, how do I put this, took the, uh, clapper outta Paulette's twanger. Oh? That *does* make sense? Right, hadda be somethin' 'that wasn't you; myswell be corn.' Then listen to this: The guy with the cure is either the one who give the guy who gave you the 500, or some other high muckety-muck *he* knows in Germany."

Burl absently searched his clothesless body for a pen before snapping his fingers and Ev brought him one. "Ah, Mr. Dave Daniels, Mr.

500 Smackers," Burl said. "No no, don't you call him. I will. I know *all* the buttons to push to get the next guy on up."

He hung up, turned to Elkins, arms akimbo. "Ev, fetch the man his key. Time for him to go to the XX, XY warehouse and get us on a weekly delivery schedule. We'll need a new DVD. And throw a half-dozen hazmat suits until we get the hang of this."

"You are certainly loopy enough," Elkins said, "to be a bird of a feather to her dominatrix-circus half-sister."

"Yes honey," she said nervously, "you're making me feel I should put my nightgown on. Like I don't know my husband."

"You remember," he said, "the dirt you had to clean off those Moorish kings?"

"Yes, I thought I scrubbed them too much and that's why they were cocoa-faced; one's sort of piebald if you get the light just—"

"Enough, Ev," Burl said, snatching the key from her. "A man can stand nakedly akimbo only so long before he has to drink some Viking blood. The point is, Mr. Elkins, there's a lot more *dirt* where they came from."

He showed the agent the door. "Oh look Ev," Burl said. "It's the new GMO snake leaving Eden; walks on two legs now. Can't shed his own skin, though. His boss will have to flay it off him. Maybe they'll name a new Hummel after him: It'll be a man with hobo stick, leaky tattered briefcase on the end of it—'Spilling the Magic Beans.'"

Elkins shook his head. "I don't know what hold you think you have."

"Oh you guys are so pure and innocent. Open a can of that batch of creamed corn that you've recalled and when you see the yellow glow," Burl said, "try to convince yourself that's just the perfect tassel color shining through. You can't, because everybody from the board room on down knew the cure would create a gold mine, with the hold you would have over all of us who ate it. Well, I'm opening a can of worms and you won't have to wait long for the results. Blackmail in White Plains is an even faster track than your Calcutta."

"We top the Fortune 500 list of companies, Mr. O'Donnelly, and our white shoe law firm—"

"—is about to get dragged through the mud. There's at least one white collar criminal I know who's not eager to play S&M Old Maid in prison. And he might just trade a steady supply of those sprays for immunity. Show yourself out."

They waited to hear the front door close, the car start. "Put that night gown on," Burl said. "I want to hoik it and overrun your paddy."

"Double yes double sir," Ev said.

Memo to Self:
Have Relationship with Self. cc: Self

Noon. Dot. Pierce caught the time clock's slightly heavier notch on the hour. And it was CJ's turn to get lunch, damn it, and he hadn't taken the order yet. Pierce had risen late—girlfriend-less the morning's hangover this past week. He probably shouldn't have backed her into proving a negative to defend their relationship; it worked back in debating class. Rushing for a bus, he had coffee in one hand and with the other jammed a bear claw pastry into the closing doors. The "five-second okay rule" for dropped food did not apply to a sticky-first landing on a city bus tread, he figured, and kicked the pastry into the street.

He then counted on the mid-morning chuck wagon but it was a no-show. Not that you can rely on a high-school dropout selling re-wrapped Ring Dings with oxycontin inside and playing turf war for the junior high crowd with motorcycle gang members. "Chuck" had derided the riders to Pierce as a "gay boutique gang" because of their clean-shaven faces, lack of tattoos, and matching purple Harleys. But what "Chuck" had heard as a warning from "The Brucers," Pierce knew, was wishful thinking, ignorant of the desire of the gang to be chromatically true—with their dark green-lettered black leather jackets and the bikes' purple paint—to their real name, "The Bruisers."

What was he doing here, big picture, playing charades with Carr during a cig break in the work yard of Water Wings, which specialized in under-20' trailerable sailboats and was located in Alexandria, a couple of blocks from the Potomac River? Four months ago he had been a creative type at a fledgling ad agency whose main client was a laborers' union that represented the lowest rung on the construction site: dirt tampers, chain sawers, hod carriers, wheelbarrow humpers. It had been a clash of classes from the start—him clean-cut "college crap with callouses on his ass"; this from the gruff first handshake with the union's hard-knocks leader. But that day Pierce was told by him to dumb down even further a training video he had written—to give equal time to the tamping machine's on *and* off switch positions—he gave notice at the agency and took this minimum wage job on a lark for a break after talking to the owner, Slater, at a D.C. boat show.

He hadn't know Corinne for long; calling her a girlfriend this early was probably presumptuous although they had talked about not seeing others. They met when she had been perusing the tech section of a bookstore. He drifted to her aisle and, looking at her chic blonde haircut and nudged to smitten-available-mode, had absently lifted the thickest book he saw off a shelf hoping to catch her attention. "There it is!" she said sidling over, "oh, and they said it's the last one in stock at the desk." He checked the title: "Oral Hygiene for Medically-Compromised Patients."

"Yeah," he said, covering, catching the authors. "Wilkens and Barrett. It's the classic. I mean, right?"

"Oh yes, like 'War and Peace' for hygienists. All happy sets of teeth are alike; each unhappy set of teeth is unhappy in its own way." She turned to go, adding "nice find."

"No, here. You take it." And she was back. He explained in the store's coffee nook that he worked in advertising and had just been irresistibly drawn to the book's "beautiful blonde cover and perfect binding." She smiled winsomely and her abashed poppy seed extraction between nine and ten took him to full smitten.

Now his work buddy Carr, the lone Water Wings salesman and the employee closest to Pierce's age of 26, looked back at the undersized showroom, saw a customer and had to step aside for Warrick on the forklift jockeying to match his rear hitch to the sailboat trailer's. "C'mon Pierce, who is it? I got somebody inside looking at a windsurfer and I'll take it; I sold nothing for 11 days," Carr said.

"I gave you—" Pierce started but remembering charades rules, silently repeated the hand turning move and when Carr said "key," Pierce gestured to draw more from him. Warrick, craning over his shoulder and seeing Pierce's hands past Carr, backed with impunity and, despite the bow being the strongest part of a sailboat, it cracked like an eggshell against the forklift's massive counterweight.

Warrick, a stocky kid who headed up the yard duties, jumped down. "What's with the c'mon back?" he yelled at Pierce, "like I had buckets of room."

"Key...Stone Kops?" laughed Carr.

"I wasn't signaling you, Warrick...and, no, Don *Qui*-xote," Pierce added to Carr.

"You're gonna have to fill this," Warrick said, putting a hand clear into the ragged hole. "You're gonna sweat your ass off inside there, layin' that fiberglass, suckin' those fumes, fibers get into your open pores, itch like crazy."

"No, I'm going to get lunch because CJ is God knows where. You back, you fill," Pierce said, feeling ad agency creative.

Carr was still chuckling. "Why didn't you just point to Warrick; he's the one thought he was tilting at a sea monster—"

"—lances ass-backward. You want the usual tuna melt?" Pierce said.

"Tell her daughter easy on the lard."

"This is gonna be your patch job, college crap!" Warrick said to Pierce, using a shared conversation against him. But he was on his way (*letgoandletgod*) to Caradimitropoulo's, the corner deli run by a plump Greek woman and her 30-ish retarded daughter whose main job was to apply the spreads to the sandwiches with the back of a wooden spoon, not being trusted now even with the metal butter knife (dropped earring, toaster, fire truck). Her mother, Marianna, would have to cut the slathering short at times and shoulder her to the old cash register where she would tap the keys with all fingers, say "50 cent 50 cent" and flick her tongue like a snake. Pierce always left enough on the counter and never asked for clarification.

The long sign above the awning was done in a finely-wrought calligraphy with gold lettering but was missing the apostrophe and "s" as, reaching up and over to paint the former, Marianna's husband—having perhaps moved the ladder enough for the day—shifted his center of gravity beyond the ladder's selling point and they pivoted to the sidewalk; though she had apparently always worn black. "Apostrophe"; from the Greek for "turning away" Pierce remembered from debating.

In the alley between her store and the neighboring duplex, Pierce saw four of the smallest Secore children—filthy and furtive as vermin—picking through Marianna's garbage cans. Making their three piles: had to be eaten now, could be dinner, could be an occasion. He had mentioned them a few times to Marianna but she welcomed the parasitic relationship and wished she could do more for those "orchins." She added "but in Greece you would weep. American garbage tops. McDonald's trash cans here even say 'thank you' on them."

The rest of the Secore clan—five more children—lived with their parents on a listing houseboat of patchwork plywood now with an anchor thrown up on an overgrown, trash-strewn vacant lot next to Ansel's Marina. Ownership of the lot was contested and lawyers tried, police tried, even the Coast Guard had pulled alongside with siren on—the kids a banshee backing chorus—but no one had the bottom-line authority to set them adrift. An eviscerated Evinrude lay on the deck next to a claw-footed bathtub too big for the doorway and Will, the father, would point to the outboard and assure any officials he was on his way as soon as he fixed it.

They would leave ceremoniously as though they had accomplished something and Will and clan would make a family picture, waving, then burst out laughing when once again clear. "I got a 120-horses Merc'ry stowed away," he had told Pierce one day. "How you think we pushed this box up from Savannah River in the Intracoastal Waterway? I wouldn't sully this boat with a Evinrude. I found this piece crap in the lot's tall grass and figured it was just the thing to show intent. The law's been using 'intent' on *me* all along; turnaround is fair play. But I'm not about to move. This the first place we ain't had our anchor pulled up and thowed rudely on board in three states. Plus, the widder likes the goat."

The family goat grazed on the lot and the "widow," one of the contentious owners, had made an on-site inspection when she saw a stray photo of it in the paper with the boat in the background. Will had helped her step over the ratty old tires ("that one's a Pirelli," he noted) serving as boat fenders to keep it from scraping the concrete seawall and quickly won her over. He asked her her name and she primly said, "Svetlana." "No," he gasped, "spell it." She officiously did and Will said, "That is crack-out-the-jug-*and*-cups amazin'; we named our boat after you!" She, flattered but wary, was led to the boat's stern. Will held her arm as she leaned over and saw "After You" in faded red duct tape. She ended up feeding her Tic Tacs to the goat, putting her hands up in surrender to its gentle butting when she ran out of them. She turned to Will, offered the same gesture before leaving and picked her way carefully across the lot.

Pierce had met Will the first morning the boat had anchored when he sauntered into the work yard wanting to trade a washing machine for a bilge pump. Pierce stopped assembling a trailer, took off his gloves—late spring was still cold for a long day outside—and wiped grease off a wrist. This was one of several mindless tasks here, like prep sanding a boat's bottom for anti-fouling paint (some were kept in the water) that subdued his free-floating axioms—shortcuts to "the way life's supposed to be"—exhorting him to follow his bliss, march to the beat of his own drum, let go and let God and on and on until they became a maelstrom. A close ex-college roommate had committed suicide and this maelstrom is what he had complained about. His note was etched in Pierce's memory: "If you can read this, you're too close. P.S. I could not make myself simpler."

Pierce led Will inside to discuss the trade with Slater. Will looked around appreciatively, approving perhaps his washer's adoptive home. He whistled shrilly and four of his boys near the front door struggled in from behind the shrubs with a chipped enamel wringer washer decades old and set it down heavily amidst the few boats on display on trailers, masts up but their limp sails negative advertising, Pierce always thought. Slater's wife, the stuffy office manager, actually wrinkled her nose at the odiferous group and Will picked at one son's ratty t-shirt: "Yep, you wouldn't think we could part with this warsher." Slater came out of his office and the two shook hands. He listened carefully to Will with his usual tilt of the head, as if discovering another dimension of you, but now he cast sidelong glances at the octopus of arms that roamed the office, latching onto the handout Hershey's kisses, brochures, pens. A customer who started in backed out as four boys ran scuffling at him toward the storage alcove with a snack machine. They started rocking and pummeling it to release its manna and Will reigned them in harshly: "Put all them geegaws back. This ain't a social call, it's business. Go on out."

Will stood back and let the washer dominate like it was a rogue monolith from "2001: A Space Odyssey."

"I can't use that," Slater said. "Could you get that out of here?"

"I'm sinkin' an inch a day. I got kids bailin', workin' harder than a packa piss-soaked matches from a nigger's pocket at a KKK burnin'—." Off Slater's wife's grunt of disgust, Will added "Well excuse me, ma'am, but that's just a back-home way of showin' you're comfortable with the comp'ny." She doubled down on her disgust. "Now you dint let me finish, cuz what makes it all, what, *PC*, is that we're the dumbasses that forgot to bring matches! Anyway Slater, I need your best pump. And my boys"—who now sat blocking the outside entrance and in fact the customer was driving off; Pierce began to see the choreography—"they're pretty tuckered. Prolly come back tomorrow fresh though take this off your hands."

Slater cut his losses and told Pierce to get a model 5620 off the wall. "It's manual," he told Will, "but it will pull five gallons a minute."

"Manual's fine," Will said, patting the washer. "We don't trust electricity; that's what comes off the devil's horns. Now let me show you how this works," and he started to take off his shirt.

"No no," said Slater and foisted Pierce's pump onto Will. "Part of the deal is you take it out of here."

Will whistled and the boys jumped up, came in and while they grabbed a leg apiece and drunk-walked it out the door, he asked Slater's wife what her name was.

"Jocelyn," she mumbled, not looking up from her papers.

"No! *Sloshin'?* We really named our boat after you!" He rolled some on his feet, took off his long-bill exfoliating fishing cap, scratched his gray straggly hair. Playing himself in his own movie, Pierce thought. "Wait," Will said. "How do y'all spell that in these parts?" and he winked himself out.

The washer made it to the far gutter where it was dropped with a crash. Will took out a lipstick tube and wrote "free to good home" on it. Pierce heard later it too had been found in the lot's tall grass, along with the bathtub.

Pierce had eaten half his sandwich walking back from Caradimitropoulo's before he reached the warehouse lunch room where Carr grabbed him. "The Potters are waiting inside for their demo sail," he said.

"They're not supposed to be here until one," Pierce said through a last, stuffed mouthful. He tossed the greasy bag to Carr who wisely stepped away and let it hit the cement. He looked inside, then used two fingers to toss it in the trash. "Jeez," he said, "you take Marianna upstairs and leave the daughter alone with the larding spoon?"

Pierce wiped his chin and greeted the couple standing next to the 16' daysailer they were interested in. Carr had told him they had never been sailing but had bought a summer cottage where the Potomac meets the Chesapeake Bay and wanted something "to 'potter' about in," stiffly pleased at their own pun. Mr. Potter worked a niche of the Social Security Administration in D.C.; "associate under assistant" something. He had on a button-down white shirt, sharply-creased khaki pants, was very clean cut, which did not keep his wife from constantly directing traffic on his being: the collar, the dandruff, the thread, the insect near his ear. Despite her slender, outdoorsy look, she was not as "pre-sold" on this concept as her husband. Indeed Pierce noticed his spanking new blue-and-white Top-Sider deck shoes; their choice of boat ironically having such a flimsy deck that Pierce knew how to straddle carefully to avoid buckling it ominously while teaching a new or would-be owner the ropes. She tended to address Pierce through her husband, making him feel their servant, and in voicing her reticence to counter her husband's enthusiasm, she told him to remind Pierce that all this still required Deidra's stamp of approval.

"Deidra?" Pierce said, checking the showroom.

"Our little girl," Potter said, cleaning his glasses before his wife's hand reached them. "She's at the marina; I parked there as Carr suggested so she wouldn't have far to walk. She, uh, lost a leg in an accident. We hoped sailing might be therapy for her."

"Some breeze in her face. She can't, you know, chase after the school bus the way she used to," Mrs. Potter managed to tell Pierce with downcast eyes.

For Pierce, who had crewed and skippered 40-footers in Annapolis-based races with Naval Academy competition at times, this plain vanilla 16' Puffer was an insult, a tub. Breeze in her face, indeed. He threw a *beherenow/letitgo* at her attitude, remembered his share of Carr's paltry commission if they bought, and ushered them toward Ansel's Marina.

"Beautiful day you picked, " Pierce said as they walked. "Do your bosses know you're out for a sail?"

"Oh no," Potter said. "I told my superior I was ill. I even walked out of the monthly tolerance seminar to make it believable; unwritten law no one's to walk out of those. That's why we were early. And Maggie here, she's got a little knitted baby toys business going in our basement."

"Oh dear," she said, "don't make more of it than it is. It's not like I import/export."

Mr. Potter struck a pose. "I always tell people interested in such potential foreign customer commerce-based interactions to go not into import/export but, rather, *export/import*. Less competition." He waited for Pierce's laugh, holding his in check, then gave up on his in the vacuum with a cough. Pierce was preoccupied, gauging the whitecaps on the sludgy Potomac. A Puffer with four people would be very

cramped and require attention to keep it "couch-like," Slater's imperative for getting newbies to buy: "Don't push 'thrills' with a family."

The bowl haircuts of a couple of the Secores were barely visible
above the grass in the lot next to the marina as they combed last
night's harvest of dumped items. Pierce waved to Mrs. Ansel, a spry
woman with sun-damaged skin who was gamely trying to keep the
business going since her husband's stroke left him sedentary. It was
a losing battle: It needed dredging, the pilings rocked, the planking
required a hopscotch or litigious mentality to negotiate.

They crossed the gravel parking lot toward the Potters' minivan
near the mossy boat ramp. There were a dozen small powerboats
squatly rocking, their mooring lines creaking the pilings. One of
them had sunk in its slip months ago and was now held by its lines
underwater, a ghostly spread-eagle Inquisitional victim.

"Look," said Maggie pointing to the dock. "There's a 'Zephyr.'
Oh, that was going to be our name."

Pierce was about to reassure her of its ubiquitous availability when
she suddenly tamped down the air a few times, a reminder not to
get ahead of herself. She opened the van's sliding door, stepped back,
put her hands in her pockets as though willfully refusing assistance.
A large head poked into the sunlight, a mass of blinking brown and
white fur now inching along the floor and ejecting itself awkwardly.
An adult St. Bernard. Three-legged, two front one rear. Saliva gob jaw
agape. A big shake to fluff is a mistake, sending her crumpling to the
gravel. The Potters abandoned their sang-froid and rushed to her side,
groaning with the lift, centering the back leg.

"Excuse me," Pierce said looking beyond them into the van, "but
I thought Deidra was your little girl; chasing the bus—, oh."

"And she is!" Maggie said, planting a noisy kiss between the foot-
wide eyes.

"But we can't take *that* on board!"

"Oh but she's very good about staying in one place," Mr. Potter said.

"And our decision," his wife added, with enough umbrage to directly address Pierce, "is based on her enjoyment. And she does love the water so, doesn't she Terrence. Oh the sticks she'd fetch from the pond...before...."

"Snapping turtle, the infection—" Potter started.

"No need to heap guilt on yourself, dear," she snipped.

"I wasn't, dear."

"Your long throws tired her—"

"Okay, *dear*."

"—and she couldn't fight off the turtle—"

"Okay *dear!*"

He reached into the van and pulled out a cap with at least captain's rank "scrambled eggs" embroidery on its bill and glared at her, then slid on new-looking wrap-around sunglasses. She brushed a nonexistent fly from his ear for parity.

Pierce thought, God, hadn't he kept this "break" job long enough? No guilt just to walk away; Slater hadn't invested in him, knowing his type wasn't going to stay menial. But Pierce yielded against his better judgment and said "well, if she lies down in one spot."

Potter locked the van and Pierce heard Mrs. Ansel talking sotto voce with her baggy-trousered handyman by the gas pump; they glanced again at this scene and both laughed, shook their heads. Here's big picture shoved in my face again, Pierce thought, suddenly regretting his acquiescence. More,—the maelstrom built—regretting all that had gotten him to here. No, that's not even enough: abnegating whatever hiccup in $E=mc^2$ was going to give him a future in this or a multiple universe. And complications were all he had, plucking the marionette master's strings: *march to the beat/it's the harder you don't try/middle path/let God/follow your bliss*...and remembered Follow

Your Bliss was the name of the tortured powerboat held underwater behind him. He threw back his head, eyes shut to the neutral sun: *"Memo to Self: Have relationship with Self. cc: Self"* came to him suddenly with a harsh bark of a laugh that even the dog turned to.

"Export/import," Pierce said, covering. "Just got it."

Water Wings' two demo sailboats, the Puffer and another model two feet longer, were at the end of the dock and even there, at low tide, they scraped bottom. Deidra had a pogo stick-like gait and the Potters steered her diligently down the funhouse planks, her wheezing heavily, bubbles popping at the mouth. Somebody—Will sunning himself, shirt off—rose up on the roof of the houseboat, took up binoculars to view the quartet, one now peeing awkwardly. Pierce moved away from the puddle and just caught a glimpse of a female, bare-breasted next to Will. I have to get these prescription sunglasses strengthened, Pierce thought, but then again all naked women reminded him of his girlfriend, the rationale for leaving Carr alone at the topless bar two nights ago.

There was a near-mishap as Deidra tried to hop over her pee and needed shoring by the Potters before she wobbled off the dock. When he looked back at the houseboat, all Pierce saw was the kids playing dangerous games (a hubcap Frisbee aimed toward one being held; dirt clod fights), the usual non-stop home schooling recess. Something gnawed at Pierce about the breasts as he remembered Will had tapped the sultry woman on the Pirelli pin-up calendar by the trailer parts shelving the day of the washer trade and said he had dreams for his daughter Belinda. Pierce had raised an eyebrow and Will said, "Oh yeh, and I ain't talkin' no 28-day month."

The Potters had not said a word to each other since mention of the turtle. This, plus maneuvering Deidra aboard (luckily the tide was very high and allowed an even step off the dock), then prepping the boat while dancing around the dog that took most of the cockpit area, distracted Pierce. The Potters had sat so they eerily mirrored the couple in one of the Puffer brochure photos—him at the tiller, her gazing at the horizon with hand shading eyes; even their clothing was a near match. Pierce was ready to sail out of the slip (the outboard engine had been stolen long before); he cast off the mooring lines, pushed off the near piling, sheeted in the mainsail and they were free.

As soon as he sheeted the tiny jib as well, a gust caught and heeled the boat sharply. Potter grabbed his cap, Maggie her chest and Pierce immediately eased the mainsheet and pushed the tiller over to adjust things back to "couch-like." He should have gotten out the life jackets before the dog blocked the cuddy cabin storage.

Maggie broke the ice. "That was quite a zephyr, dear." A wave slapped the bow and sent chilly spray over all. "Ooh, I got a frisson, Terrence. Did you?" He just wiped his glasses with a bandanna, squinted needlessly into a darkening sky.

No other boats were out at this weekday hour. After work some fishermen might go out to try their luck and indeed a catfish breeched nearby; "coming up for air" the anglers' rueful punchline about the pollution.

Pierce dispensed some sailing basics, checked the lowering clouds, decided to cut to the chase. "Mr. Potter, you might not be interested in racing right now"—this got his attention and he quit folding his bandanna—"but most owners find their skills accelerate by putting a boat through its competitive paces. One couple, your age, bought one of these a month ago and already has a trophy. Third place, but still." Pierce probably didn't need that last lie because Mr. Potter had a look in his eye that precluded any input from a dog. Even Maggie gave him an "oh Terrence you've already got the shelf. Just take those dusty Lionel locomotives to the consignment shop. Some child will—"

Potter held up a hand in disregard.

The toy-like bobbing, the low boom, and having to pick his way over Deidra made it awkward for Potter to squeeze next to Pierce. He put his hand on the tiller as instructed, matching Pierce's. "Now our hands dance," Pierce said, "I lead, you follow, to feel the changes in heading—. Whoop!" he said as a gust caught them and Pierce had to fight Potter's arm gone rigid. "That was a puff and when that happens, don't tighten up; you ease the mainsheet, except the dog is now tangled in it—my bad seamanship—or just push the tiller away from you and the boat heads into the wind and flattens out. Either one works. I'll be right here," and Pierce perched himself on the narrow strip of deck behind him.

Potter snugged his cap down, settled in.

"Now Terrence," she said. "I know that look."

"Just you hold on, Maggie. Let's see what this baby can do."

"Terrence."

"Kidding."

The dog moaned and rose quickly and Potter, in making room for her, didn't react to the gust. Pierce was looking over his shoulder at the front moving in and listening for thunder. The Puffer's quick heel nearly flipped him over backwards into the river as he yelled "push the tiller over!"

The dog was standing, gulping air, and there was no pushing the tiller past her. The boat kept heeling; Deidra slid, claws scraping and she threw up into Maggie, both going overboard, followed by Potter holding his hat. The mainsail scooped water and Pierce knew it was too late to recover. He was able to hold on and avoid full immersion but that became quickly moot when the boat "turned turtle," its mast now pointing straight down. He crawled onto the hull by holding the centerboard and looked around.

"Stay with the boat!" he yelled. "The boat has flotation." He swam off to round up three life jackets; a fourth had blown too far away. The water was already numbing his legs; he tensed to stop his teeth from chattering. "Put these on!" he said when he got back.

"Where's Deidra?" Maggie yelled, whipping around and knocking a jacket from Pierce's hand.

"She's there," he said. "Take this!"

The dog was perfectly camouflaged in the brown river with whitecaps. It looked like a crocodile, just flaring nostrils and eyes out of the water.

Potter had lost his sunglasses and captain's cap. "Where's *her* thingy?"

"It floated away," Pierce said.

"How do you know it was *hers*?"

"You two! Put those jackets on now."

"The boat's sinking!" Maggie shrieked.

"No," Pierce said treading around to see, "it has flo—" and he saw the hull washed over in increasing murk. He kicked it before it was gone from his reach.

They all put on vests. Deidra tried to climb on any jetsam; rag sweatshirt, ice chest lid, Puffer brochures which her pawing caused also to sink. "We're going to have to swim to the marina," Pierce said. "Nobody's out here." He talked over the distant thunder but saw their panic.

"Oh God, there's going to be lightning," Maggie said, "and we're in the water. Up to our fucking necks!"

"Deidra's struggling!" Potter said.

"We have to swim," Pierce said.

"It's her fur her fur," he said. "She won't make it; each on a leg each on a leg and push."

The Potters reached under her but it was Pierce the dog tried to climb on. He was scratched and swallowed a mouthful of foul water. He gagged as much of it up as he could. "Listen you two. You're going to die if you try a stunt like that. Already we've drifted away. I am going to swim and I want you to follow." Pierce began a breast stroke, the best way to make progress with the restrictive life vest.

"Maggie, where are you going?!"

"With him," she said. The first lightning sheeted behind the clouds giving the whitecaps a stroboscopic stagger.

"Don't you dare leave me alone with her. She needs us."

"That dog can either sink or swim," she said.

"I've read about this. If we make it, I'm taking her from you."

Pierce stopped, turned his back to the smacking waves. "Potter, cut the shit! This is no soap opera. Anyway, look." The dog had passed Potter unnoticed.

Pierce undid his belt, removed his shoes and pants, looked just to look at his dead cell phone for a message from Corinne. He and she, feeling their way through this raw, uncertain separation—encapsulated by her frustrated "F U future!" exit—had resorted to leaving messages when the other couldn't directly answer. These vapid "sorry I missed you"s crystallized for him now when he hit the functionless Send button and let the phone sink.

The stinging rain was even colder than the river but they swam steadily, occasionally mis-timing breaths and coughing up God knows what pestilence, Pierce thought, until Maggie's legs cramped: "I can't...I'm freezing."

"C'mon. Look how far we've come," Pierce said, another sales lie. The marina's swinging Gulf Oil sign was fractionally larger. "Mrs. Potter, we only have strength enough to save ourselves—"

"We're saved, we're saved!" she yelled.

"I've read about this too," Potter said. "Hypothermia hysteria. She'll feel hot and take off her clothes. Last stages last stages!"

"Shut up you jerk, we're saved!" she said and Pierce followed her finger, wiped his eyes. Between bobs he saw a rowboat being lowered from After You, a large and smaller Secore getting in. Lightning silhouetted the large one now rowing furiously; the other working harder with a bilge pump.

"I'm here! Help me!" she said into the maw of the wind, no way she was heard.

"*We're* here," Potter said. "Deidra and me. *That* we."

Incrementally the parties met. The rower shipped oars and drifted into their midst. The bailer had the model 5620 and was working it like a race car's piston, siphoning water in spurts over the side. The Potters grabbed the rowboat gunwales and tried to lift up but the rower smacked off their fingers and shoved their heads down.

"Keep out!" he said when they surfaced. "You caint just climb in. Me and Twerp barely sank ourselves. Just hold onto the edge and I'll row you back."

"What about Deidra?" Potter said. "Can't we put her in?"

"Can you handle it?" the rower said. Twerp smiled back at his brother and Pierce saw the bad teeth that were a Secore hallmark. "Molasses-soaked rag pacifiers," Will had told Pierce one day at the marina, explaining his own false teeth. "Wordsworth—yeh I know my poets—says 'child is father to the man' and as I was raised there ya go for my kids. Though it was the wife, this's back in our trailer days, come up with the cavity-free substitute for the outta-control bawlin' ones—holdem over the stove with the pilot blowed out." Pierce shook his head in disbelief and Will said, "oh don't fret; just a dose and they'd nod right off. Anyway, we're all Dr. Spock now, what with Community Services showin' intent, visitin' regular. That sneak photo of the goat and boat in the paper didn't help none, put us on their goody-good map. We ain't in 'plight'; bite me."

"I guess so," Twerp said, water running off his quivering chin. "Get in lady."

"Not the lady," said Pierce. "That." Pointing to help them spot the dog.

"Jeez, that's a bigun," the rower said. "We gonna sink if you're feelin' puny."

"Shit," said Twerp, who couldn't have been more than ten. "Pops said you folks was sartin fools and I share that. Put him outta my way. I got to be a blur."

The dog was dead weight. It took a few tries; the Potters counterbalanced the rowboat as Pierce dove under and pushed while the boys pulled. Twerp grabbed the handy ears first, eliciting a tired woof of objection. He checked the solo back leg as she flopped like a played fish onto the flooded floor. "What'd I tell you Gatlin," he said. "Pay up when we get back. There is teeth creatures in this river."

But for Twerp's winded, mantric cursing and the creak of the oarlocks, plus the elements, it was a silent ride. Maggie tried resting her head on her clinging white fingers but that exacerbated the nausea. Potter put his arm around her to help ease her shaking to no effect. The front had luckily moved through with no more lightning; it wouldn't have needed to be very close. Pierce had had a bolt strike near him sailing in the Chesapeake Bay—a huge inverted Hiroshima blast into the black water hundreds of yards across that lingered before dying out. He wanted to help the straining rower by kicking but he had nothing to give; the river had fused with his lower body. Lost Carr's sale, lost a boat, nearly lost lives—what if two preservers had blown away—and a big picture tried to focus through his fatigue. He put his face in the water to ward it off and imagined he was Houdini escaping.

The Secores mustered on their stern deck, Will dancing a buck-and-wing and yelling encouragement. The rowboat bumped hard; Gatlin was on automatic with his back turned and Will said "mind the finish!" and cackled. The only covering on the houseboat's plywood was green slime, barnacles, and a NASCAR bumper sticker. Gatlin slumped and checked his bleeding hands, then put one on Twerp's shoulder and he, too, ceased. The rowboat filled less quickly once those two stepped off. Mrs. Potter's weakly swaying arm was grabbed and her soddenness rose with her. Mr. Potter, then Pierce were lifted by viselike hands; his briefs slid to his thighs and there was tittering. Mrs. Potter turned too quickly away from the sight and fainted, caught by two tomboy girls—these were all sinewy, strong kids.

Pierce saw a woman with unkempt gray-and-white hair, a gentle face with a bemused smile—Will's wife, he guessed—looking out a paneless window near the bow. He pulled his underwear up and sat next to Potter. Deidra, lying down, was just keeping her head above water in the rowboat when Will and three boys stepped onto the thwarts. The leak now burbled up under the weight; they lifted the dog, gained purchase and balance, then rolled her onto the houseboat. The rowboat sunk under them as they stepped off, shaking their wet legs.

"We'll pull it up later," Will said. "Lena, run tell Ma we got company. Caleb, draw some water (Pierce wondered vaguely from where since there was no shore power electricity either) and Pecky don't just stand there, grab some blankets for drapin.'"

Three thin American Airlines blankets—more the size of shawls—were placed over the trio's shoulders. Will ushered them inside the sliding glass door and the background Potomac smell yielded to this one. Mrs. Potter gagged violently, covered her nose, and Will gave her a look and headed back out. The one room had a curtained off corner, no furniture but for a couple of folding chairs and card table, mattresses and covers scattered about the mold-snaked plywood floor. Fishing rods were propped in a tangle by the propane

WHERE I'M CRAWLING FROM

camping stove on the counter; the freestanding dented stainless sink drained to a bucket. There was, incongruously, a newish Culligan water dispenser that looked like the one missing from Water Wings' warehouse. Pierce figured they just filled the water bottle from a dock hose. Two doorless cupboards held a rainbow of bowls and plastic glasses amidst canned food.

Pierce started breathing through his nose to avoid the smell of dank decay. He could see chinks of daylight all around the walls. Gnats backlit were hovering over a pile of loose potatoes near the sliding door, a poster of Jesus in his seamless robe above them with his emanating rays merging with the chinks', his arms beneficently spread offering more infested potatoes.

Will's wife gestured for them to sit, primed and lit the camping stove. Will struggled in carrying the dog and set her on a mattress.

"Cripes," he said holding his back, "that sumbitch is a anvil." Twerp and Gatlin came in shivering, sharing a Hilton Hotel bath towel. "You pay your brother," Will said pointing to the dog. "Twerp were right about them teeth creatures" and he winked at Pierce.

"Maybe he's inna fight and the other thing's dead," Gatlin said.

"No," said Potter. "It was an accident."

"Nobody's fault," his wife offered weakly and got a weak smile back from her husband.

"This your boy?" Will said to Potter of Pierce.

"No."

"Dint think so. Little big for your blood. Unless the best part of you dribbled down your wife's leg during the monkey jumpin'. Now Varnie, that water on the boil?"

She shook her head without turning to him. Her gray shift and mismatched bright flip-flops. Pierce couldn't get over the softness to her face, its symmetry not common among her children's faces, her smile that imputed a come hither look gone by; a minor crowning for her way back when, perhaps, during a rustic tryst as someone's Feedlot Princess. What on earth had she given up for the promise of this life, he wondered.

"You kids all scoot," Will said, "ceptin' Gatlin and Twerp. Go on, scout that grass for night crawlers. We got parlayin' to do with the fishermen round here."

They exited reluctantly, sneaking superior smirks at the unfortunate sailors.

"You want coffee too, Will?" Varnie said, spooning instant into cups.

"Yes but hurry up and get them theirs. They're shiverin' like hot owl shit."

Mrs. Potter looked up. "That's twice you've been uncivil—"

"They may do it to us out *there*," he said sharply. "You're in *my* home. You don't hold your nose and retch like a sick cat! Not in my home!"

"Will—." Varnie handed the first cup to Pierce and when she bent over, he saw her full breasts hanging free, black pubic void. She handed the next cup to Potter and he too looked, set the cup down, coughed.

"Oh," Varnie said. "Would you like milk in that?"

"I would," said Potter quickly, wiping his regular glasses for something to do. "Yes, that would be…please."

"Wind's still strong out there, no?" Will said to his boys and they nodded.

"My manners, my manners," Varnie said. "Be right back."

"You're lucky I was on the roof grabbin' the last bit of sun," Will said. "Otherwise nobody'd seed you go belly up." He put a finger in his mouth and popped it out four times, ostensibly four bubbles drowning. Pierce felt the choreography coming on; he had to respect this redneck with savvy homespun ways, crude talk with Wordsworth thrown in. Somehow he kept this string-for-shoelaces clan together. The older kids certainly could have run away; wherever they anchored—certainly Alexandria, even this seedy section—would have enticed them and likely afforded subsistence. What sententious aphorisms has he triaged (the way I have, Pierce thought, when one of mine is too wounded to carry any weight) along the way to grace him with a core belief in his own persona? Or was it even cerebral (and now Pierce felt jealous; if guys like Will "dint need no shrink; you just gotta bottom out bootstraps-wise") for this hick; was he somehow atavistically ever-present—*was a caveman ever not there now?*—

—*the part a caveman doesn't understand is still the Buddha; there is no other*—

—*let*—

—*now is the first nanosecond of ok on out*—

—*be your own crying shoulder*—

—*cherish*—

—*zeroes and ones*—

—*hey*— Pierce gently cocked an ear: —*"Didn't you get the memo?"* And the clench of his teeth came from the shivering but also from a surge of adrenaline; he had bottomed out, damn it.

—*then again*— as Varnie re-entered leading a black-and-white goat. The dog growled, more a soggy breath.

"Oh my," said Potter as Varnie took the cup from his hand.

"You did say milk?" she said and Pierce was sure she felt no irony in her role as hostess.

"Of course he did, woman," Will said. "Don't interrupt my flow."

She held the cup under the goat's udder and started a rolling squeeze. "A lot or a tetch?"

"A tetch…a touch," said Potter grabbing at straws. "Just the teeni-est…oh that's way too much."

"You want sugar with that?"

"God no!" he said, pushing the goat from his shirt. "I mean, no, thank you. No sugar."

She handed him the cup. "You two?"

"Black."

"Black."

"Twerp, fetch Pepper outside before she gets into somethin'," Varnie said.

"He stays. Let her roam," Will said. He put his arms around the boys. "Mighty proud I am. Gatlin, I believe you coulda rowed all day."

"Well my hands was—"

"—but it were dangerous out there. And Twerp, you coulda bailed all day."

"I guess so, but my neck cricked—"

"—but it were dangerous out there."

"Will," Pierce said, catching on, "I can patch that leak in the rowboat, make it good as new."

"That'd be fine." Will looked expectantly at Potter, who took an obliging sip of coffee.

"How about that watch? Still workin'?" Will said.

Potter took it off, shook it and water dripped out. "No, it was cheap—"

"Those army khakis kinda ruint, ain't they?"

"Certainly are."

"How about givin' them to me?"

"What?!"

"With cash money in the pocket. Always useful."

"What are you talking about?"

"Mister, what the hell you think I'm talkin' about? I'm talkin' about compensation for sendin' my boys to haul your ass outta the drink."

"Of the drink?"

"Of the drink. Compensation."

"Compensation?" He put the coffee down with a shaking hand.

"You applyin' for a job with the Grand fuckin' Canyon as a echo? Compensation, yeh," Will said.

"I…I wouldn't have asked you for compen—"

"You'dve gone nowhere near that river to save me, don't pull you own leg. You're damn lucky I was here; you'da drowned. At least your dog woulda."

"Give him something," Pierce said.

"My wallet's in the van." Potter looked at his wife, who nodded.

"He didn't want to get it wet," she said.

"I'll go get it," and Potter stood.

Will moved to him. "No you don't. I'll just take the khakis."

"My van is right over—"

"I say no."

"Are you *crazy*—. I mean, it's the light blue one right over there. I'll leave my wife and dog here."

Will snorted. "*Leave* is right."

Potter firmed up. "I'm not going to *leave* them leave them."

"Rado Parker," Will said. "When I was 19 I was gonna beat him senseless but he walked his wife and dog to my trailer, said 'stay' to both while he went next county over to his uncle's for what he owed me for splittin' his wood. Well dint he never pay plus they both run away—not back to him—so deal was done far as he's concerned. Now Shakespeare says a man's only as smart as as many times as he makes a mistake over. You callin' me dumb?"

"You said yourself," said Varnie, "Rado was peculiar, prolly a homo saper. Pooh poohed the Bible on that count many a time. Wife's no collateral to a homo saper."

"True. Then again, he might just've had a case of the outsmarts," Will said. "Now Potter, I got a good wife, and Pepper would back that cripple of yours down a sinkhole in a mole dick second."

"Give him the pants," Maggie said wearily.

"What am I going to wear to the car?"

"Nothin'," Will said. "Part of the deal. You stirred me."

Potter disrobed under scrutiny. Pierce saw Maggie reach for his hand to steady him pulling the clingy pants legs past his new Topsiders he didn't want to remove for fear of having them taken as well. Little while ago she was leaving him in her wake. Now she whispers she loves him and later she'll say the pants were ruined and nobody noticed your burgee pattern boxer shorts. The banished couple rallied their dog and to the snickers of the kids, they stepped to shore, Gatlin and Twerp giving Deidra a leg up over the gap.

Will wrung water from the trousers, shook them out.

"Vest woulda been nice," he said.

"Somethin' in a red," Varnie said. "Go with your cap."

"I'll be over soon to fix that rowboat," Pierce said. "I better go tell my boss what happened."

"I bet you're wonderin' why I was petty and took his pants."

"Not really."

"So he knew we was equals. Whatever twisty story he tells on out, we'll be equals in his mind. Hell, I'dve saved you all regardless."

"I know that."

"Shit, son. I couldn't let you drown out there. Shakespeare says when you see your brother in trouble, extend a hand. Then ask for coin."

Pierce laughed. "Can I borrow the blanket?"

"Keep it. Somebody keeps thowin' a bundle every week or so into the lot, I guess for us. By the time we bring them in, about three Pepper ain't sampled to scraps."

Pierce was trying to it knot it around his waist and when he looked up, Corinne was standing by the wall.

"That ladder's a little loose coming down—" she said and saw Pierce. "My god."

He was smitten all wrong, knees gone weaker. "I sent you a message—" all he could manage, thinking of his sunken phone.

"You two know each other?" Will said.

"I could say that about you two," Pierce said and sat on the wet mattress the dog had used, feeling an uncharted part of himself had been amputated.

Now the babble from the duo was a bull rushing him; Pierce shook his head, wondering what the goring would feel like—

— the free dental clinic I volunteer at
— just up the hill
— in came three boys and Will
— Fettle had this abscess thing like a mouth fulla chestnuts
— carrying in an old washer with smeared lipstick on it to barter
— she said they all three needed work and, who even knew about gums disease
— he said all told he had nine but no way he'd let me treat them, against the Lord's plan, only reason he brought this one was the bawling and he was too big and squirmy to hold over the propane gas or some lunacy
— gave her a proposition, she comes to the boat we play doctor strip poker, she wins she plays doctor, I win and I play doctor
— well he wasn't going to win because I loaded my hair with bobby pins
— I hadda cheat so hard, false shuffle, second card deal just to get her top off
— we played until the storm and he quit, saying he had to deal with a river incident
— I took my binos, set the boys loose, kept an eye out

— I put my glasses and top back on, Fettle came up
— nothin' I could do out there if Jesus chose
— I started cleaning, best light was up top, under a tarp thing

Pierce looked at his cold coffee.

"I could heat that," Varnie said.

"From the look in her eye, I'll bet *she* could heat it," Will said of Corinne, who had put a hand on Pierce's shoulder. "Well ain't all's well that ends well. My granddaddy said he woke one mornin' with a cravin' for fried chicken and women and knew the Lord had called on him to preach. I guess I got a tetch of him in me, bringin' these two together."

"We were together…uh already," Corinne said, rising. "I…I am so late for my appointments." She stepped toward for the sliding glass door and a girl in a tank top came from behind the curtain and cut her off, leveling the shotgun. She was backlit, long brown hair a nimbus like Jesus's on the wall next to her. She kicked at a soft potato and the top half came off on her shoe; Pierce didn't like the imagery. He saw that she was the pretty eldest girl, about 16, he had caught once stealing nickel deposit empties by the warehouse Coke machine.

"Now Belinda," Will said. "That gun is primed for muskrat and low-strollin' Negro."

"I saw you on the roof. Comin' back early from the libary. Horses don't have druthers!"

"Darlin'," said Varnie and the shotgun swung around.

"Stay out!" Belinda said. "You *been* out all along!"

Pierce rose off the mattress shielding Corinne. "No," the girl said, "she stands by him," and poked Corinne with the barrel toward Will.

Will had no backpocket savvy for this, Pierce saw, his distress making him look furtively around, checking his life for loopholes. Belinda squinted, turned and fired one barrel at the poster of Jesus, splintering plywood and spattering light from the outside.

"*He* don't dwell in this house of sin," she said, then patted her belly. "One other thing in the libary books. I am *pregnant*. I got the devil's child."

"Gimme my gun," Will said and yelled at the kids now looking in from the stern deck to scram.

"I'll cut you cards for it," Belinda said. "Or you wanna *woo* me, take your time gettin' me naked with strip poker?"

Varnie looked at Will, her mouth open. "Belinda, I dint know—"

"Well you shoulda," her daughter said. "Under your nose, him on the roof, workin' his hand up my leg toward my sluicy, one time tellin' me the parts of a horse: fetlock, hock, *druthers*." She stepped to Will. "Havin' your fun. Then you got the crinkly balls to tell this one," and she shook the barrel at Corinne, "*she's* got alabastard breasts. Those were mine; I was the one you had calendar dreams for."

"I never said—," Will tried.

"I *heard* you. I snuck back in and got behind the curtain. It was so easy catchin' you, you all cocked up." She was near tears. Pierce saw a chance to tackle her but she stepped to the boat's side.

"I waited, wanted to see how this rescue played out," she said, "if there was any cash I could take offa you. I'll be eatin' for two, the books say, where I'm goin'. Nuh uh, no way I'm stayin'."

"But dear," Varnie said, "you got a home—"

"I'm gonna ruin *all* of it," Belinda said. "'After You' is *nothin'*." She shoved the barrel into a gap in the floor and fired, blowing a hole below the waterline. The brown river started climbing aboard. Twerp, who had lingered outside, ran in yelling "that's her two shots" and grabbed the gun, ran back outside and came in with the bilge pump but saw the futility.

Pierce told Corinne to leave fast and they mimed calling each other with worried nods. Varnie hugged her daughter long and hard; the water reached their feet and they headed out herding the onlookers with them to the lot.

"She's going down fast," Pierce said seeing the angle to the shore shift, the shadows change, the water climb to Jesus's feet. Then even he began to sink.

"Not built for Shakespeare's drama," Will said and Pierce, seeing his crestfallen look, didn't know if he meant his boat, his daughter, or himself. He rallied, smacked his thigh: "Well you're off the hook patchin' the rowboat. Go ahead, you gotta abandon her afore I do."

The sirens wound closer and the first police car billowed dust sliding into the marina, obscuring the second and the TV van following. The cops ran over, guns drawn, but sorted it out quickly, telling Will he had to come with them for illegal firearms possession and discharge; he had taken the blame. He asked for a minute to watch with his family the undignified sinking into three feet of water. "You kids have a indoor pool," he said to the stoic bunch.

The reporter and cameraman were trying to get something on record but Will just smiled grimly as he started past. Then Fettle stuck out a dirty hand and a jar with a few worms. Will chucked his still-swollen jaw with his cuffed hands then took the jar, held it up to the camera: "Secore's night crawlers, best money can buy. As seen on TV."

Pierce answered police questions, left contact information, and walked barefoot to the bus stop in an American Airlines sarong he had to hold closed; he figured his look alone would get him a free fare. He'd call Slater in a while and explain. But first, he'd wallow in this clearheadedness, this imperative—this *simplification,* thinking of his ex-roommate's last note.

After you is nothin'.

Maybe You're There

The first sign was right before the rust-streaked gate on the dirt road there for no reason as she could just skirt either side. She waited, though, and it opened electronically with spasms after the closed circuit surveillance camera on a pole gyred amateurishly around and finally found the low-slung sports car. But it wasn't until the second, about 1/10th of a mile beyond the gate and nearly identical in every aspect—spindly-legged, knee-high, white script painted by hand on plywood ("Maybe you're there")—that she remembered the Burma-Shave signs on the hick highway just before her parents would pull up to an Ocean View, Virginia, bungalow ("Breeze-cooled!" over the usual "Vacancy" sign) each summer for their chintzy two-week vacation.

Her jaded cousin Althee, whose divorced mom got the trailer not far from the water, never wanted to go to the only lively thing there for 12-year-olds; the amusement park with its ancient roller coaster, wooden scaffolding like vertical pick-up sticks. It swayed noticeably from a ground's eye view when the cars took the tight top turn after the initial drop, clattering like un-oiled bearings were grinding their teeth. She always thought it was ironically named "The Hurricane" because of this sad, ghostly sway and otherworldly creaks mixing with kids' shrieks, with all of its windage reeling as though from the gusts of one of the "big ones" well before they started naming them. Of course Althee would label "ironically" one of those "Yankee words," like "soda" for "pop" or "colored" for "coon."

The drizzle was just enough for her to turn the wipers on and off manually; there was no fancy intermittent setting for a car this old. There was no CD player, of course, and the AM radio now only received a Christian station that was so clear compared to the rest of the static it had to be nearby, likely some two-room cinder block building with an "all-Jesus-all-the-time" format.

Then the third sign, "Maybe you're there." There were two more equidistantly placed with the last one under the homemade-looking porte-cochere. She drew on unpleasant snippets of amusement park to override an incipient panic attack—using distant, faded, discomfort to supplant that more immediate—now that she had arrived, actualizing her rash decision. She grabbed at the blueish drowned man, no shoes no shirt, pulled from the leftover storm's pebble-chocked big waves as she soared in the Galactic Whirl above the Midway's rubber-neckers, interrupting their sucker games of "skill" to watch the EMTs carry the uncovered stretcher past. The Whirl was best at night, our bodies untethered (no seat restraints back then) inside shiny sheet metal open space ships more like Cadillac convertibles, with red seats, huge fins and single yellow and blue bulbs blinking out of sync on each prow (how un-sci fi, even then). All the ships tugged at cables as the necklace of them twirled through the wind, and each time around the waiting ambulance's rooftop pimple red light was a streak in her tearing eyes. She grabbed at the dirty swabbie's hat with RIP in black letters nailed to a low crossbeam on The Hurricane as a reminder not to stand up during the ride. She grabbed at the power outage while riding the House of Horror teacups, having to walk out, tripping on greasy rails in the black, landing in eons of oily funhouse debris, sending thematic rats scurrying…and these thoughts drifted her back to simple unease.

Her hyperventilating had clouded the windshield and she turned up the meager defrost. "*This* is why you've come, this distress," she said, shaking her head in the car's mirror. She remembered her friend's take on her recent weekend retreat here: "My brain, guru told me, 'is like the skull was lifted, revealing all the snakes, and then red pepper was shaken on them.' And now, snakes in there, sure, but asleep in the sun." "Well that's my brain too," Evelyn had told her, "but I can't help holding a magnifying glass to the snakes."

She hadn't told her friend in Seattle she was going to visit. It had come down to a harsh, private acceptance that her daily life—with no anchor to it, human or otherwise, notwithstanding the first gulp of morning coffee imbued with a caffeine snap that this day might posit who knows what—was now aimlessly encapsulated into a 30-minute TV show called "The Conjecture Hour." "Hello again, I'm your host Evelyn Beech and I'm often asked about the discrepancy between the name and length of the show. I say *hmmm, tautological conjecture, perfect.* Next, how do ants sleep packed in the colony? If one has restless leg syndrome are they all kept awake? *hmmm, perfect.* Does the Russian army have the equivalent of our alliterative 'shit, shower, and shave'? Something like 'drekashinski, dryblyatzoff, drabowvilli'? *hmmm, perfect.* Do one-armed people say 'three fingers wash the other two?' *hmmm, perfect.* Why do they say 'if you see the Buddha on the road, kill him'? *Oh, I know that one. Just kidding. We're out of time.*"

Her back was starting to spasm from the cramped seat; her Volvo was in the shop. She was two decades too old for this "Cuban whore red" MGB her father had called it. He had traded in his Chrysler LeBaron, traded Mom for a perky nudist girlfriend, and literally topped off his late mid-life crisis with ugly, raw hair plugs. His sudden coma, suspicious to all but the authorities, had left her, the only close relative, with the MGB and a two-fold decision whether to pull the plug(s) to prepare for the open casket viewing.

She was still slender, had no stretch marks to go along with the no children, and only occasionally needed a touch up to her graying hair. She had promised herself she'd never yield to what she called Hollywood Zen: the ability to "empty the mirror" not as a Zen step toward enlightenment but, rather, delusional vanity—emptying the mirror by becoming the "after" in your plastic surgery procedure. And she was *certain* she would never opt for the apocalyptic die job that looked like the colorist had poured black enamel paint on your hair. Her mother got one of those every other month at the rest home.

Physically, knew she wouldn't feel at a competitive loss this weekend if there were yoga classes ("competitive? check that karma, darling," she told herself), though her friend had said the guru considered yoga postures "slow-motion slapstick." Any attempt to get more details about her visit went for naught and when Evelyn finally said "so it's a cult with skull-drunk blood oaths" all she got back was "I don't know what happened. I was overwhelmed; in fact, I nearly fainted on the porch soon after meeting him; he just *knew* stuff. They helped me to my car and I left that day. They yelled 'good-bye number 17!'" Her newly-serene look was such an abrupt change that Evelyn would have attributed it to snuck, quickie, Botox injections but for her friend's phobia about needles, inexplicably tied to her chewing half a splintered green toothbrush in her Mexican restaurant entree. ("It was dark and I thought it was celery. The handle half, thankfully," she had told her as though only the bristles half would have kicked in a lawsuit.)

Despite the ivied porte-cochere, which she now saw had a painted plywood roof dripping where poorly joined, the run-down house held no imputation of amenities, possibly including plumbing as she saw an outhouse in back. She squinted to catch movement against the tree line; a milky shape floating in the mist, a pale box kite lolling against a string that led in past the outhouse door.

She was startled by a mostly-bald man trundling his bulk awkwardly out the door, putting on a thin green vest over a flannel shirt, tightly belted pants cinched low, like holding back the dam of his pot belly. He looked like he could be leading drinking songs at Oktoberfest in the old country. He told her to leave it running just as she turned the car off.

"Damn, I said—," and he slumped. "These English cars don't start worth a butt fuck in the damp. Like Jaguars. I had one, walnut dash, practically gave it away. Brits should have known, most cats hate water; call them Junkers. I'll bring your bag."

She was too tired to fight herself; the long drive, the poor directions that had her ticking off unmarked railroad crossings she had gotten off the most rudimentary web site—kc.org. Not much more than a home page with a blinking "17—the number of people who have lived after visiting." Her friend had assured her not to be put off by that or, indeed, the lack of any business protocol. The repetitive desolation into the high plains three hours east of Seattle—past the Cascade Mountains where the drizzle had become icy on the passes— had almost caused her to turn back.

She got out of the low seat with difficulty, her skirt riding up enough to draw the man's creepy rosy-cheeked leer; her father's look a couple of times when she squirmed out of his grip off his drunken lap. She drew the skirt down, meeting his gaze. "Look," she said in a stilted manner, sliding easily into a full backstory. "Has been long day already and I don't appreciate? yes?"—her English was adequate, having been a librarian in East Germany. When the Berlin wall came down, she got her hopes up but when she read her file kept by the Stasi secret police under the unified country's new "sunshine" policy, she left her husband of four years. She told him when the taxi to the airport arrived (she had said almost nothing to him for a month since the discovery of his being paid to inform on her), "Of course I knew a Holden Caulfield. I'm a *librarian*. If you got a bonus for revealing that subversion, this country is sicker than I thought."

"Such language," she said to the man approaching the car door, straightening his vest; he took a mincy step back.

"Excuse me, you don't have *those* where you come from?"

"Of course we do," she said still in character, "we're no peasants. But we borrow of Czech word—*lomcovák*. Means 'sudden headache.' About as romantic as 'butt fuck,' no?"

He smiled with tobacco-stained but fine teeth and nodded for her sake to the fifth sign as he got in the car with surprising grace considering his size. He handed up her pocketbook, ground the gears, jolted forward, stalled. It took a few tries to catch, him nodding accusingly at her in time to the cranking.

She started another backstory and imagined he was once quite trim and fit—had been a back-loader at the circus, the euphemism for the guy with the broom and folding dustbin who punctiliously cleaned up after the performing elephants, horses, bears, dogs. His breach was trying to clean up Yamba's mess right outside the cage which threw off the tiger's concentration on the burning hoop and he went around instead of jumping through. His excuse to Gunter, big cat tamer and part owner, was flimsy and Gunter scoffed, "you can't *sneak up* on a tiger. You're history." He took out Gunter's firing with a hard kick to the back leg of the tamer's wife's star waltzing poodle, Primo.

She saw him park nearby so she waited, checking around the side for the box kite but, now with little breeze, it was gone. She guessed it landed in the high grass that stretched primitively—no telephone or power lines, no houses or farm animals despite some strung wire fencing. She knew for the last hour she had no cell phone coverage but she checked again, pushing her writer's notebook aside in her purse. She was a script doctor with, as she liked to add, a specialty in "back-story surgery." She was able to work as a freelancer (with occasional flights to LA) mainly over the phone—and extemporaneously if need be for a director thinking of adding a character or twist on the fly on the set. She could whip off two-three mini-bios based on the barest details. Joel Coen had called: "Evelyn, he's got to be a fat-ass since I'm going to have him—this is killer—he's going to get stuck head down and die breaking into a mob restaurant through the grease duct on the roof. Why was he there? Did he have a phone; did he hear something? Play with the greaser angle. Call me right back."

It unnerved her that she was unable to slide into that "fourth dimension," she called it, about the kite operator inside the outhouse. There had been odder vignettes to delve back in time for. Peter Farrelly had called: "Need this by the afternoon: particulars about Gina reversing a sex change operation she just got last week that turned her into Gino because *now* he wants to be the number one girl again in her old gig, a Saudi prince's harem. Work the 'getting her slot' back angle." Quentin Tarantino had called: "Evelynhowareyoudon'tanswer, need it post haste: why would the priest's double cross have to happen during the funeral of the wrong twin? Work the double, the double, the cross, the cross and a beginner thereminist trying to play 'Amazing Grace' angles."

TV gave her additional work explaining an egregious incongruity ("jumping the shark" in the industry) that was used to bolster sagging ratings. She was paid decently (when the director remembered the conversation!) but was creatively stymied since most of her ideas were tossed as costly or time-consuming or unnecessary when the director, or more likely the dollar-watching producer, remembered H.L. Mencken's "nobody ever went broke underestimating the intelligence of the American public." And she never got a screen credit; not even in the list of "Special thanks to...." She was ostracized by the real screenwriters who wanted no part of her and called her a "quickie brain fuck" at best.

The valet returned with her overnight bag and offered a meaty hand. "*Gas*ton. Not 'Gas-*tone*,' I don't know how many times I have to say it."

"Jitka," she said, slight roll to her "k" for some reason.

"No. You're still number 18 pending. Let's get you settled," and he held the door for her, then put the bag down in the foyer rubbing his hands from the chill, all host now. She already wasn't sure she would spend the night. Firstly, there had been no payment extracted or written confirmation of anything. There was no reception desk; no sense of this being a business. A regal black standard poodle walked down the stairs and confronted her as the thick smell and taste of ash in the air caught up to her. She coughed and sneezed in a fit so severe she realized she had been parsing her breath for minutes from anxiety.

"Only the truth!" Gaston said sharply. "Once you step through that door, only the truth! You can't be allergic to a poodle; hair not fur, so no dander. You have scissors where you come from?" She nodded, stifling her cough. "So fucking cut it out."

"It's the ash."

"We have fireplaces in every room. That's the heat. We try to keep everybody from shivering." He raised his hand quickly and grunted and the poodle instantly dropped its regal stance and slunk away, looking over its shoulder. "See. No shiver."

The ash was lighter as she ascended the stairs and she was able to blink away some irritation. His bulk swayed oddly as he carried her light bag and she now noticed his gimpy leg. Gunter's circus goons had gotten payback for him kicking the waltzing poodle.

He waved to the bathroom off the landing then, remembering, turned back to it. "Of course, my manners, women want to see how their ablutions will go."

"Why you have—how you say—night soil? outhouse? when you have this?" she said, pointing to the toilet with her shoe.

"Come come, Miss Jitka. *We're* not peasants. There are even rare books downstairs that haven't had their pages cut." He pulled out a switchblade and the blade snapped open just as it cleared his pocket. He sawed the air carefully as if splitting pages: "First edition, 'Crime'..." and with a fillip at the "top" of the page, "...'and Punishment.' Of course, once you use the knife, 'elle n'est plus vierge'; she is no longer a virgin." He folded it back into his pocket.

No, he was in the circus but an aerialist and had started an affair with their catcher's wife, all part of The Intrepid Trapeze Trio. Fooling around in practice when her husband was elsewhere, she'd slip the crotch of her spangly red leotard aside while swinging from her knees as Gaston, standing on the bar, pumped and filled the tent with beer drinking songs from the old country. She could be as flirty as she wanted; no one from below could see. One night Gaston's twisty fall (caused when one arm is let go by the catcher before the other) broke both his legs. Their act dissolved—she accused her husband of dropping him purposefully—and Gaston rushed into knife throwing to stay with the circus and keep close to the wife. With his atrophied leg muscles, he had to sit close to her as she spun spread-eagle in that spangly leotard while strapped on the wheel target. He was wearing a see-though "blindfold" hood and clumsily more or less stabbed knives around the whirling woman. Talked into it, Gunter had given him a sparse matinee audience to try it out and said after that performance, "people should not titter at 'death-defying.' You're history."

She had expected the bathroom to have the same dilapidated character as the living room with its water-stained ceiling, lightbulb-less chandelier (there must be a generator since the ochre-tasseled figurine table lamps there had been on). And one glimpse of the kitchen had been sufficient: stained porcelain sink, avocado cabinets against salmon walls, colors from the 50's. The poodle was standing tall at the sink lapping at the faucet drip. She thought Tarantino would want the dog's penis out for the tableau and started reeling back the miles to when she last saw a place to stay overnight.

There was a jury-rigged shower curtain inside the tub, suspended from a ceiling ring; a hose to hold from the faucet. The medicine chest was empty and clean and a spotless glass sat on a doily next to the cold water faucet. The wallpaper was a pink and pale blue confetti of tiny poodles, with red blips of tongue as they ran in a thousand directions; "chiens dans le parc" in crimped brown script threaded throughout, like sticks they were chasing. Despite the disconnect due to a lack of benches, flowers, grass, trees, people, it was the first whimsy this house had offered. It distracted her enough that the bolt on the outside of the hall door Gaston led her to didn't really register. He set down her bag: "I have you in here."

He slid the bolt quietly and as the door opened she saw a half-dozen poodles—from puppies on up—on the bare feces-spotted floor come running. In a corner by the window in the near-empty room illuminated only by the outside grayness was an elderly couple who turned their age-mottled faces up from the bowls in front of them to the closing door.

Nonplussed, Gaston tsked and mumbled "our computer. So!" and he moved to the next door with a forced smile, shuffling her bag along with his foot. Before he could even slide that bolt, she said "excuse me, but I'd like my keys," forgetting Jitka's accent. Feeling faint, she leaned to pick up her bag; it was all the movement her knees could handle and she leaned against the wall. Reflexively, with a cold sweat coursing her, she thought, My god, Mr. Spielberg, why do you even have to ask? They're his parents and he's giving them tough love to get them past their incapacitating agoraphobia. They'll be champing at the bit to get out and about—. Oh, it's not a comedy? They adopted him and they're senile—"

"And the dogs?" a hazy Spielberg asked. "Okay. Here," she thought numbly. "The elderly couple, their macular degeneration, but they always wanted to run the Iditarod together and they're training a seeing-eye sled team—. No, they have no fur; they'll freeze—"

Gaston looked at her with genuine confusion. "Your keys? You'll never make progress if you can't face the truth." Now he was all bluster again, as though he wasn't going to acknowledge how much she had let him down. "Well it's your ass," he said searching his pockets for her keys. "I must have left them downstairs." He pulled out a linty dog biscuit, brushed it on his pants, slid open the first bolt and flipped it through the door's crack.

"And the *floor*? C'mon Ev, time is money, this is not like you," Spielberg said. She thought, feeling nauseated, "he, Gaston their adopted son, never liked his job as 'back-loader'—"

She tried to go first down the stairs to make sure he wasn't between her and the front door but he did a nimble juke move, grabbed her bag and led the way. He taught polka lessons during Oktoberfest to the tourists—; stop it! she told herself and shook her head tightly, a shudder of defiance to keep from sitting meekly on the stairs to gather her wits.

The keys were on a side table and she plucked them from his hand before he turned to her. She watched him over her shoulder as she pushed the heavy door open and in the gloaming stopped short of tripping over a pale white box kite.

A slight man, as old as the couple upstairs, partially turned with stiffness from his seat on the edge of the porch to her presence. He was rolling on a stick the string which looped into the tall grass toward the outhouse. His arm moved slowly; she imagined it might take half an hour to reel it in. He faced away and she saw his wrinkled neck under a tattered ball cap gathered heavily in the back due to its cinch on his small head.

It was raining harder but that's not what held her. When he turned his body more fully to her, he grimaced from the effort before smiling unselfconsciously despite random teeth missing. He pushed his glasses back up his nose, displaced from looking down at his work. Like his denim shirt and corduroy trousers, they were too big for him, framing his frailty.

"You flew this?" she said. "From the outhouse?"

"Sure." His voice was higher pitched than expected and was subsumed in the rain, no breath behind it. The door was still open and the floor behind her creaked as though Gaston shifted his weight. She heard the poodle's nails approach.

"How—. Why fly it from in there?"

He stopped spooling. "We're not going to get anywhere if you're from Seattle and don't know how to keep dry," he said. He slowly stood, an origami crane on a shelf loosing its binding creases to the sun's warmth; a wing, a leg, the neck. He wasn't much over 4' tall, his shins like white tubing above the socks; he steadied himself on the railing. "Low blood pressure," he said. "Dizzy when I get up too fast. Hah."

He offered his hand: "K.C." His hand was frightfully cold but the rain, wet string couldn't have done that—. "I know," he said. "Raynaud's Syndrome. Old geezer's thing. Feet too."

For the second time, now not anonymously, she tried to add a fourth dimension to the man and kite. Nothing came; there was a void. She looked to her car; it better start in this damp.

"Come inside," he said.

"I'm *not* going back in there." She saw no one in the doorway.

He sighed. "We're not going to get anywhere—"

"Why does everybody keep saying that? Like I have somewhere to go with you!"

"You don't understand. It was not a request."

In her fingers she singled out the ignition key; it would save five seconds. She could easily overpower him but where was the dog?

"'We're not going to get anywhere' is the *answer*," he explained. He seemed to tire before her eyes and sat, plumping a pillow first, on a rusty loveseat glider. "Your car's not going to start now," and he patted the seat next to him, only his toes touching the porch. He turned his cap around, bill backwards. "Does that help?"

"How do—. My car—." She stared at him.

He tilted his head, gave a goofy smile. "Do I have to swing and clang my feet on the glider until you tell me to stop, it's giving you one of those migraines?"

She involuntarily swiped at the encroaching darkness, as much to draw a curtain on what was sinking in. Now she saw him as the boy he was, maybe 12 or 18 or 8. His laugh was an effort, part wet cough. He took his cap off to set it aright; he was completely bald. He seemed like a gnome that had served most of a life sentence in a damp cell—

"Don't call me a gnome," he said, reading her mind. "Is that what you busy yourself with? Labeling? Movie shorthand? '*Moby Dick*. The whale kills Ahab.' '*Love Story*. She dies.' You know, you pussyfooting about here on the porch has cost me, say, few hours easy. I don't like doing the math."

She had felt threatened inside but put down her bag and sat next to him, the rain sliding back and forth in sheets, a kite of weather.

"It's progeria," he said. "I'm 15 and 70-some days. I try to lose track. It's accelerated aging. I'm the oldest one of 28 in the world with it. No one has made it past 16 and a bit. And no, we don't keep in touch."

She wanted to hold him, to rock him. She wanted reality from him.

"You came for something," he said, "but the source of all problems is looking for answers outside yourself." The woman nodded out of an old habit that agreement would serve; that assertiveness, identity, would be punished by her alcoholic father. He was an artist and entered coloring contests in her age bracket for her—a van Gogh-esque purple-and-white portrait of the evil Cruella de Vil for some grand Disney prize, for example, so vivid it gave her nightmares. She signed the entry form placed in front of her, adding a flowery "12" on the age line; a slim attempt to reveal herself, not to feel a cheater. She won a stupid fourth prize AM radio and had to go pick it up at a participating theater for a photo and her mother kept warning her "if asked to draw something tell them you only use Caran D'ache pastels; they won't have them." There were other contests for a year or so until it got embarrassing even for the cover of liquor and she wondered how these "museum pieces" never won. Therapy had revealed to her that she had signed off more and more childishly on purpose to quash hopes of winning. It got to where her father made her practice her "mature" signature beforehand but once on the original entry, it was too late to change. Further, she figured this warped symbiosis with her father was the reason backstories came so easily and rang true for her: There was no "kidnaping" of her imagination.

"Of course," K.C. said, "*I*—someone *outside yourself*—just told you not to look outside yourself, so, blah blah circle endless circle. The reality you wanted from me—" and again she was unnerved by his words to her thoughts—"okay, how many eggs can a giant eat on an empty stomach?" She shrugged. "One, because then it's not empty anymore. Please put away your keys; them clicking makes me feel more temporary than I do already."

"Oh I didn't know I was—"

"Just leave it at 'I don't know.' Isn't that what your friend told you? About what she took away?"

Evelyn stood up. The poodle had taken an bristling stance in the doorway.

"Don't worry about him," he said, "he won't be what stops you. Back to the eggs. The point is, add something and it wrecks it. The point is, add anything to enlightenment and it's wrecked." She wanted to slow him down, presenting this bolus to digest from on high; she wanted him to laugh when she said "you're wise beyond your years."

Instead, he stood to confront her, barely reaching her ever-barren breast (it struck her). "The point is," and he smacked the back of his hand into his palm with hardly a sound, "enlightenment is knowing that *maybe this* is enlightenment! Thinking 'you're there' defines, narrows, pigeonholes the infinite—." He coughed from the exertion, walked toward the dog, raised his hand and it ran into the rain. "Go to hell," he said. "*Not* the dog. You." He coughed his way to the door, bent, moving too fast for him, staggering. He returned immediately to the glider. "I can't make it. I need a glass of water." She hesitated, looking at the doorway. "Or do you want me to just lean back in the rain, a face swimming in a pail? *Do you?*"

She yielded and when she stepped inside, saw Gaston in the kitchen. He took a glass filled already and held it out. She held it to the light, then poured it out and re-filled.

"You don't trust me—"

"I know I know," she said, "'we're not going to get anywhere.'"

He applauded silently and bowed slightly. "He's good, isn't he?"

"Quite a psychic scam you're running. I can't wait to let the Better Business Bureau and Chamber of Commerce know all about it."

He laughed from the belly. "Oh my, we'll have to remove their decals from the window. And, what, you're going to say we wouldn't give you your life savings back after you brought us the bag of 'tainted' cash and we pulled the 'clean it with rooster blood' switcheroo? Grow up."

"Maybe the police."

"What. That old couple? My parents, well, adoptive. They're senile and the dogs, eh, keep them young. The dirty floor? I hated my job with the circus and I didn't even last the week it was in my home town—"

She blanched; somehow the glasses had been switched. Some hallucinogen...the smell of burning thai sticks hidden by the ash? Thankfully Gaston rambled on: "—K.C.'s my boy, sort of. I took him from a cousin who was going to have a drowning accident because of his disease, on his first birthday."

The water in her glass was quivering yet holding her up. "I...I...I..." was all she could manage.

"That's what we're here for," he said and left.

She went outside and K.C. sipped from the glass like a humming-bird, dipping back and forth. "A bundle of nerves inside you, right?" he finally said. Before she could answer he added, "Maybe you're there. The only way to know you're enlightened is to know *anything* could be it."

The dog came out of the rain and shook itself off. She looked to her car and remembered her car seat was likely wet from a leak.

"English cars and rain," he said. "It will start now if you need it to."

"I don't know if you expect me to fall for this mumbo jumbo, this psychic scam, and empty my bank account, with your haunted house or fake hostages or some nonsense—"

"*My* face in a pail."

"What?"

"C'mon, backstories is what you do. If I can somehow remember it...."

She grabbed her bag, ready to go. "What are you talking about?" but she tapered off her harshness when she saw his tears welling.

She hadn't given a thought to the Pennsylvania farmhouse for decades. Between drags, he said he indeed was a doctor. He made her go last when she was 80 dollars short (her freshman college roommate said he would take it, it's still a crime in this state without your mom signing off, he's in no position). She heard the two other girls' screams through the thin wall; they walked past her one by one holding their bellies to the odorous cots. When it was her turn, she would have backed out but it was his driver brought them from the shuttered inn's parking lot.

The heartfelt anguish of her long talks with the engineering student with a future—the love between them on the rack being stretched and tortured because of her own choice—would make her howls no more sanctimonious than the others' when it came down to the shared padded table, the obvious dentist's lamp, fear-moistened stirrups, the purity of pain to her core. She was just another source of "road kill" he called it when it went from her to an organic sploosh somewhere beside her. Helped off the table, she was told she would have no rest, to get in the car, she should have paid in full, and the driver would not slow for bumps. When she forced herself to look in the pail—

My god.

It was him.

"It was me," he said.

It is him.

"It is me. *Don't* tell me you see a resemblance," the boy said with a wry smile.

She walked into the rain for something real, felt the mud suck into her shoes. All she could do was mutter "I don't know, I don't know." She looked at him, striated through the gray rain, her hair matted and clothes soaked as they were back then from fearful sweat; the boy on the porch an old black-and-white TV picture full of static like the one in the cot room. "Say something."

He pointed to the sign.

"I have snakes in red pepper," she said.

He gave her time to absorb this. "Think…obituary with the last line 'he is survived by himself.'"

Nothing came to her, no fourth dimension. She wanted to bray with Hollywood excess that this trip, this day, was not even the meaningless void of swirling bad poetry. But his encouraging look, a labyrinth in the wrinkles, stopped her and she began to realize it was *her* void, her void to fill uselessly or keep empty. She knelt in front of him and took his cold hands folded into a gnarl. His progeria, she now knew to her painful core, was the curse she had imbued into his cauterized spirit, the "pre-face" in the pail. She had created an imperative for his next incarnation to short circuit fate, to palliate the uncertainty of life by harshly compressing it. That's why he said "go to hell," she thought.

"But how did this," and she embraced the grain of sand of the universe the two shared with her pleading arms toward the sky, "come to be? Today?"

He shrugged his slight shoulders. He was a lost kid being asked where he lived, where his mom was.

She stepped off the porch into the rain, crouched to the mud, squeezed it through her fists until there was nothing left. She walked to the fifth sign and muddied over "Maybe"—finger painting, it struck her; what she might have done on her own for the contests. His head drooped as a nod or he might have been dying again, another limbo, as the rain eroded the doubt and restored the "Maybe."

Dementia Dialogues, or,
The Last Fill-in-the-Blank

The kitchen looked as if the portable TV on the counter corner might just be able to pull in from its memory a faltering black-and-white grainy broadcast of a moon landing decades ago. It was not the messiness that time hadn't caught up to; it was as if time itself had been hoarded through the avocado green refrigerator, goldenrod linoleum floor, burnt sienna accent wall, and the turquoise-painted birch wood cabinets with ecru—not ivory, she would have said—knobs…all the colors held together with a tablecloth of Mondrian's early "Dunes with Beach and Piers, Domburg." It said "modern" years past.

The wall calendar, themed "Carpets of the Maharajas," was a subscription service she didn't have to think about. The years came to her door. It had the bygone dates X-ed out—*au courant*, she would have said—but for today's, and that one had one diagonal in place. The second would be drawn just before turning out the ceiling light for bed; she must have mentioned the dead fly there.

Desmond slid two days' unwashed dishes to make room for the cutting board. This meant fancy dinner, she thought, and not something from the freezer—with us stepping up from déshabillé. Except he was wearing some smocky work shirt like he should know where the stepladder is to reach that ceiling light. She checked herself with a bit of an air and brushed at the stains on her nightshirt.

He got a cucumber from the fridge and as he peeled it started humming "Red Sails in the Sunset." I'm old enough to remember that, she thought, and joined softly in the humming.

"Hmmm?" Desmond absently droned and Kate was sure she had mentioned the fly.

"'Red Sails,'" she said.

"Surprise, surprise, how you 'Red Sails in the Sunset' out of the blue drifting. Quizzical?" Desmond said. He re-started slicing: "Wistful when people danced with their arms around each other with no knives hip hop today violent rap kill cop song on the charts with a bullet next to it didn't used to mean the rapper was dead entirely new world consternation drifting? Quizzical?"

He turned to her, shrugged as a question, but got no response. He looked in the cabinets and Kate got up to dance slowly, a eurhythmy-esque solipsism, wafting a napkin as if waving bon voyage to Queen Elizabeth II passengers.

"Dance of the Veils, see page 93 for that 'bedroom eyes' look."

"Well, that's way back," he said, "but sure...perplexity, skillet?"

She pointed in a different direction from where he was looking, which he didn't catch. He stood on his toes swinging his head back and forth slowly to look in the upper shelves. "Confused, confounded...," he said.

"Conning tower," she said, mimicking his swinging head. "Conning tower. No new drapes on a submarine, see page 128." She walked to a cupboard behind him and as she reached for the knob he noticed and jumped in ahead of her.

"In here?" he said. "*I'll* flippant disingenuous gratitude, annoyed."

She pulled the door open and was in his way as he reached for the pan. Flustered, he shooed her away.

"Annoyed! Fussing room," he said.

"Fuss, fusty."

"Yes, give me fussing room so I can get supper on the table."

She reached past him for the skillet. "My job," she said.

"Indignant petulant would have found it," and he stopped her. She reached again and he pushed her back and she dragged a pile of pots clattering to the floor. She laughed tentatively, then plopped down amidst them.

"Indignant! Peevish blaming," he said.

Kate held a pot atop her head. "Laurel and Hardy."

He lifted the pot from her and smiled. "Laurel and Hardy."

"Got it right."

"Yes, dear, Laurel and Hardy got it right."

"Hardy was...hearty."

"And that's a...?"

"That's?"

Desmond drew her out. "Engaging, helpful...*helpful. Encouraging.*" He could see something click.

"Mnemonic!" she said.

"Dismay if you can remember that why on earth can't you curious slugfest drifting."

"Laurel was skinny."

"Yes," his wiggling fingers asking for more. She indicated the mess of pans.

"They had it right, right?" suddenly raising her voice in a plea. "Why else? *Right? Or else why else?*" She scattered the pots with her foot.

"Okay, okay," and he helped her up. As he picked up everything and put it back, she went to the counter, put a few tomatoes in a pot on the stove and sliced at them with the knife.

"My job," she said.

Desmond saw the knife. "No! Give me that!"

"My job!" He took it and her shoulders slumped. "My kitchen."

"Testy rebuttal nostalgia say goodbye to sharp hot burning things when you have a big summer issue of trust." He extended her arm to her side and pretended to slice her palm, the tomato leaving a slash mark. She didn't recoil. He nodded, superior: "Unctuous, smarmy, ambulance you can't be trusted. Rhetorical. Insistent rhetorical?"

She extended her other arm crucifixion-like and he hesitated, then pretended to slice her other palm, again leaving a red mark and getting no reaction. "Unctuous be dead and not know it," he said.

She dropped her arms, started to wipe her hands on her nightshirt but he got a dish towel.

"Unction, finality," he said.

"My own good," she said handing him the reddened towel. "Be dead not know it."

"Yes!" he said supportively.

She stepped to him, touched his cheek. "Godsoloved," she said, making it one word. He shrugged. "*Godsoloved!*" she said.

"Me?"

"Sure."

"*Me?* Desmond?"

"You Hardy," she said and picked up wooden spoon for approval.

"Wait. Me *God*? So loved? Or just me, godsoloved?"

Kate grew more exasperated. "Hardy had it right. Skinny one was Laurel; skinny one on a laurel crucifix—no, pine—pining for God, pining for holly bush—"

"Okay, stop there," and he put her wooden spoon to stirring the tomatoes in the pot.

"Stew of holly blood, see page—"

"I said stop there! Just...stir."

She went rigid. "And don't stir up," she said giving him a hard look.

"You and words," and he urged her back to motion. "Oh, and don't let me forget 'anything trash day' next Tuesday."

"Don't forget anything trash day next Tuesday," she said simply.

"Not now. If I forget. Come the day."

She plugged "if you forget the trash sails without you" into the "Red Sails in the Sunset" tune.

He laughed. "Is that a joke or...?" She looked at him blankly. "Never mind," he said. "Singsong butter unless drifting? Also, I'll boil some eggs if sunrise set a place. Three."

She went to the refrigerator, took out three eggs. Desmond took them from her, squeezed the two ends of one between his fingers, grimacing for effect. "Ovoid perfect geometry can't crack."

"Why godsolove if something strong just cracks another way?" she said.

Desmond waited, as he found himself doing more lately, for something from her; a tipoff from anywhere but the miasmic ever-present. Then she cupped her groin and pulled out the butter.

"Imprecation!" Desmond shouted and she turned around. "Chastise Kate a no no finger in the dike!" She guiltily removed her cupped hand. "Redundant over this."

Kate was embarrassed. "'Pleonasm,' noun, redundancy," she offered as if to a parent.

"What? Neo-plasm?"

Now she laughed but again as a child. "'Neoplasm,' noun, tumor. Confusing."

"Redundant been over this!" and he cupped his groin.

Now she was her own mirth. "Re-redundant?"

He pointed out of the kitchen. "Pouty big girls bathroom by herself."

She put the butter dish on the table, let out a quiet gasp as she remembered the butter knife in the drawer. She placed that and left the kitchen.

Desmond took out half a bottle of red wine from a cabinet, uncorked it, tried a taste and thought about pouring it into the sink but stopped abruptly at the knock on the door. He parted the curtains warily, then took out a key from his pocket to unlock it. A middle-aged man in suit and loosened tie, a tan from somewhere else, didn't wait for Desmond to invite him but his first steps slowed as he took things in.

"Surprise surprise," said Desmond flatly. The man lifted a few of the dirty dishes with a finger as if uncovering archeological clues and Desmond locked the door surreptitiously. The man cocked an ear to the sound of the key turning. He opened the refrigerator door, shook his head. He looked into the tomato pot and scoffed, "No, I can't stay for dinner." He noticed a stack of mail and riffed through it, separating it into two piles. "Where is she?" he said.

Desmond moved to take the mail; the man, while not a boxer, had the look of someone who could turn any four walls into a ring, and he elbowed him back. "Kate?" he called. Desmond offhandedly pointed out of the kitchen. The man tore open an envelope.

"I sent this three weeks ago," he said. "It's her birthday card. She *did* celebrate her birthday? Does she get out? What's with the inside lock, that's new, you some kind of jailer now?"

Desmond muttered to himself: "For her own good."

"*What?* Speak up, old man!"

"For her own good," he muttered again and picked up the bottle of wine to drink.

"Oh no," the man said taking it. "Happy hour is over. Now, does she get out? Does she see friends, that woman across the street? You have her *ostracized*?"

"In the *street*?" he said, glaring at the man. He grabbed the bottle by the neck, met resistance, then tilted both their hands to pour it out in the sink. "Be dead not know it."

"You treat her," the man said taking out a handkerchief to wipe splashed wine droplets from his hand, "like she's some second-class piece of—"

"Fudge!"

"What?"

"Fudge! Her birthday gift; I didn't forget. Plus 74 spanks! Why are you *here* Cal?"

"I've tried to call but the phone company keeps telling me...." He went to the phone on the wall, followed the line down and held up the cut end.

"She did that," Desmond said.

"I don't believe you."

"By inference. Kept trying to call Holly."

"Holly?!"

"Your sister."

"I *know* who she is!"

"So I had to."

"I see your point," Cal said sarcastically. "You wouldn't want her to talk to Holly, would you?"

Desmond squared up. It would be no contest but Desmond had acquitted his share of those. "What do you mean by that? Listen, whelp, you come into *my* house—," but he stopped his finger jabs just short of the jacket.

Cal removed his glasses, purposefully folded them, set them aside. He straight armed Desmond back from him. "You don't want to connect that last inch, bud. Let's get this real clear in everybody's mind. This is *her* house. You're just a guy can minute waltz a widow."

"Four years I'm here!" Desmond said, spinning away and flinging his arm in dismissal and nearly hitting Cal's face.

"Bud. Next time you do that, I better see a taxi you're hailing." He put on his glasses.

"It's 'Desmond.' Which you know."

"What are you hanging around for *Desmond*? The bloom is long off the rose, so all that leaves is motive. You going for common law, where you end up with half this place? Or re-write the will and get it all?"

"That's you, isn't it? Mr. Bottom Line. Mr. Time Equals Money. Hey, you're so concerned about getting ahead, why don't you just make time equal double money? There's a quality concept for your next meeting."

Cal took in the sink mess for Desmond. "Like you know a damn thing about quality."

"We try."

"No no no! This is not *her*. Her sense of style set trends. She was the editor-in-chief at one of the glossiest fashion monthlies. She is meticulous." He went around flouncing the curtains on the windows and door. "Hell, I'll bet these cafe curtains each have the same number of stitches...."

Kate entered, drying her hands on her soiled nightshirt. Seeing Cal she stopped, then with a lost gesture ran a hand through her hair.

"What the—. Mom?" he said.

Desmond tried to usher her to the table but she stood firm. "Cal here just flew in for business and decided to come over. No reason—"

"Quiet," Cal said and handed Kate the card. "Happy birthday stamp of approval."

She looked at the card but didn't open it so he opened it for her.

"She goes in and out like a radio station—," Desmond said.

Cal wheeled on him: "Shut up!" Kate dropped the card, shaking, which Cal picked up. "Apologetic soothing dulcet," he said to her.

"You can't pop in and expect to get through," Desmond said.

"What have you done to her?"

"*Done?* I've done nothing."

"I was here, what, eight months ago?"

"Dutiful," Desmond said.

"I mean, she was vacant, but she was helping the church, some fund-raising sale. Does she still bake?"

"*Bake?*" he said. "Yeah, right after swapping out motors in the dehumidifier. Alzheimer's is downhill, fast or slow. Ain't no rope tow back up."

"But that was June, for chrissake—" Cal said.

"Our biggest issue," Kate said. "Garter belts say bye-bye."

Cal stepped to his mother. "Quizzical. Insistent quizzical."

Desmond said "*You* are not getting through to her. Her biggest issue of the year would be June, with the weddings and swimsuits and travel, whatever." To her he said, "Right? Buy buy up those garter belts."

"You think *you're* talking to her?" Cal said.

"Yeh," he said. "She picks up emotions and…some thoughts. I mean, I, you, we're both talking regular sentences to her but, what she hears?, she's got some 'filter' that fucks—"

"Typo!" she said. It was word she always used with enthusiasm. She added, "try flocks, foxes maybe…but bad mix those two."

"—some filter that *mucks*," Desmond corrected himself, "everything up but I, anyway, get through, yes. We pass the days."

"You're joking," said Cal. "When she doesn't even recognize her son?"

"Sunny," Kate said, straightening the straight napkins on the table.

Cal leaned into her. "Mom? It's me, Sunny."

"June. Sunny," she said. "Two hundred twenty-four pages. Bouquet, piquet, élevé, plié." She pliéd and sat in the chair.

"Wha—" said Cal, exasperated.

"See," said Desmond. "'Bouquet.' They had four perfume inserts in that big June issue. She talks about it like it was yesterday. I found a copy in the closet last month, so many smells mixed together even now. It was like, um, or as if—"

"Simile 'like,'" she said. "Metaphor 'as.'"

"Then," Desmond said, "*like* Godzilla stepped on perfume factories all the way to Tokyo." He took giant awkward strides to Kate, his arms outstretched. "Right, Godzilla?"

She faux recoiled and laughed. Desmond smugly smiled at Cal.

"There's no way you two—" Cal said. "Summer solstice," he said to Kate.

"Biggest issue," she said.

"Winter solstice."

"Biggest issue."

"*See? See?*" Cal said to Desmond. "I mean, you can put an aboriginal in with a Russian in a space station and something will, I mean—." He made a series of clicking, clucking noises. "Enough of those," he said, "and the two of them will know how to say 'goodbye' or 'pass the salt' to each other after a while."

Desmond held up his hand. He faced Kate and mimicked those clicks and clucks.

"*Do svidaniya*," she said, and started to pick up her napkin to wave it.

"No need. We all know it means goodbye," Desmond said, resting his hand on hers. He cocked his head to Cal and walked backwards a couple of steps as if he had bowled a strike on the beer frame.

"*Do svidaniya* bath salts, see page 56," she said, "for that 'bedroom eyes' look."

"Yeh, I thought so," said Cal. "You're deluded. And she needs care." He helped Kate from her chair and held out her nightshirt. "She wouldn't be caught dead in this, this stain-palette *thing*! And her hair, her nails…."

Desmond ushered Kate out of the kitchen. "Okay," he said to her, "change, change in the air."

Cal got out his cell phone, took off his tie, and gathered up one of the piles of mail. "Barely a signal," he said. "Ah, hello?"

"What are you doing with those?"

"I'm going to…yes, hello, I need to change my flight reservation—. Hello? Damn, the call dropped."

Desmond grabbed the mail from his hand. "Routine around here is bills get paid end of the month."

"Give me those, they are addressed to her."

"You don't live here. We got laws. Snooping laws."

"Oh I've done the snooping. I know you. I know the downtown corner you came from."

"It wasn't pity!" Desmond said.

"She stopped the car every morning at the light on her way to work and gave you $3 for lunch."

"You don't know the core—"

"I know *you*, you shabby homeless riffraff—"

"No, there was, there was—. It wasn't pity."

"—with your sign, with no hyphens between 'prisoner-of-war,' which she first rolled down the window to correct. Her friend across the street there told me the whole tale. So. Sir. As far as 'routine'? I suggest you get a fresh piece of begging cardboard to re-write your POW camp sob story; maybe you can get your old street corner back."

Desmond made sure this wasn't a question. "What are you going to do."

"Tomorrow I am going to Social Services to file a complaint or restraining order or, or 'overstayed his welcome' execution or whatever the fuck-all form they have get *you* out and then put her in a care facility."

"You can't do that."

"Wanna bet? I'm her son."

"She's my, she's my—"

"She's your *what*?"

Kate stepped into the kitchen for approval, her hair brushed, a clean-looking nightshirt on.

"There you are," Desmond said, "looking fresh for dinner. Hey, aren't you my 'runway girl'?"

Kate did a model's walk perfectly, one foot smartly in front of the other, a "book" suddenly atop her head. She whirled in front of them and walked back, revealing the stains and that the nightshirt had just been turned around. Cal glared at Desmond.

"I'll get her in another outfit," Desmond said.

"Leave her alone," said Cal, drawing her to a chair. "You don't live here, remember?"

"Calvin, don't do it. There's not much makes me smile these days, but she does. We get by, *more* than get by, really. I mean, you did drop in unexpected."

Cal weighed this, opened his mouth to speak but held off. He pulled up a chair next to Kate. "Mom," and she looked up. "We always did these at the dinner table slugfest. You're the wordsmith, right? Fill-in-the-blanks? Puzzlement?"

Her engagement wavered; she fought for an atavistic tendril to her womb. Then: "Hyphens, not dashes!"

"Of course," Cal told her. "Now. Focus—"

"Pocus."

"No. *Focus*. Okay, like a *blank* of lark…exultation of lark. A *blank* of lions…pride. C'mon, here you go. A blank of crow…murder." No response from her other than a wrung smile. "Okay, Mom. I'll give an easy one, okay? Okay?" He shook his head when she looked away. "Hopeless," he said to himself.

"Where's the blank?" Desmond said.

"Quiet," Cal said, "that wasn't it."

"A Zen of hopeless," Kate said.

Cal sadly hugged her. She fingered his collar missing a tie. As he started to the door, Desmond stopped him and said, "look, that's probably a story headline, she's always spouting those: Zen of Hopeless Everyday Thong Wear, see page—"

Cal moved around him. "Wait, she's all I have," Desmond said. "When she stopped one day, she had all these belts she wanted to give to the bunch of us under an overpass from the rain. To hold our pants up instead of rope and such. Dozens of them left over from photo shoots. All colors—ecru, not ivory, she said—and all widths, vinyl, leather, sashes—"

"Belts are a Cinch," Kate said, "see page—"

"Hey," Desmond said gently, "I'm telling the story." To Cal he said, "Later, we—she and I—brought sunglasses for the guys. The fanciest names. She had drawers of them, taking up space. I helped her get her life in order here."

Cal tried the locked door. "Open it."

Desmond stiffened. "You not going to toss *me*. No hobo corner. I got roots here! No fucking way!"

"Typo!" Kate piped in.

"Open it. Or I'll rip the key out of your pocket. Believe me, she'll understand that."

Desmond unlocked the door, closed it behind Cal, locked it with a covering cough and slowly returned to cooking. "Well," he said, "knives, forks..." and Kate headed for the silverware drawer.

"Trinity," she said. She set two place settings at the ends of the table, then added a third.

"Three people?"

"Guess," she said.

"Cal left."

"Cal sayeth 'exultation,'" Kate said and Desmond peered for clarity.

"Muddled," he said.

She returned to arranging the table. "Not 'guest.'"

"Who?"

She patted the third place setting. "Holly."

"Adamant repressive tongue-tied she's dead!" He reached to take the place setting away; she stopped him. "Been dead," he said.

"Doesn't know it."

Desmond took a deep breath. "Reproach a year ago drifting the car?"

There was no mistaking this recollection. "Pills!" she said.

"Yes! Pills, the car, the garage?"

"Reds, Tailpipe into the Sunset," she said, adding matter-of-factly, "possible headline."

"That's your *daughter*—," he started angrily but relented when he saw her eyes well up. "If you want a Seconal place for a ghost, this one time mind you, be my dither."

"Holly ghost."

"Rueful resigned," he said chuckling. "Jocular, joke coming, always wanted to see a classified ad, 'For sale, the Holy Grail. Beautiful condition. Must be *appreciated* to be *seen.*'"

She doesn't get it.

"Echo redundant," he said: "To be seen?" He waited. "Reassuring nobody gets it."

"Grails," and she opened a cupboard, closed it, looked distressed.

"Quizzical."

"Grails!"

"Oh, goblets?" he said. "They're for special occasions."

She walked in a tight circle, reaching in the air for the cabinet knobs. "Grails! Come on, getting warm…."

"Getting warmer," he said as she scouted, "colder, warm bath salts, warmer, hotter, hot!"

She opened that cabinet and proudly pulled out a tarnished silver goblet and raised it over her head in victory. "Aha!" she said. "Some game in a church!"

He applauded. She took another goblet out, closed the door, placed the two on the table, headed back for the third but stopped, changed direction, stopped; lost. She opened the wrong cabinet and slammed it in frustration.

"Move for chance of helpful temperatures this sunset," he said.

She took the same door and slammed it several times.

In starting toward her, Desmond bumped the hot pot on the stove, grabbed it before it fell and burned his hand. "Loud loud loud loud!" he said, dancing and holding his hand. She tried to help him and was bumped to the floor.

She laughed and said "fussing room." He ran his hand under cold water.

"Laurel and Hardy," she said.

"Got it right, yes."

She stood and examined his hand, kissed it. He kissed her forehead. She grabbed a nearby pot and put it over his head.

"Hardy," she said.

"Denying," he said playfully, "defensive accusatory antithetical fault yours."

"Antipodal fault yours."

"Yes, even better. I'll give you that one. I guess being an editor for 15 years you always nebulous with words what Beethoven was to drifting, drifting."

Kate made two fists. "Finish my thought," she said. Desmond cleaned up the spill on the stove.

"Finish it!" she said.

"Hmmm?" he droned.

She looked at the fly in the ceiling light. "Finnish boats have red sails!" She waited. "Gone," she said. She walked to the right cabinet and got the third goblet. He put food and rolls on two plates and brought them to the table, sat and started eating but she held back.

"Hmmm?"

"I wish you wouldn't say that," Kate said.

Desmond pointedly enjoyed a bite, then held a forkful out to her. She pushed his hand away.

"Re-proach," he said and tried again. This time she pushed his hand and the plate.

As though coaxing a child, he circled the fork in the air and said, "Reproach cajole wheedle guilt."

"*Reproach cajole wheedle guilt?*" she said angrily.

"What?! That's not what *I* said."

"It's what I *heard!*"

"Well what I *said* was—"

"Who knows what you said? I'm tired of it!"

"Tired of what?"

She grabbed at the sand, wrinkling the Domburg dunes tablecloth. "How I *am!*" she said. "A radio in and out. Picking up pieces, emotions, *smatterings.*"

"This is good. This is the to and fro, back and forth the doctor said we need."

"Post and riposte."

"Yes! Sally and forth."

"No 'and.'"

"Right, you're the editor. Give and take, toss and flotsam. Generic? *Generic?*"

He gave up. Kate slid her plate to the third place setting and stared at him until he noticed.

"Bring her back," Kate said.

"Finality."

"Then take me to her."

"Confused, dismissive."

"What?" she implored. "Make sense."

"Unintelligible," was the answer.

Kate thought even pinballs know where they'll end up and shrieked "Aaahhgg! Godsoloved!"

Desmond slid the plate back in front of her. "Overbearing adamance one thing to set a place at the table another to pretend she repetitive to death."

"Your fault," she said sharply.

"What."

"'Don't let me forget to hide the car keys, Kate; Holly sounds serious tonight.' I reminded you. I'll never let you forget! Criminal."

"*What?*" he said rising.

"Shabby homeless riffraff!"

"Ohhh. You heard that *just* fine. Then you heard me tell him just like I tell you, I got fucking boots here!"

"Typo!" she yelled, adding "your fault, you didn't hide the kingdom keys, your fault" and he yelled over her "how dare you blind fury refutation hopeless bleakness imprecation imputation see this to the end of strength!" He stood over her and cocked his arm to slap her.

"*Godsoloved.* Take me to her," she beseeched, "or, or—." She sent her plate to the floor. "I starve."

Desmond pulled his plate over, grabbed a fistful of her hair, shoved a forkful of food at her. She ate it but started choking, then worse. He moved behind her chair and before beginning the Heimlich maneuver paused with his clasped hands at her chest.

A locomotive idling in the yards, its steam eddies seamlessly into thick fog. Boxcars to oblivion. Sobbing, shouts, dragging feet. A dog's freewheeling nastiness. Desmond reached instead for the napkin in her lap.

Kate, coughing, managed "Heimlich."

"Heinrich."

"Heimlich."

"Himmler."

He used the napkin as blindfold on her. He strutted, slapping his thigh. Her coughing caught his attention.

"Surprise surprise," he said sympathetically. "Someone's not well."

Kate stifled her gagging in fear. "Not me."

"Yes you," he said, lifting her nightshirt off her lap. "A gypsy."

She batted it back down. "Not gypsy. Just rags."

"A sick gypsy...Jew."

"No, no. Pink sails."

"What?"

"Healthy. In the pink."

"You have a *yellow* star," he said. "Pinks are for others. Unless we have not fully *appreciated* you on our paperwork. Hmmm? So. 'Homosexual sick colorblind gypsy Jew'? Is that you? Oh come now, just whisper in your obergruppenfuhrer's ear."

"I just—"

"Guard! Take this woman behind that building! Save room on the trains for the healthy."

Kate grabbed blindly as if pulling someone toward her. "Holly!"

"Separate them!" he said pulling her arms apart.

It started as an inchoate wail but moved into certainty, falling into the pulse of the locomotive. "No more no more no more, no more, no more...no more...no more," she said.

He moved behind her and untied the blindfold, put the napkin in her lap. There was a residual cough and he placed his hands near her chest, then moved them to her neck and squeezed. She swallowed hard in fear past the constriction, raised her hands to resist but faltered.

"Singsong singsong singsong," Desmond lulled.

"Godsoloved singsong into hands commend," and she relaxed into his grip. His upper body cocked minutely, the irreducible shift from stasis to imperative—the way he, an old man, he thought, bent before committing to step off a high curb. He released his hands.

"Fussing room," he said and headed to the stove. She floated her napkin over the mess on the floor, brushed table crumbs onto it as the first dirt onto a casket. He fixed another plate of food, brought it to her along with the pot of tomato sauce; held the dripping serving spoon.

"Tomato blood perplexity?" he said. "Gravy train?"

"Typo," she said to herself. "Grave."

Where I'm Crawling From

"**H**e's in my lap!" came her hushed yell from the back stoop. That drew the two men, one setting the table, the other chopping zucchini for the frittata, easing to the open window. It had been a few months in the making, starting with anonymous plates of expensive cat food left out, to a snuck stroke, to last month's burr removal.

"Gonna be a momma's boy," said Coop, shaking the zucchini as admonition. "I can pet it but it won't lollygag like that for me." It was black with a James Bond white bow tie. "Maybe he's there because he knows she's missing some fur," he laughed to Moss.

"What was *that*?" she snapped. "What was that?"

"Don't worry, Krissy, we'll always have Paris," and Coop went back to the stove.

"I heard that!" and she got up fast enough to send the cat heedless through thick brush. She let the screen door slam. "And your pal did too," she added, thumbing to Moss who made himself busy micro-straightening the flatware he had placed. He had come over to help dig post holes for a new fence section to replace what a downed oak had taken out. Moss had dissuaded Coop from dealing with the diseased tree—"the next nor'easter will take it out"—and assured him it would fall parallel to the fence. He had worked half a summer logging in British Columbia but couldn't take the hazing as the rookie. "I guess it yawed," Moss had told Coop, using his limited lingo.

"So what," Coop said to Krissy. "He heard. He's clueless."

"I need a fourth salad bowl," Moss said.

"See?" Coop said, looking at her but punctuating with the back of his hand to Moss's chest, then turning to him: "Krissy went to Paris to have her pussy shaved. Now you're not clueless."

"You dare to make that our dinner conversation," she said. "With him?"

"I thought our lunch repartee flagged, finger sandwiches notwithstanding. Wasn't that a Sylvester Stallone line in 'Rocky'?" and he snorted at his own joke. "Anyway," Coop added, "Moss is the one who said to me 'what's going on' last month!" He banged pans around more than necessary; he had a flair for cooking (one semester Culinary Institute instead of college "where I'dve flunked out even sooner"). His current job—"inventory control," a.k.a. forklift driver—and this live-in relationship were his two longest commitments so far, about eight months apiece.

"What's *that* mean?" Krissy said, taking the paper towels Moss had wafted like bombs to the table adding muffled explosions, and folding them in half.

"You got more questions than a stutterer on 'Jeopardy!,'" Coop said. "It means, *il*—Moss—put '*duh et duh*'—French for 'two and two' or English for 'duh and duh'—

"Don't patronize me," she said.

"—together when you got all made up for *take-out* Chinese that night. Hair washed, eye shadow, liner, fuck-me-red lipstick...telling me 'hey it's Saturday night' when I said what's all that for. Then we're re-heating the take-out and clearing the pot off the table and he sees you Skyping in the steamy bathroom, all angelic, looking like hell from the tits down but who knows that on a smartphone."

Moss put his hands up to disavow that last bit.

"Having that pot in the house—" she said.

"We were just measuring on the kitchen scale, which out of respect for your AA, we don't knock beers back during."

"If you understood AA rules—"

"Don't change the subject!" Coop said. "I will not be cuckolded by a 2" dick in my own bathroom, or whatever the size of your screen is. All whispery."

"It was three in the morning there," she said.

"Oh, right. He's a DJ," he said to Moss, "so the dance club was closing and his ears were all tender. Give me a break, Krissy, you grabbing a plane two weeks later." He threw the last chunk of zucchini in the frying pan without chopping it. "We're having scrapple with this," he added angrily.

"I don't—" she started.

"You know how they say 'scrapple' in Japanese, Moss? Anybody? 'Sklappa.' They don't have a word for it." He pulled a gray loaf out of the fridge.

"I don't eat that junk, you know that," she said.

"Fine. More for me and Mossy. 'Gejigeji' is 'millipede' in Japanese."

Moss had pulled an ammo reloading magazine from under the rifle on the table, one of three subscriptions Coop had on the subject. Target shooting at the range got expensive with new bullets when you shot as many rounds as Coop did, especially to prepare for the annual meet. Although his participation had been in doubt when a vote went against him to change the targets from turbaned shadows to bull's-eyes. It wasn't a humanitarian thing; rather, where did the forehead stop for scoring purposes?

"Actually, Coop—" Moss said.

"Oh, what, you don't eat corn?"

"Yeh—"

"You don't eat spices?"

"Yeh—"

"You eat roast pork fried rice?"

"Well that is not—"

"And you," to Krissy, "if it moves, the French eat it. Didn't you pick up on that? So, here *le scrapple*."

"Get it out of my face," she said. "It has about as much to do with a pig as head cheese has to do with cheese. No wonder they flunked you out of the culinary school."

"No, I left. It was a decision. Just like you made a decision to follow some Altoona High alum at your reunion to Paris."

"What was their mascot, Charlie Tuna?" said Moss trying to lighten the mood.

Krissy pushed by Moss to remove the fourth setting off the table. "You know what? I'm not inviting Kaf over for a blind and *dumb* date."

"Maybe I should just boogie," Moss said to Coop.

"No you don't," he said. "We've got more holes to dig—. Oh fuck!" He jumped for the rifle and slid out the narrowest possible opening of the screen door, an assassin's move, damping the slam, snaking the long gun's encumbrances without bother; a natural third arm. The gun snapped to his shoulder and the shot cracked immediately. He didn't surveil; just turned back inside, leaned the gun inside the pantry.

"Possum sushi anyone?" he said.

"You could have hit Tux," she said.

"Who the hell is Tux?"

"The cat. In the bushes?"

"I thought we said we weren't going to name it until the vet cleared him. Besides, I don't miss. Plus, what do you know about *bushes*?"

"I told you, nothing came of Paris."

Coop ignored her. The settling sun had gone under the treetops now spare of leaves and the ridge would soon cut it off. Coop shot at all manner of wildlife—deer seriously, for the venison—knowing that the ridge behind the bungalow would keep stray bullets from the neighbors, even when going for the squirrels running the phone line. Krissy didn't mind the guns. She called them one of his "macho billet-doux," her oxymoron for the pursuits of Coop's that he called "the price of admission to my life": kayaking, dirt biking, rock climbing—even caving sodden through a long, dripping, crimping tube called Rifle Barrel where one shoulder had to inch forward at a time.

The rock climbing, however, was dropped over a trust issue: On the crux ceiling move on a climb back in the summer, Krissy couldn't pull herself over it and, arms pumped out, she hung on Coop's belay like a rag doll, slumped, slowly twisting in the air under the gibbet-like rock so long his back began to spasm.

She kept saying "lower me" and "my arms are noodles" and he refused, finally tying off his belay to a tree, walking off the small crag and around to stand under her until she noticed him. She cursed, he gestured to the heavens, and when the tableau become intolerable to the nearby climbers, Coop hiked back up and helped haul her, scraping, over the crux. He told Moss the sex that night was the best since she had moved in—tied by the same rope to the bed. But *that* was where the trust issue had boiled over because he had left her tied while he drove for more beer, then joked he was going to "trickle some down her throat; 'beerboarding.'"

His belated contrition barely kept her from calling her brother to help her move out that night, swung ultimately by his confession of a panic attack—coming with more frequency—that week that was "out of control" and that maybe controlling her put him back in a comfort zone.

"Well you're sick," she had said, still with an ice bag on her wrists.

"Not really. I took the 'Rate Your Kink' quiz the Cosmopolitan had while waiting for a haircut and I was closer to Mr. Rogers than to OJ."

They had shared the beer and he backpedaled that the panic attack, while definitely out of control, did not cause him to "lose it altogether" and she started listening with less hope of an epiphany for him. "Anyway, I was in the DQ parking lot and it was boiling in my car—the hot day last week?—and I'm trying to stay ahead of my dripping cone. And this big black woman with a service dog, with the vest, except it was young, in training, all flouncy because this *other* woman's dog was nipping at it while they stood talking. And the second woman—she was white, not that it mattered—had this teen daughter who was a sexpot, like Jon Benet Ramsey had made it a couple more years. Okay, I guess it does matter. And the black, she was big and ugly with a folksinger's hat on like Pete Seeger, which made no sense, and that whole picture started the angst trickle—"

"'Trickle'?! Use a different word."

"—the angst *flood*, okay?, and her dog is jumping up on Jon Benet, all this is in front of my car which I had washed the day before. And the black woman is doing the hand jive, whatever, service signs, for him to stay down and I want to—. Okay. I'm *attracted* to this girl, she's got shorts tight across…and the mother's regular but real frumpy and I'm thinking this fucking flouncy dog is going to jump on my hood with its claws and my ice cream is running on my wrist and she's saying 'down down' for nothing, then to frumpy she says 'I need him to pick up things for me because I can't bend' and she drops her Pete Seeger cap as proof and she's got that weird woman bald thing going and gives a hand jive and the dog grabs the cap but shakes it like a rabbit so he doesn't get a treat so he whines and then there's the irony of this girl—the angst is now pulsing, like a *reactor*—this girl, who no way God can make her look like the mother when she grows up but no doubt He will, and I'm positive I'm going to have to tongue-lash this black bitch when flouncy scratches my hood and I throw my cone out the window to make sure she knew I was in the car and the other dog dashes for it and pulls frumpy almost into my side mirror, for which tongue-lashing I'm completely unprepared, and I'm seeing spots I'm so angry at the tableau—. You were talking before about *your* tableau with the rope, feeling at the mercy of fate. Well, I had a tableau, too."

"But nothing came of it, right?" Krissy had said. "How *could* it? It was *nothing*: The service dog's a puppy, the girl's a bush-less kid, the black's a human, and the girl's 'regular' mother is a, a, metaphor for the normal childhood you obviously missed." She laughed as she added, "the other dog's a red herring you shoot." They went to the range the next night to try out the his-and-her Colts they had bought that day at a Delaware gun auction they had ridden their other motor-cycles to despite the calls for rain.

Moss, still in sweaty clothes from the branch removal and the digging that had started late morning, thought about changing shirts with one he had brought in the car. But if there was no blind date, why bother? Plus he he still had sawdust in his hair.

Coop had ignored it as long as he could. "Nothing *came* of Paris," he finally said to Moss, "because he's a DJ in a hot club meeting five honeys a night and he didn't want the herpes."

"For chrissake, Cooper," she said.

"Sklappa's going in the frittata," he said, mashing it into the fry pan and flaring the heat.

"Fuck Cosmo. You got some real control issues," she said.

"Okay. I'll leave it in chunks; you can pick it out."

"I'm *talking* about playing the truth game with Moss in the room so you can take pot shots and I just have to be too embarrassed to say anything. Well. Fuck you. I have herpes, Moss, not that you know-ing it is anywhere on my radar. And DJ Bona Party—his high school name was Bennie Kramer—prefers his women smooth. So yes, I went that far but, no, he kissed me not on the lips after my 'late breaking news' and foisted me onto his Moroccan friend to see Notre-Dame and the Louvre where Mona Lisa—well, you might as well go buy the postage stamp—and I came home a week early."

"So we don't talk much from the airport," Coop said, "because I found a receipt for lots of expensive lingerie and Mr. Pinkie—the sex toy—is gone from the nightstand so this was not a whim—"

"Why was a picture of me in that drawer when I came back?" she said.

"What."

"The cameo of me. Why was it in the drawer, hidden? Was somebody here?"

"Don't try to make *me* embarrassed," Coop said. "For nothing. Who would be here?"

Moss coughed and spoke a line he had heard his ex-wife say at their last couples' therapy way back: "I am not comfortable with this tone." She had separated about the same time as Coop's wife had, which had thrown the working buddies into more time together than either welcomed at first, with lots of "fuck her, right?" cutting short any real introspection. Moss knew Krissy's sudden trip had not come out of the blue; the rope episode was just the beginning of the fraying. And he knew Coop had Takuri-proofed (the name of his covert Japanese girlfriend) the bungalow more than once so she wouldn't try to break another framed picture of Krissy, yelling "bitch." He even had to take a photo of the cluttered fridge door so he could re-assemble the collage after she left.

Takuri and her young son lived with her parents, Coop had divulged one of those beer nights now that he and Moss were sloppily sharing everything that didn't matter (two mugs clink: "Only the end of the world is the end of the world"). "Takuri's 40," Coop had said, "but it's an honor-your-elders Japanese thing, living with them. Maybe some repression, but that I like in the bedroom."

"Abused women make the best lovers," Moss had said, trying to hang in Coop's breeze, but that shut that night down when a perturbed Coop took the mug from Moss's hand and poured it out.

Krissy was older than Coop as well but in terrific shape, recently taking a job as a trainer at a gym. Plus she had what she called a degree in reiki—what Coop called "voodoo healing, just uggabugga believe" and would wave his arms like a hummingbird doing martial arts. She was an exercise junkie and, with their stress lately, was unable to call it a day after the evening's thumping spin class. "That's why Takuri fits in. Krissy's got nothing left in the tank for me right?" Coop had said (clink of mugs) when she took off on her late-night jog, an over-the-shoulder wave to the two men at the kitchen table. Coop had taken a photo of Krissy's long blonde hair for the fridge before it went down to a buzz cut because she showered so often now.

Coop had met Takuri when she had Iko with her for "Bring Your Child to Work Day." Coop, in the warehouse by himself since Moss was on a delivery, saw the woman from accounting gently pushing a mop-haired shy boy forward. She wore no make-up, unlike Krissy—already he was making comparisons—but her lips were an inviting flush.

"My son Iko"—he bowed on cue—"wanted to see the forkerift," she said with an effort to cover her Japanese accent.

"Sure, sure," said Coop and got him a hard hat that wobbled on his head.

Her name was paged and she asked if she could leave him a few minutes. When she returned, Coop had Iko on his lap and was whipping past shelving, the forks snapping up and down. Out of breath, he pulled over and Iko jumped down.

"I was Gojira in Tokyo!" he said, stomping around. "Yaaa!"

"*God-zirra*," she corrected for Coop.

"I figured," Coop said. He waved to the vastness behind him. "We tried to knock over everything made in China" and she got the joke, laughed shyly, eyes lowered, like a geisha. That's when his comparisons ended.

Krissy knew about Iko (and his single mother) because Coop took him on some of the same outings ("just couple of boys") he used to share with her—the shooting range, the crag—not mentioning Takuri's tagalong and details such as why he knew the Japanese word for "millipede." (Takuri, having to pee once, went behind some bushes and came running out screaming "gejigeji," pushing her skirt down, having disturbed a nest of them.)

Krissy wanted a cigarette but did not want to step outside and lose this focus: "So Moss, you're 'not comfortable with this tone.' Why would *you* be queasy about my cameo in the drawer?"

"No, I'm—"

"Talk about queasy," Coop said, trying to change the topic. "She comes in after her shower, right after the airport pick-up from Paris, I'm lying in bed, she steps to me, unwraps the towel and presents it shaved, eye-high like John the Baptist's head on a platter."

"Yes yes, can I have a 'glory be, hallelujah,'" she said, now blowing smoke out the window. She thought she saw the cat stalking in the twilight.

Coop added "so it all comes out; the lingerie receipt, Mr. Pinky getting his passport stamped—"

"Praise the G-spot, Jesus, and pass Mr. Pinkie! *Something* ought to get to the Promised Land!" she said.

"—and she's standing there, looking like a sexless marble statue, and gives me a half-ass apology, 'I guess I didn't think it through.' I say, 'so I get the gift that Bennie didn't want.'"

Headlights swung across the backyard and the cat became a trundling skunk. "Damn!" said Coop and made for the pantry. "Krissy go out the garage and head off Kaf."

"I never called her over," she said.

The gun was all that mattered now; putting things at the mercy of his slightest touch. "Moss cover that frittata" had no irony for him. He slid onto the stoop.

"It's too dark out!" Krissy said. "First rule, know—"

"Shut up!" he hissed at her. "I told *you* the rules!"

The motion sensor turned on the floodlight; he wheeled back, assassin again, but couldn't spot it. The rustling to his left yawed his trunk, gun at shoulder, and Takuri, holding a platter, stopped short. The light went out in the stillness.

"Oh my," Takuri said. "Firsta rule…."

Something—he was stock still; maybe her trembling—set off the sensor and in the light she stepped forward offering a pie. "Fuck me," he said to himself, "John the Baptist on a platter."

"Sklappa quiche," she said, coming up the back stairs. "From the deli you say slaughter his own meat—"

Krissy opened the screen door and Takuri entered warily. "Why don't you put that gun away?" Krissy said to Coop as Takuri set down the dish. "And you are….?" she addressed Takuri, adding "never mind, I think I know."

Takuri hadn't let go of the dish; she smashed it on the table, cracking it. The escaping quiche had chunks of scrapple, Coop saw, big enough to pick out if they were sharing. "Why is she *here?*" she said. "You say she in Paris." She eyed the fridge door. "So *that's* what it rook rike!"

Krissy half-laughed as she sat and brought out another cigarette. She'd smoke this one right here.

"Huh," Moss said nervously. "So this is not Kaf."

Krissy deadpanned over to him. "Asshole. Turn off the helpful fret and turn off the frittata. You and I don't do coffee in the future and snicker at this."

"Why is bitch *here?*" Takuri said and the quivering tautness of her face reminded Moss of the concern Coop had for her "Bruce Lee temper" he called it: "First she coils, then wipes out anybody in the room."

"I *live* here, bitch!" Krissy said. "So you take your clacked prate—." She stubbed out her cigarette in the quiche.

Takuri turned to Coop who had leaned back into the corner with no slouch, relaxed but not. Moss saw a crooked post, one that would need its hole re-dug, rocks and roots cleared, tamping—a lot of work just to get something back to the way it was. The rifle was behind Coop, a parallel lean; his finger absently flitted in out of the muzzle.

"Why I do *this?*" Takuri said, patting her crotch. "You shave me in fleezing tent and I have to pee in gejigeji for *what?*"

Krissy headed to the bedroom. They could hear drawers opening and shutting. Takuri went to the fridge and swiped all the fruit magnets holding snapshots to the floor. "Nice hair," she said kicking at that photo of Krissy. "Everybody shave for you?" She passed Coop still in his corner and set off the motion detector as she rounded the garage.

Krissy came back with a handbag. "Do me a favor. Don't come to me with 'contrite' again; you were just re-packing an empty shell."

"This is where I'll be crawling from," Coop said as the light outside went off.

She left by the front; there were cars doors slamming and two long wails of horns down the dirt driveway, a ghostly claim to evanescing territory.

Coop jerked his head precisely an inch, flicked a switch by his shoulder and the floodlight came back on, fixing the cat in mid-stride in the yard. He shouldered off the wall, pulled the gun silently from the closet. "*Looks* like a skunk," he said with his toe cocked against the screen door. "I could tell her that."

The Last First Black Man

The eights were the most misshapen. Next, the zeroes were hardest to carve. Those with the bad luck to caddy that slow, very rainy summer of '08—known ruefully to the rich club members who measured their lives by consumption as "when the cup on 15 stayed half full" or, for the less philosophical, "when you literally sank a putt"—had more time than they wanted to smooth their initials and numbers in their shack's scarred walls.

Only a portion of the wrap-around bench was under leaf cover so the veteran caddies took the shade or the dry. Most were college kids; a couple of high schoolers. You had to be 16 and in great shape to carry double bags—usually with a rule-bending excess of clubs—over the hilly 6900-yard course. They all knew of some legendary tips; the day Mr. W's profitable skins round, for instance, was $500 in the caddy's pocket.

They heard the scuffed steps on the crushed oyster shell walk and they put down their distractions—phones, magazines, knives. This seaside course near Marblehead, Mass., had plenty of two things: shell walkways and sand traps (21 of those on hole 11 alone). It was one of the few remaining courses that still mandated caddies—carts were a rare exception—and while not exclusive, you wouldn't know it from the whites-only photographs adorning the club house interior walls.

Bunny Haire, the black caddy master (here "since the slave days" was a members' joke he would nod too agreeably at), slammed the shack's saloon-style single door without entering. It was an early morning habit to get any sleepers upright so members looking in wouldn't see his crew slacking off. But Dash, applying liquid white polish to black-and-white cleats jumped and slashed white across the black kiltie top protecting the laces on one.

The door opened part way revealing Bunny bent over laughing silently with his big body. "No I hadn't heard that one, Mr. H," he said. "Don't tell your wife that one, that's a good one, yessee, have to remember that one." He slammed the door again without entering. "Let me see who I got for you, Mr. H. Be right out."

Dash rose from the bench and said, "Could you not slam the door?"

Bunny looked at the cleats. "You done with those yet? Mr. L gonna be up on the tee any minute."

"I was almost done when you made my hand slip—"

"Jackie!" Bunny said ignoring him. "You're up. Take Mr. H and Mr. A's bags—" and when Jackie rolled his eyes added, "now don't give me guff. If you want to sit, fine. I know Mr. A slices and Mr. H hooks. Zigzag, just figure that's how you walk today, zigzag. You want to be paid by the mile, go drive a cab." Jackie shut off his phone and headed out. "And check you legs for ticks when you come out the woods each time. All you. It's high season for bloodsuckin."

Dash used his sleeve to wipe the stray polish; held them out. "These are done."

Bunny brushed by him and exited. Dash wheeled and flung them at the closing door. "What kind of faggot wears white-and-black shoes with this flappy crap, look like doilies, on top?"

"You better get those," another caddy said and Dash glared at him. The door opened and swept the shoes; Bunny waited and Dash grudgingly picked them up.

"Patrick," Bunny said, "you're takin Mr. B and Mr. G. Now they're playin skins—$200 a hole—that's right, if you got it, flaunt it. The point is, stay out of their heads if you want a nice tip from the *loser*, too, not just the winner."

Bunny followed Patrick out, hung in the doorway as a member approached. "Mr. R, oh it's a good mornin, yessee. Now you're doin 27 today, are you? Well, that's givin some notice to the rest, ain't it, for the club tourney, yessee." He looked over his shoulder. "Well I got Petey in the shack…I know you ain't crazy about him, but the only other one is a little green yet behind the ears." Dash started to object; thought better of it. "Petey it is then," Bunny said, "and I will mention that to him for sure."

He stepped in and caught Petey heading into the side kitchen entrance from the shack's back door. "Hey, quit moochin that buffet stuff. And latch that door, they got air conditionin in there. And throw out that Butterfinger. Jesus! That's exactly what I'm gonna talk to you. You got Mr. R as a single, 27 holes. He's givin you another chance but don't be unwrappin candy on his backswing. Get out there." To Dash he said, "I told you hurry; Mr. L's up next. Let me see those."

Bunny took the shoes and pointedly held them under Dash's chin. "I guess they got a *shine* in them," he said.

"The fucks that mean?" Dash said.

"Don't use that language in my shack."

"But callin me 'shine' is okay?"

"I didn't call you nothin."

"You kiddin me?"

Bunny headed out but Dash grabbed his sleeve. "Speakin of callin, I been here three days and ain't been out yet."

Bunny brusquely lifted Dash's hand off; the discrepancy in size gave Dash an insight into how powerful the man might have been before he went heavy in the footfall. "Day one you walk the course," Bunny said. "Everybody does it. Day two you walk the course. Everybody does it."

"Like hole 14 don't follow 13 all of a sudden? Like 15 don't follow 14—"

"You count strides, measurin from the bunkers to the green; you measure from the drop zones; you measure pin placements; distance from one edge of the lake to the other—"

"I know my way around."

"I *know* what you know. There ain't no damn windmills out there, no clown mouth to putt into. This is the Marblehead Links Country Club, maybe the uppityest club on the east coast, and one of the last places to give caddies a job. And I'll tell you this just one more time: pull those pants up on you black ass. Nobody wants to see your crack. You walk the course when I say so."

Dash adjusted his pants, re-tightened his belt. "Marblehead. 'Nappy Head' more like it." He slid to a Stepin Fetchit impersonation. "Yassuh Mistah B, lemme fetch that club you threw for ya. Oh, Mistah K, you got goose shit on you shoes; lemme wipe that for ya."

"Number one, they're not shoes. They're cleats. You know your way around like hell. *Maybe* if you sprayed some arrows with a can a Day-Glo."

"Fuckin fetcher."

"Fuckin tagger."

"Stepin Fetchit—"

Bunny got in his face. "My name's Bunny Haire. And you a ass-flappin tagger from the Roxbury Projects, happy to piss paint all over town and say, 'lookee, that's me.'"

"I don't have to take this. I don't have to be here—"

"You're right, cuz the judge said where you *should* be is slaughter-house mop man in that stench hole backside of Boston! But, somebody here sponsored your ass for 'alternative community service' or some such. Figured bein out in nature be good for you. I personally think sloppin entrails was your justice cuz otherwise this is just one more thing supposed to be handed you by the white man."

"Only thing they hand me is shit to keep me down. Food stamps, welfare...like that."

"You cash it?"

"Fuck yeh!"

Bunny looked him up and down dismissively. "Like I said, handed you." Someone called for him outside. "I'm in here! Be right there." He stopped and checked the earth floor, picked up slivers. "These from the bench?" he said. "Don't be pickin at my woodwork here." He walked slowly, examining them. "Yeh, Bunny be right there."

"Fassas I can shuffle," Dash said. Bunny wiped his hands and sped up but Dash caught up to him at the door. "Look," he said, taking in the empty shack. "In case you ain't noticed, whichever Mr. X is out there, all you got left is me to tote him. So all this talk is mute. Right...*bro*? I mean, bottom line?" and he tried to engage Bunny in an elaborate handshake series which he ignored, slamming the door behind him.

Dash scuffed the dirt at the man gone. "This place even look like jail," he said to himself, waving at the stockade-style fencing. He sat and absently picked at the bench, flicking splinters. He stopped when the door opened and the greenskeeper, a wiry white man in his 50's with sun-damaged neck and slight stoop, sidled in finishing a conversation. "That's a good one, Mr. J! 'A black man walks into a Marblehead bar....' Have to remember that one. Now I'll have you ready in three shakes of a jig." He stepped into the shack.

"Shakes of a *what?*" Dash said.

The greenskeeper looked around the empty shack so long that Dash followed suit. "Okay Askew," he said, "guess it's you."

"Name's not Askew."

The man waited, looked past Dash. "C'mon, you're up for Mr. J and guest!"

"Name's Dash."

"Askew!"

"Who you *talkin* to?"

"Last chance Askew. You don't want it? Okay, let me see if he'll take Perkins."

"Perkins?! Ain't nobody—"

The greenskeeper exited. Dash paced and the man quickly returned.

"Who *are* you?" Dash said.

"Greenskeeper."

"Where's Bunny."

"He's busy."

"Doin what? *I'm* his job."

The man gestured and spoke to the air. "Then forget it Perkins! If you can't go out now, maybe Mr. J'll just play *after* lunch to suit your schedule!"

"Look," Dash said. "Nobody in the john! Nobody mooching the buffet items in the kitchen! *Nobody* in the shack!"

The greenskeeper seemed to see Dash for the first time and matched his aggression. "You saying I see nobody?"

"A golf ball dimple your skull once too often, man?"

"Excuse me...man?"

"I'm sayin, there ain't no Askew, no Perkins. I'm up to tote."

"We're saying the same thing. *Nobody's* ahead of you." And he left.

"The fu—?" and Dash started after him but the door opened and a young man with carefully mussed blond hair messily finishing an "everything" hot dog walked to the caddy wash-up alcove, and re-entered drying his hands. He sat on the bench, belched with no filter, pulled out a tee and started picking his teeth, making loud sucking sounds. He opened his shirt and basked.

Dash sat in the shade that remained. "You got to do that noise?" No response. "Then use somethin that works," he finally said, "not a damn tee." He pulled a long sliver off the bench and tossed it into his lap, receiving a nod of thanks.

"We don't get many of your kind around here," the young man said.

"Fucks that mean, 'my kind'?"

"I meant a guy nice enough to splinter a bench for a fellow caddie with gristle in his teeth. You *are* a caddie?"

"I ain't tryin for a suntan."

"What's your name?"

"Dash."

"Dash."

"Yeh."

"Dash?"

"*Yeh*, I said," and, as though it should be obvious he added, "cause everythin that comes after me is death."

"You mean like 'dash somebody's brains'?"

"No."

"You mean, what, on a tombstone?"

Dash was honestly impressed. "I can't believe it; you got it. Nobody gets it!"

He spit out some hot dog. "Technically, I think that's a hyphen."

"Techni—? No way." Then recovering, "Whatever. Same diff."

"No. Two separate things, grammatically."

"'*Grammatic*—'. We still in *grammatic* school? Anyway, theory still holds." Dash waited. "Real name's Tyrole."

"Rhymes with 'parole.'"

"No it don't. What's yours?"

"Smyttee," he said, matching 'mighty.' "S-m-y-t-t-e-e."

"You mean 'Smitty,' Dash said. "Rhymes with 'shitty.'"

"No," Smyttee said. He was done with the splinter and flipped it away. "It's one of those old names you can't mess with. Been passed down for generations. You know, forged in feudal battles and secret pacts and marriages of nobility. It's a mix of Smith, Smythe, and D'Arquis."

"The fucks that mean?"

"'D'Arquis'?" he laughed. "Part of a French-English bloodline you can only be jealous of. I guess I'm one of those people you hate."

"Hate?" Dash suddenly had no clue how to compete in this conversation; he felt the person opposite him held facts he had to improvise about—a dossier, they called it at the police station. "You mean paint fingerprint expert?"

"What?!" Smyttee said.

"Nothin."

Smyttee took out baby oil and spread some on his chest. "Of course, maybe I'm being hasty, making an assumption about your hurt feelings as I was, vis-à-vis my lineage. It's a habit since I am privileged, but you also could be some rich kid headed to an Ivy League school in the fall, doing this caddie thing as lame punishment."

"Yeh," Dash said, backing out of this.

"Oh. Which university? Brown?"

"The fucks that mean?" he said, back in.

"Cornell, Princetown, Brown? Ivy League?"

"Oh," backing out again. "You wanna bond? Let's bond over the 'lame punishment' part."

"I'm here since my dad said I have to"—now with a patrician tone—"purchase my own wheels." He scoffed. "I know mom will pick up the tab but I've got to at least make it look good."

"You're not gonna make any cash showin up at lunch time. Probly only get the afternoon round, if that."

"Doesn't matter when I show up. Bunny's on my ass; he won't send me out."

"Tell me about it," Dash said sarcastically.

"Well I gave him an IQ test last Wednesday—"

"I didn't mean I really wanted to hear it—"

"Wait, I'll give it to you." Smyttee got one of the scorecards and snub pencils from the tray and sat next to Dash, drew something quickly. The sun had slid to where there was now no shade and Dash wished they gave the caddies a hat from the pro shop, least they could do.

"What's the matter with this scene?" Smyttee said, holding up the card.

Dash stood, losing patience. "The matter is I'm broilin in this goddamn stockade, playin another man's doodle game!"

Smyttee started to pocket the drawing. "I heard IQ tests were scary for some types."

"The fucks that mean? Gimme that."

It was a quarter moon with a star between the horns. "Star's in front of the moon," Dash said. "Ain't no star in front of the moon." He crumpled the scorecard, let it fall.

"According to Bunny there is. I had a sheet of paper and drew a night sky, big quarter moon with one star right here like this one. Bunny says, 'if the moon's full, you don't see that star.' I told him he's about 85."

"That's moron level. Normal is a hundred."

"You're pretty quick. I figure you for 110."

"The hell you get off bein my IQ?"

"But I am, if I want to"—now street-black accent, head bobbing—"go all *solipsistic* on you ass."

"Go *what?*"

"You don't know what it means? It was on the English SATs."

"Sure," Dash said, releasing his discomfort by grinding the bit of meat Smyttee spit into the dirt. "Go whatever, *sobsista* on me. Do your best shot."

"It means, I am the center of the universe. Everything revolves around me. I don't have to 'do' anything to you. Sorry."

"*Sorry?* You think you can disappoint me?"

Smyttee laughed, flipped the pencil toward the tray. "You're right. How could I possibly disappoint you. So. What is your IQ?"

"No idea."

"Mine's 131. Top two percentile of the population. Just missed a partial scholarship. Not that my parents minded, of course, but money's money."

"Partial's just chump change," Dash offered, keeping up.

"So you get a basketball scholarship?"

"No."

"Track? You look like a track and field guy; lanky—hop, step and jump?"

"I ain't no *fetchit.*"

"Too small for football...."

"Look. I'm more what you call artist than a jock."

The sounds inside the kitchen were ratcheting up, lids and pots slammed, the Spanish losing its mellifluousness as the workers felt the extra heat and chef's daily ire with the lunch deadline nearing. Seeing as this was a rare sunny day, the buffet would likely be moved onto the patio, adding cleaning those tables and cushions, opening the umbrellas, to the logistics.

"Let me guess," said Smyttee, stroking a non-existent goatee. "You got in on a découpage scholarship. No, you're more the picassiette type."

"I didn't get in on any scholarship, period. I didn't get *in*, all right. I never said I did. I'm here, that's all."

"*Here?* You say that like it's a future. Not unless you plan to end up like Bunny."

"No way I end up like Bunny, droppin trou, kissin white ass."

"'*Fucks that mean?*' Smyttee said. "I mean, you're mixing your metaphors. Either you drop *or* you kiss."

"Oh, we back in grammatic school."

"Now me, I'm on track for a diplomatic posting. First it's international service school, which is basically learning how to hold your liquor so you can drink like a fish and get other people to spill secret shit. Even if I get posted to some no-alcohol towelhead hellhole like Saudi Arabia, it's still, believe me, cocktails, white tie, cocktails, black tie. Hmm. So you messed up in high school and weren't college material?"

"Oh very diplomatic," Dash said. "You *definitely* got the flair."

Smyttee slapped his thighs. "I just haven't had enough to drink" and he pulled a flask from his back pocket. "Screwdrivers. Nobody can smell the vodka on your breath." He took a swig, offered it to Dash. He moved over, wiped the top, and took a big slug.

"Whoa," said Smyttee grabbing the flask. "This has to hold me over until I get back to daddy's stash." He wiped the top, took a nip and pocketed it.

"So when the guidance counselor talked to you about your future—" Smyttee started.

"What are you, broken record? My future's today, man! I didn't get no guidance counselor, no camp counselor, no whack off—oh

excuse me—masturbation counselor. My dick is in my *own* hand. I
control my *own* fate. I'm just doin time here for some 'malfeasance' or
some shit and I'm outta here."

"You broke the law?"

"Oh, you don't want to *ssociate*?" Dash spat on the floor. "There's
your swig back."

"Relax. I'm just asking—"

"Hey don't get off on my havin a real life!"

Blue smoke poured out of the kitchen's screen door accompanied
by the smell of fried chicken. Dash's stomach growled. Yesterday the
dishwashers tossed stale bagels to the caddies.

"Okay," Dash said. "What I did? I was dry humpin yo mama's
butt in Tiffany's. Maybe you heard it over the store PA: Clean-up in
aisle six."

"Aisle six?" said Smyttee smiling. "Right next to the express check
out?"

"Whatever."

"They don't have 'aisles' in Tiffany's. You never been in the store,
have you?"

"And yo mama got no butt. What's the point?"

"Just be real, man, you with your 'real' life. What did you do? Are
you embarrassed because it's too big…or too small."

"Too *small?* The hell—. Oh I see. Maybe you will make diplomat;
gettin me to spill. I was caught taggin." Off the quizzical look, he
added "'usin aerosol paint containers in a unsocietal manner,' is how
you'd put it. Least the judge did."

"White judge?"

"Why d'you think they wear black robes?"

"It goes back to the pre-colonial English system—"

"Fuck that. It sets off they bein white, that's why! Eleven more
days here, keep my nose clean, then they wipe my slate."

173

"So they have a file on you."

"Yeh, dossier. Chickenshit excuse to keep tabs on the black man."

"Oh, the black man in *general* did it, not you."

"I did it, but that don't matter. What matters is some white woman, quote, 'saw a black face and I look like somebody,' the cop said."

"So, *you* knew it was you—"

"Exactly! But they didn't. I was just somebody, not even somebody suspicious."

"Except for the fingerprint."

Dash chuckled. "Yeh, the fingerprint. That tore it."

"All a cozy tête-à-tête at the station, until that."

"Be on my way, until that."

"So what are the repercussions?"

"Reper-*whats?*"

"To not keeping your nose clean," Smyttee said.

"You mean if I 'recidivize'?"

"Recidi-*what?*"

"I guess you don't get everythin from the SATs. Maybe if you had a 'truancy counselor' when you were growin up," Dash said.

"Man, your kind can sure dance."

"The fucks that mean?"

"Dance around the *issue*. Never mind, Tyrole. I really don't need to know you for the future." Smyttee went back to the sun. There was a metallic clink of a struck ball and the standard murmurs of approval from a tee nearby.

"I go to jail," Dash said. "Repurcussion-wise."

"Jail?" and Smyttee sat up from his slouch.

"County time, not state!"

"Oooph. I thought maybe a fine or—. Man, jail. On a resume and all? I mean, you don't want gaps, missing years to explain."

"The hell you know? They don't give *years* for taggin. A month, max."

Smyttee took out the flask for a swig. "Even a month," he said, "when you're on a life track." Dash reached for it after his swallow but it was pocketed quickly with a "shhh!" Smyttee opened the shack door a crack. "Oooh, I thought I heard her. It's Mr. V and his daughter Lara. Does she look fine today. We both got into Yale." He stepped back to button his shirt and Dash snuck a look: "Oh my," he said. "She dropped her keys."

Smyttee pushed back in, then slowly pulled back. "Whoo am I a sucker for that."

Still peeking, Dash said "puffy titted 17-year-old skinny tan blondie in a kilt thing, ass in the breeze, at the uppityest club with daddy's valet parkin the Mercedes SL550 convertible with custom saffron gold fleck paint job? You a sucker for *that*? Imagine."

"No mommy. And daddy with a quadruple bypass. Not supposed to even play golf. That makes my dick the shelf that trophy wife is going to sit on."

"Shit!" and Dash softened the spring door closing and quickly stepped back. Bunny entered.

"I got Mr. V and Miss Lara up next," he said. "God knows she'll be off in the woods half the afternoon bent over lookin for a ball. Dash!"

"Right here Mr. Bunny!"

"How about we steer you well clear of that," he said, "and you clean some clubs. Smyttee, you're up." He left.

Dash stood transfixed and Smyttee grabbed his hips from the back and shimmied them. "Oh I'm up, I'm up! 'Miss Lara, let me hold your hips, help you line up that putter while daddy takes a knee and clutches his heart.'"

Dash shook free. "Bunny's a goddamn 85 IQ moron! He think I'm gonna rape the bitch? With white guys fulla clubs runnin around?!"

"Don't show your ignorance. They're not the right clubs."

"The fucks that mean?"

"Got to go. Got some tawny downy thighs need to be checked for ticks."

Smyttee exited, squeezing past Bunny with a bag of clubs who said "they're goin off number 10. Hustle yourself over there." He plunked the bag down, unzipped the cover to reveal very muddy club heads.

"Oh no," said Dash.

"Mr. E is eatin lunch and these need to be in the trunk of his BMW before he finishes and heads to the airport."

"The hell he try to do, dig a ditch?"

"Bag must've fallen off the cart where they're layin sod on 6. Cut short his round."

"Cart? So you didn't give him a caddy?"

"Come to think of it, he did ask if there was anybody new in the shack could tote for him. Nice guy that way."

"So you skipped me."

"You were doin shoes."

"Cleats."

"Don't tell me my job. I caddied here before you were born."

"And that makes you what?" Dash reached under the bench for the scorecard with the IQ test. "Other than a ignorant fetchin nigger thinks there's a star between here and the moon."

Bunny knocked the card to the ground and in a forced whisper said "and I'm just about one nigger too many here. Last thing these members want is some ratass tagger on parole—"

"*Not* parole; community service. After that, the charge comes off, my sheet's clean."

"Meantime you're the reason any shit happens here. If a Rolex goes missin from a locker, finger points to you. And then it swings so easy right to me. If they're twenty bucks short in the pro shop till?

Finger points to you, then me. Now I got this job since I knew this course inside out as a caddy and I made sure every member I toted for knew it. When the white caddy master moved to Florida, the committee asked me to step in. It's okay. More than okay. Less cash than caddyin but it's less humpin and you get paid when it rains."

"Well don't you sound like the lord of the fuckin manor." Dash closed to him. "They give you this 8-by-10 shanty; they let you hold their clubs, shoes, car keys for a little while. Man, wake up! You in some kinda Hell's lendin library where they say okay to stick your head out once in a while and look at the good life, then shove your ass back! I pity you."

"I don't take your pity!"

"Oh yes you do. You take me mine and you *suck* up theirs. Tell me you never heard them stop short when you come round the bend, like in the locker room, and they quick change the topic?"

"There's instances maybe when stuff's bein said, they stop. Don't mean it's about me," Bunny said.

"Oh no. It's somebody rowin a whole other slave galley."

"Watch it."

"They ever cozy up to you sayin, uh, 'hey Bunny, slow down, you're workin harder than a pair of jumper cables at a nigger's funeral.'"

"What?! Nothin like that—. Why would they?"

"Because they turn! People turn. And before they do, they *practice* turnin on you all the time, to see what's gonna be required when the time comes."

Bunny seemed to want a hail from outside. "That's not how they seem to me—"

"That's cause you turn with them! Stand still you feel their slap. Give them time to know you and they'll turn, oh yeh, or even they just can't wait and a damn *stranger* says somethin to your face you can't get rid of..." and now Dash had made the shack's confines his own measured cell as he paced, oblivious to Bunny. "I don't *care* if it was back when you was a kid and he was a kid, somebody new in the hood standin on the sidewalk with a vanilla cone and you say 'hi' and I don't care if it was a cute-ass white kid, you can't get rid of it, you hear what he said outta the blue and you never will shake it, that's why my guard is up!"

"You're mumblin, Dash. I don't know what you're talkin but sounds like you need some self-respect—"

Dash coiled menacingly. "*Don't* be another shiftless tells me to get some self-respect! Like you got anything in the human bank to give me."

"Don't you judge me."

"Well at least I ain't wasted my *entire* fuckin life. Here you go, for one: They *ever* take notice of you? Besides makin you the chocolate egg piñata or whatever the hell they bash for Easter at Marblehead? Better yet, they ever give you a Christmas bonus?"

"Was just last end-of-season they gave me somethin for caddy-masterin, yessee. I mentioned it was 10 years comin up and they got me a wrapped gift."

"You had to remind them? What was it? I hope a trip to Hawaii."

"It was like a cologne," Bunny said, embarrassed. "Committee gave it to me. Nice."

"*'Like'* a cologne?"

"It *was* a cologne. French. Means 'Water of Man.' The guys were jokin, sayin 'parlez-vous,' messin around like that, callin it 'You Da Man' perfume, or 'You d'Homme'—e-a-u, d-h-o-m-m-e—which was on the label. Except I heard the lady in the department store later, she called it 'Oh d'Homme.'"

"And you didn't put two and two together," Dash said, outraged. "The committee tellin you thanks Bunny for wastin away 10 years; here's a supply of 'U Dumb'?"

"Just shut up! I was the first colored to get this job. And I tell you, it's a hell that eats you every day when you think that maybe, if luck grabs your bootstraps, you're gonna at least be the *last* first black man; that all the slots were taken by the first black astronaut or senator or hockey player, or mayor or *deputy* in Texas, or loan officer at a crummy mobile home bank, or dog catcher for chrissake, or, or—I saw the picture in some PTA newsletter—'school's first black crossin guard.' And down you go on the 'last gasp' list. So I took 'first black caddy master' slot here. That means there's one less slot out there for you and for that I'd pity you, except I see you. Oh yeh, I see you clear. You the slow nigger fate runs over while you try to carjack it." Bunny stood up the club bag which had fallen over. "Now clean these." He also picked up the IQ test scorecard, nodding. "This? I was makin a fool outta Smyttee."

"Talk about self-respect. You don't grasp it, do you?"

"I know that star's not there."

"Well that's the one he hitched you to."

"Let him be stuck on that childish trick—"

"You his drownin *boy*, grabbin for a white star not even in heaven."

Bunny looked hurt. "That's low, son."

"Tell me if it's true and I'll tell you if it's low."

"I got to get back...to the members."

Dash mimed shaking out some cologne, patting it on his face. "You got to get back to *somethin,* man! Talk about self-respect."

Bunny stared at the IQ test all the way out the door. Dash looked over the muddy clubs; shouldered the bag and walked around, vaguely pointing out things and nodding sagely. He set it down, brought out the driver and handed it to the absent owner.

"Now Mr. E, this hole's 446 yards from the white tees but playin longer with the soggy fairway. Why is that, you say? Simple. You don't get no loose change; no *roll*. See, you toss a body outta car doin 60 into a river—no roll. Toss a body outta car doin 60 down Broadway—loose change."

Dash took a clumsy golf swing; peered after the "shot." "Oh, Mr. E, that's a lost ball. Wha'chyou mean I gave you the wrong club? You just jerked it left, clean off the course. You lucky some white kid wasn't on that swing set or it'd be a *drive-by* killin. Get it?" He smacked his thighs in faux laughter, then stopped suddenly: "No I am not goin to look for it! You're out of bounce; suck down the penalty and hit another."

He pulled out an iron. "You wanna try this one? You got to carry 175 over the lake if you're tryin to cut that corner." He put that club back and pulled another.

"I thought so. Need a lot more club for your droopy white biceps."

Dash took a swing, dropped the club and made a plopping noise with a finger in his mouth.

"I sure hope your dossier got stock in Titleist, Mr. E, at the rate you losin balls. Wha'chyou mean, I gave you the wrong club. You hit the ground first, is all. Look at the shit on this club. What? *'Wade'* in there? The hell. You put it there; you fish it out." He called after him: "Better roll up the sleeves, too, you gonna get your hands in that muck; it's like entrails, right? Look at Mr. E punchin in for a shift at the slaughterhouse."

Dash leaned against the wall, laughing and pulled his hand away quickly, sucking it. "Damn nail." He pulled out a fairway wood. "This looks like the right club." He hammered the nail flush with a chopped baseball swing, looked at his work, held up the club: "Man, the tool user." He brushed at the nick on the club face. "Oops," and he slid it back in the bag. "Oh you back already Mr. E. And you found a couple extra balls in the pond? That's called 'vig': you was owed one but collect three. You kiddin? You never heard of 'vig'? Don't go low IQ on me; you just call it somethin else, like 'easy terms' or 'no cash down' but it's all just workin a poor black sucker. Right. Now I got to 'shhh' 'cause you got a tough ass shot."

Dash took out the driver again. "You got a dog's legs right with a big-ass maple in the way." He bent the club shaft way off true and offered it. "There. Just take your natural swing, Mr. E, and you'll go right round that maple. Wha'chyou mean I'm the one with 'natural'? I ought to wrap this club like a rope round your Adam's apple—. What's that mean, 'be like a lynchin'? I'll show you a lynchin, what I shoulda done back then, when that little white kid's scared momma come runnin over, droppin her groceries afraid for her *po' baby* when I done nothin to him, shoulda strangled him with his ice cream, say such a thing to me, can never can shake such a thing, what, you never seen a *colored* kid before in you life?"

Dash was smashing the driver against the nail head: "The fucks that mean, how can I tell when to stop *wipin?* Him pointin that vanilla cone to my asshole, sayin *it's* all brown and *you're* all brown, how can I tell when to stop *wipin?* I did nothin to you, and you *turn* on me—" He stopped, hearing people approach the door. He threw the clubs in the bag and zipped the cover.

"He's likely done, Mr. Edwards," Bunny said, still outside "but your clubs were pretty goddamn muddy."

"There's no need to swear," the man said. "And you usually call me *Mr.* E."

"Well Mr. *Edwards*, maybe we're a little tired cleanin up after you each round," Bunny said.

A polished throat clearing. "Perhaps we should change the subject."

"Fine," Bunny said, mock upbeat. "Let's change it: Uh, how was the veal putanesca at the buffet?"

"Quite zesty."

"Oh, *zesty*. I never had no veal, zesty or otherwise. Matter of fact," Bunny said sharply, "I never had no buffet here. Look, why don't you just yell in the shack—. Better yet, get your own damn clubs to take to your car. Me, I'm gonna go piss in the members' toilet."

"Ever the joker, Bunny," said Mr. E as he walked in. He had obviously just showered, wavy black hair glistening, some moisture on his monogrammed shirt. He was squat and looked more like a rugby player or catcher than golfer. He preened, as though shaking off the last conversation. "Ah. These all ready for the next round?" he asked Dash. "I'm flying out to play in Raleigh and when I say 'I'm flying,' it means I'm the pilot so, one drink max." He finished the highball, started to hand the glass to Dash then set it on the bench. "Cessna 152. Two-seater. Know the plane?"

Dash glared. "You got a nigger in the shack!" he hissed.

"Well. We could use one."

"Angry nigger!"

"That's what it takes. After last year's fiasco."

"Fias—. What the fu—?"

"Oh right. You weren't here then. Our caddies played the Breton Pines lads at the annual outing for bragging rights. They had a ringer in their midst; our caddies lost four and two."

"I said, you got a nigger in the shack!"

Edwards looked confused. "What's a 'ning-er'?"

"Fucks the matter with your ears?"

Edwards brushed at them. "What, is there something on them? It's not blood from shaving; perhaps tomato sauce from the putanesca—"

"Okay, let's talk 'puta.' I can say 'whore' in lotsa languages. You got a daughter? Goin to college maybe?"

"She's home for the weekend, but yes."

"Pretty as Mr. V's baby girl?"

"She is quite fetching."

"Why don't you fetch her here and she and I can go in the woods."

"Or, you're an ornithologist?"

"Man, you guys got a word for everythin. Horny-thologist, that's me."

"*She* is too," Edwards said. "She'd love to practice some new bird calls."

Dash stepped into his chest. "I guess I got a few 'screeches' I could teach her."

Edwards patted him on both shoulders. "Fine, fine. You look like an upstanding young man, knows what he wants in life. It would be an honor to have my daughter meet you."

Dash had the feeling some member's son was behind him in the kitchen doorway; he turned and saw no one but, unsure, said "This is *me*, right?"

"Who else would there be?"

"No Askew, no Perkins. Some 'nobody'?"

Edwards laughed. "Don't go slippy-solipsistic on me. Be the center of the universe, nothing less."

"I don't know your game—"

"No, no, buck up!"

"You callin me a 'buck'?" Dash said.

"You da man!"

Dash felt like some secret rank was being pulled on him: Smyttee all over again. "You mean like 'U Dumb,' that cologne game? You're not gonna turn?" he said.

"Turn how?"

"The way it happens, in the blink of an eye?"

"What happens? To whom?"

"To me! To me! Who else is here?" Dash said.

"There you go! Back to being the center of the universe. That's self-respect."

"People turn on me and that makes me the center of the universe?" Edwards put a shoe on the bench to re-tie it. "I'll get it," he said.

"What? Your *lace?* You expect—"

"I am so glad I talked to the judge about sponsoring a black scofflaw here at the club. I said you would straighten up and fly right. I like what I see. Matter of fact, I could use a mover and shaker like you in my shipping department."

Dash felt a wave of dizziness; where was today's bagel? "Hold on, none of that. Me bein a mover and shaker means somebody yellin 'move that crate and shake a leg.' I'm done with totin."

"No, you're right, none of that for you, a guy with a brain. Let's take you out of the warehouse and put you on the paperwork side. You'd cause a stir, you would, with that clique of old white biddies yak-yakking in the office all day. You'd be the first black man there."

"The last first black man," Dash said, more to himself, looking at the dirt floor for steadiness but the ants on the hot dog were more spots showing up in his vision.

Edwards looked at his watch. "Yep. Credit to your race."

Dash sat. "The fucks that mean—. I mean, what're you implyin?"

"Your race to get the delivery order picked every morning for the trucks. Early hours no bother, right? If you're a horny-thologist, you're used to those."

"I guess, yeh, early bird. That's me."

"Pay's pretty good. There's a health plan, 401K for your future, chance to move up the ladder especially if you can give Clara, she'll be your boss, give her some heart palpitations. She just needs to be provided any excuse to retire."

Yielding to the flow, Dash said "'Excuse provider' is definitely one of my job skills. Sir."

"Well," Edwards said, clapping his hands. "I believe a deal's been done. Can you start tomorrow?"

"Tomorrow? I got this 11-day...commitment thing."

"I'll talk to the judge and fix that. So, unless you have matters to wrap up here...?"

Feeling less dizzy, Dash too clapped his hands. "Consider that we're, uh, in one of those, uh, win-win matters wrapped up..."

"'Paradigms'?"

"Yeh, pair 'a dimes, that's us. Rubbin together."

They shook. "I'd say this is awfully white of me," Edwards said.

Dash slowly pulled out of the shake. "White like a new sheet of paper? Startin fresh?"

"Just...'white.'" Edwards pulled his clubs to him. "You all finished with these?"

"Yeh, uh, well...."

"Don't be modest. I'll bet you put a *shine* in them."

Dash backed a step. "Tell me you're not turnin."

Edwards unzipped the bag cover.

"About those—" Dash said. Edwards held up his hand to stop him but his plea, Dash realized, was always part of the bargain: "Don't turn, Mr. E, don't turn like everybody when I drop my guard."

"What?" Edwards said distracted, wiping mud off his hands from sorting the clubs. "*Me? I* turned the golf cart?"

Dash latched onto it. "Yeh, maybe sharp like. Maybe on a hill down to the new sod; you turned and clubs flew off. And then you backed over them. In a haste. To make your plane."

Edwards pulled out the bent driver. "Hmm. Shaft looks off true... and it's got some nicks on the head."

"You coulda hit a rock? On the follow through when you was watchin the ball?"

Edwards patted Dash's shoulder, left mud. "You certainly are a good excuse provider."

"Oh yes, the best! You'll see."

Edwards pulled out a folded bandana to wipe his hands; he hardened. "But I didn't. Hit a *rock*. Or back over them. Isn't that true, son? Sonny...*boy?*"

Edwards waggled the club at Dash with one hand, like a riot police baton. Dash placed a hand above Edwards' on the shaft and stopped its movement. Each of them ritualistically placed a hand around the other's throat.

Bunny opened the door, addressing a golfer outside. "*No*, Mr. Atkins," he said, "I am *not* headed to splash some 'U Dumb' on my face. Why don't you come up with a new way to disrespect me, huh? That one's as old as your wife's beef-jerky pussy. Yeh, well fuck you too!"

Bunny stepped in; the two had dropped the club and were using two hands to strangle. Despite the menace, there was almost no violence; just a circling, more a test of wills riding the cusp of subjugation, a double lynching, horses stamping to unseat this weight. Bunny grabbed the club on the ground, lifted it high over one man's head, then the other, wavering.

"*Daaaaasssssssshhhhh!*" he bellowed.

The Zen Fake

"You're going to sit? *Tonight?*" my girlfriend Merci says.

"*Again?*" her twin sister Patti says, not looking up from her beginner's sudoku puzzle.

"It's a process. If you don't keep at it on a regular basis, you get nowhere. Besides, it's called 'just sit,'" I say.

"Oh, that makes it official," either one of them says.

I had my windbreaker on but I thought it premature to zip it. Show some openness, like uncrossed arms. Yesterday I was sitting in the meeting room at my Internet job with eight other Sales Livers (vs. Killers) when the promised new v.p. over from American Express ("Damn, shape up time," we had worried) strides in and catches me with my arms folded. "You," he said ignoring my Welcome name badge, "you've got the body language of a Biloxi jail guard. Do I want to talk to you?" I started to give him one of my sure-fire cold call ice-breaker lines, this one about Missouri being the Show Me State and Mississippi the Show Me Again State. But he puffed up alpha male and I yielded, him in a pinstripe suit and corduroy vest, conflating his old corporate tower with our casual cubicle mindset.

"I thought the whole idea with this Zen was to go nowhere, or be nowhere," Merci says, picking at it some more.

"You're the teacher then," her sister says.

"They're called roshi, and they're not 'teachers,' per se."

"Oh yeh. 'Enlightenment is in you already.' I've heard that," Merci says, faux remembering what I had told her. "You have to not grasp it, it just has to be released. Like the trash to the curb or Deena's upchuck this morning."

That's her six-year-old.

"My niece," the twin adds.

This "visit" from Patti, now into day five, is really an "intervention escape" (if there is such a thing) from her husband. They're in their rocky first year and she didn't think his drinking would get in the way when they got married. Anyway, it made the sex all they could handle, which I can't help hearing about through these thin interior walls when the twins have their regular heart-to-hearts in sleeping Deena's bedroom. That's where Patti's inflatable mattress is but it's more that they force themselves to stop smoking when they're in with Deena. I'm not as priggish as Freud but I can't help but wonder at the subliminal effect Patti's sexcapade details have on her niece's sense of self. Although for me to pretend to Merci I contribute more than cursorily in the Deena arena would be a stretch, as I am reminded perfunctorily by my delay in asking about the upchuck:

"And I don't ask you to raise her or give me money except for your share," Merci says, "but if you live here, there's a certain nuclear reality. Like if you were in Bolivia and there was a curfew, you'd stay in the house."

"Or at the however you say *flophouse* in Bolivian," Patti says, "if you didn't *own*." She's done with—and graded A—the sudoku but it's only 3x3 square and half the numbers are filled in already so it's as hard as a four-letter TV Guide crossword clue missing the word

"Show" ("Hour"?). She takes one of Merci's cigarettes, stands near the sink and they share drags; they're both quitting.

"You could be even more like twins if she inhales and you exhale," I almost say but zip my jacket instead. I don't need my sarcasm labeled again as "oh, one of your koans" ("It's ko-an," I always have to remind them, like Jo-Ann, not Joan). And yes, my roshi uses those time-honored "unsolvable" riddles to addle one's brain toward gaining the highest spiritual insight (*satori*). The koan given me was "pretty straightforward" I was told (but then again they all are if they're not what you personally have to sweat through in front of roshi): How do I stop the oncoming Tokyo-bound bullet train? But when an earthquake tore up the tracks, my koan was revoked in a short ceremony. I am now koan-less, which these two would certainly make fun of, and I don't need that lorded over me, although that makes me seem grasping at a nullity (wait, is that a koan; having "nothing" have a hold on me?).

We now four don't live on the wrong side of the tracks, although you'd hardly know it except for the new avocado electric stove the landlord had to install when Merci started her list of code violations. Deena's into doll coffee klatches and this burgeoning sociability on her part is inviolate, which means stepping constantly around her Stonehenge-like tableaux. It's not just that we're cramped; it's Merci's clutter, including the sentimental Pez dispenser collection from her mother (each one is from a different drive-in movie date). Merci got them all, being two minutes older, and her mother insisted that none of her bric-a-brac be broken up.

That's one reason I took to the zendo where we just sit: bare walls, bare floor...pretty much the spirit of a log cabin, which is what it is. Well, a scaled-down version more like a kid's backyard hangout. It was a kit the roshi and his students built and while I know the kit's early-hours TV spot with Tab Hunter doesn't mention "zendo" as one of its many uses, our roshi, as usual, recognized its "innerness."

"If this Zen stuff—," Merci starts.

"An oxymoron," I counter. "Zen doesn't have 'stuff'—"

She rides over it. "—is supposed to 'make you one with everything' (she's amping up because she sees I've zipped my jacket and am taking the last two fig newtons so my stomach doesn't growl and distract others), why can't you *just sit* here?"

"'Make me one with everything,'" Patti says, "like the hot dog vendor" and they laugh coughing out their shared drag remembering the joke about what the guru orders from the street vendor.

"Sit here. We can turn the TV way down—"

"On the visual quiz shows, not Jeopardy!" Patti says.

I can't tell them they just don't get it because of their ignorance, a word they would only hear with its throwback pejorative connotation (vs. what roshi calls our "launchpad" ignorance). The last thing I'm supposed to do is use my teachings as one-upmanship but it sure would be like shooting koi in a barrel in this case. I bow from the waist to Merci, palms together as obeisance/see ya later.

"Oh don't give me the Weebles wobble but don't fall down silent treatment," Merci says.

Patti has had enough; she suddenly crumples the empty fig newton cellophane noisily in my face. "Presto? *Sudoku?*" she says.

"That's the puzzle—," I start but give up. I made the mistake of sharing my initial enthusiasm and reading a poem by Basho to them from the 17th century, about the deep woodsy silence broken by a frog's "ker-plop" in a pond leading instantly to his *satori*.

Patti leaves the kitchen with, "besides, what if enlightenment is all there is!"

I take advantage of the room's parity and step to Merci to give a hug. With Patti gone, she'll yield. It's like she has to show solidarity toward her sister's plight and lump me as "bad guy" in with Manny, the 1/6th Choctaw—I never did understand that fraction;

something about a bartered pinto—who can't hold his firewater. And after downing a few and chucking the TV remote, he'll usually start a purging weight-lifting session in the den. If Patti doesn't hear clanking and satisfied grunting right away, she has learned to get out of the bedroom and forget something at the 7-Eleven.

I don't drink or smoke (now, both) and I steer clear of reminding Merci about these Zen "gains" since I am unsure whether I would be one-upping her or successfully "jettisoning the non-me detritus" (have to ask roshi for less literal translation from the Japanese). Besides, when I did invite her to the monthly guest night (when the roshi's wife bakes a gluten-free sheet cake that frankly could use some harmless frosting), Merci said afterward, "well, having a six-year-old keeps me in that 'here and now' thing."

We hug near the kitchen door. Even kiss and she grabs me below my tanden (Zen breathing core, lowest chakra for yogis—you get the idea). "It's all an illusion, right big boy?" she says stepping back but delaying her hand's release. "Oh, *he* doesn't think so. But now I'm, gosh darn, *grasping* again" and she adds a painful twist when the phone jolts. It's probably Manny, home alone, post one-pot dinner, pre-dishwash, when the bleakness sinks in. I bow my way out again and get a backhand wave.

———

I take the Vespa since parking a car after 7 p.m. is tough, by resident permit only for blocks around. Mostly garden apartments engaged in their balcony clutter wars, some duplexes, and a few holdover cottages near the lake that have been winterized from their Methodist campground days; those owners claim the neighborhood's bygone cachet with their Annual Lantern & Piccolo Night.

I thought my leather gloves were with the scooter but I wasn't going back inside for them so now my fingers are cold and the zendo will be chilly—kept that way to stoke our "fire breath" which roshi said actually can raise our body temp. A fellow student had whispered to me that he'd sure like to see some science on that and that was enough to make even the prospect of a placebo effect difficult.

It's a sparse gathering tonight, only six of us. I'm one of the youngest—and newest—and my friend Zak who brought me on a guest night (he said Zen made him a more "here and now" tunnel toll taker so I took him seriously, though it sounded like a mixed blessing to me), no longer shows up. Zak got discouraged when, after an intense six-hour meditation *sesshin,* all the others felt they had "jumped in the pond, *ker-plop*" or similarly joyous, if temporary, immersion in the experience and Zak, who didn't, couldn't stop feeling competitive. "When the back-slapping sounds hollow," he told me, "and it's not because you emptied out anything, you'll quit too."

The roshi is late, which never happens, so there's some zendo gossip during which I learn that my bullet train ex-koan had previously been issued to a woman (alpha female Ivy League professor who had done well enough by her divorce that she "would include it on her c.v.," she had joked) who literalized the koan (but sidestepped the bullet train component) to the point of one night standing in front of a rail yard switcher doing about three miles an hour wearing all black and holding a penlight she flashed on and off in Japanese Morse code. Even so it stopped the way trains do; down the line.

The roshi's high-school age daughter blows in and apologizes with a bow. "He'll be a minute," she says, swallowing her last bite of dinner and calling us to non-order.

She takes the roshi's embroidered red cushion, places it as we place ours and we all settle down. Her name's Aya—"uh-ya(h)h"—with some delicate aspiration we never could master during roshi's first and only Sanskrit lesson; it was dropped with us stuck on the vowels. She floats to the cushion doing a slow-motion plié right into a half-lotus, then tucks the other ankle to go full lotus without using her hand to place it. It's like something a praying mantis would envy. I lower myself like a pack mule with lopsided prospecting gear, try the half-lotus but it quickly hurts and I go to sitting on my heels (roshi calls it the "Devil's Island shackled prisoner pose"—I forget the Japanese word).

Aya leads us in our first cleansing breaths and I'm front and center because usually nobody wants to be in the roshi's "perfection" shadow and the other spots go early. My shoulders always relax first, then my gaze—which now travels past its usual point on the floor, toward her diaphragm and, well, saucy ("non-pal" thought surfacing) breasts as they rise and fall. She's purposefully unattractive in the weird way high school peer pressure can work but she probably doesn't need to enhance the downside. She knows this, I think, because she said at a guest night her goal is to become a "parts" model: "Hands and legs. Do TV spots for arthritis cream, Isotoner gloves, stockings, depilatory gadgets for anywhere but the upper lip."

I'm thinking "after" in a bra commercial. Our two breaths have slowed and synchronized, although I get light-headed matching Aya's extended exhalation. "Our tandens are in tandem," I want to whisper, to breach the purity; she'll smile without shifting her gaze and whisper, "you're my first."

Chip the Monk scuttles through, tail high, looking for old sheet cake crumbs. I maintain synchro with Aya; in fact all of us seem to be "bowing the walls" in and out a millimeter, our tidal breath eroding the boundaries, losing even the seamlessness of the seamless flow—

Of expletives! Coming from roshi's cottage, him to his wife. Their screen door slaps shut and we hear his footsteps near. There is a cacophony of breaths now.

He hisses "Buddhadammit" just outside and enters, first forgetting to remove his slippers. "Thanks Aya," he whispers and she unfolds her infomercial TV legs and floats off the cushion. She slips out and he takes her place, forcing some foamy pug-like cleansing breaths I presume to catch up with us?

The settling of our disturbed "mind-silt" has not gotten very far when roshi ("Tim-o") stands and says "this sucks." He composes himself a bit which entails, even though there is no mirror, a glance to the side window and his hands ruffling graying hair. It's hard to ignore his L.L. Bean catalogue, new-football-in-hand (can't they ever use a scuffed one?) rugged good looks, but I'm sure we are all, including him, supposed to.

He sits down again, heap-like. "I know who I am," he says, putting his head in his hands. "I'm a Zen fake. The real thing."

We've stopped our pretend breaths at this point. Is this last statement his own high-irony koan he's been working? The stray cars, dogs, music, and my tinnitus are flexing now, not the log walls. I'm trying to pigeonhole the last minutes into some salve—crazy ward haiku?—because I liked where I was and am annoyed now. I devolve to my fig newtons.

"No snacking," Tim-o starts but waves himself off. "I *know* who I am. What a cock up—." He looks at us as if for the first time tonight. "Most of my adult life I've been, you know, emptying the mirror. Stripping away who I *was*, to be who I *am*. I was not *so many other* 'Tim-os.' Rigorous. I was rigorous." We nod like unsure zombies questioning a mission more complicated than eating people. "Then one phone call. Fuck! Yes, I am one with 'fuck me' right now!"

No one knows what to do with the tension. The elderly couple who are near neighbors have huddled a bit. Roshi sighs, an orphaned breath, lost, amorphous. Ugly.

"The Tim-o I've nearly emptied from the mirror—you should watch me shave sometime—is now the very one I am defending to the death, apparently, judging from using the 'f' word in this zendo. A word that wasn't even allowed during its building, with plenty of cuts, blood blisters, splinters...my god, the splinters in a log cabin."

The elderly man clears his throat. "What on earth, or wherever, happened?"

"I've been hacked!" Tim-o shouts. "Not just my computer, mind you! Me, I, the quashed—nearly—ego of me. By some Serbian gang-bangers or whoever. My identity has been stolen. All of it and I want it fucking back!"

A chorus of "oh nos" is meant to soothe but roshi will have none of it. "Checking account cleaned out, Visa, MasterCard both maxed, a $10,000 CD cashed in early *and* they avoided the bank's penalty. They are good," he snorts. "Oh, and they hit you guys too."

Chip the Monk starts another pass but yaws way right as we all quickly rise, sending cushion flak in his path.

"Yes. Any of you who gave me social security numbers for, whatever, insurance coverage, or paid by credit card—"

Now we're a meandering Alvin Ailey modern dance for six called "DEFCON One Denial." The elderly woman, who has always been on the fringe, tells her husband "but I won't be able to change my mother's maiden name." We stumble, our legs still half-numb, and press in on roshi, seeking un-koan-like unambiguities.

"This is all very fluid, very new," Tim-o demurs. "My wife is..." and I don't hear the rest because I remember answering her email re: Acme-me Zendo Gift Shop special offers. For Merci's birthday, I bought a "babbling Buddha" (better translation needed?) fountain from Japan. I secretly hoped it would double as bedroom white noise and let me sleep through Deena's frequent checkpoint "mommy" visits during the night. Since my wallet had been stolen from the gym, I answered the email with Merci's MasterCard figuring to pay her back when the bill came.

There is chaos: voices rising, flapping jackets, shoes sorted in haste. "Remember," Tim-o says, trying to calm things down, "for instant anger just add anger to any path you're on." We'll have none of it. All six of us it turns out are on the hook to some degree. There are dozens of phone calls facing us that will be a stew of frustration, punching numbers, being on hold, being disconnected, getting the supervisor. All to reanimate the "straw person we've been scything at the roots, hacking up until the pieces can't find each other," Tim-o actually said once.

Roshi holds the door for us, head bowed, all as usual, but now it seems he's just avoiding the shaking heads and mumbles. I start to ask about the Acme-me Zendo Gift Shop return policy but remember I modified the fountain's babbling flow beyond its last setting of "verdant hubbub."

I grab a fish sandwich from McDonald's, sticking to the drive-in (it's all the color saturation there I can handle), eat the non-soggy half and throw the rest out the window. By the time I'm back at the apartment, Merci and Patti are bookends, asleep, on the couch and the TV talking heads cover me to the bedroom.

———

For some reason, I've never needed an alarm to wake up for the twice-weekly 8 a.m. sales meetings. With my commute, I'm up at 5:30 for car, train, subway, subway, walk/bagel stand. I was going to leave Merci a note about the credit card but it's too complicated and she'll want to vent. But I am a good listener: I once brought home the dentist waiting room copy of Cosmo. "Test score highest bracket:

'enlightened male'" I showed her, to which she snipped "next time your ears are close, try to listen to my G-spot."

Alex, the new sales v.p. from American Express, is all over our case (this his first real day on the job) at 8 sharp; anyone late is excluded. "We have the latest, hottest Internet thing; you've all been to Pasadena corporate for five days of training, so why are we bucket lapping?" he says. And, not that he'll add this, but Alex wants his signing bonus of stock options to kick in before the Internet IPO bubble bursts.

I know he has waited for my mouth to fill with coffee and bagel before sandbagging me in front of the nine of us. "Pascal, you've got the most robust territory in the city; 8 futon shops alone. Get one and you get 8; they're all related by blood or hate. But *nada* this month."

I couldn't say anything in my defense if I wanted to so I hold my finger up, which he ignores. "So I'm splitting sector 11 in half; you keep north of Houston St. and Ben will add Houston south onto his sector 12." Ben, of course, is good with that. "Also, you and Kumar (who nods to alert at his name) are on probation until my discretion; and there may only be room for one of you." (This is the "damn, shape up time" I feared). "I suggest," Alex adds, directing everyone's gaze to the tally board, "that if you two want to get out of the cellar, you work your territory harder. If a prospect tells you he has time near closing at seven p.m., you work until seven and beyond. If he says his brother has to be in the meeting and he's not there until seven, you work until seven and beyond."

I've spilled some hot coffee onto my tan slacks. I bolt upright to daub it before it burns and this action takes on a life of its own. I see Kumar is now all twinkly and bushy-tailed and I realize he's going to kick my ass to make the cut; he has a pregnant wife.

This was inside of me already, it dawns on me; just needed to be released. "Okay Alex," I say, "I'm willing to work to seven but what am I going to do with a four-hour lunch?" No one is sure if this is a shootout, gaffe, or what, so I tell them. "It's a shootout; laugh at him." I crumple my meeting agenda, hit the three-pointer, and my out cocky as a man can with coffee groin.

It's raining so sideways when I head home that all of us Sales Livers would have had a hard time this day keeping our computer laptop for in-store demos dry through our backpacks, even with the cheap garbage liners they give us. I'm not concerned about a new job; I have a desirable skill set for anyone who thinks the Internet is not a fad. And the piddling IPO stock options I walked from are now the junk they almost certainly were inside themselves.

I hope when I get back to the apartment, all have left early and I can have time to "sort out which ends of the spaghetti platter of my life are attached" (a work-in-progress koan of my own making).

———

"Soak-ed socks gruesome," I say to myself, starting a new haiku as I fold my umbrella in the apartment lobby. There are raised voices behind our door but by the time I get it open, I face a museum diorama—Merci, Deena, Patti and Manny, and a standard poodle so skinny its head could pick skeleton locks. The only thing moving is cigarette smoke. I step in and apparently trip the light beam that kicks the diorama into its animatronic set piece: "End of Merci's Nuclear Reality, early 21st cent."

The lull bursts; they all re-activate, glaring at me and each other, flopping on the couch, gesticulating in disgust. The poodle mashes through one of Deena's Stonehenge-like doll klatches on the floor so she's the only one now speechless and as Merci pulls herself out of the vitriol orbit, she says to me, "Just the fucker I'm looking for." She grabs a notepad by the phone.

"I'm not taking it back," Manny tells Patti, kicking toward the dog. "That's fucking final. Unless you come with it."

"You found that dog, you brought it home so I wouldn't pester you for a baby for another couple months, you fuck you," Patti says.

Deena smacks the dog with a doll and the poodle becomes a Möbius strip of skulk, avoiding her then Manny like an obstacle course of palpable fear.

"Aunt Patti fucking until she's full of come," says Deena, singsong, "come to her gills."

Merci rushes over. "Where did you hear that talk," she says, holding Deena tightly.

"I don't know," she says, now scared. "What are gills, mommy? What did I *say*?"

"She heard it in her sleep," I say, "the same way I hear about Patti's bionic beaver through the walls. Leave her alone."

Merci turns on me. "Don't you ever fucking—. Don't you ever tell me how to raise my child."

"Oh," I say taking the room in for her. "I wouldn't presume."

Merci flails the notepad. "I got a courtesy call from Mrs. Acme-me Gift Shop about their little hack-a-poo. When were you going to tell me you used my credit card for that fake jade fountain?" The dog is lapping out of it.

"Mommy, what is come? It sounds like an ice cream cone."

"It's *okay*, honey," Merci says. "It...*is* from an ice cream cone you put in...your gills." She whips back around to me: "I'll never lie to my child! Unlike you. To me. You out in your alternate universe while everyone in your orbit on earth has to pick up after you."

Manny is giving Patti prison guard body language. He is what the gym rats would deferentially call "big"; just shy of the muscles-as-crustacean look. "That dog stays here with you or you bring it with you," he says.

"That dog is not staying in this apartment," Merci says moving in front of her sister. "I'm allergic to fur."

"Poodles don't have fur," I can't resist. "They have hair, just like Deena."

"Shut up, you're not helping," Merci says.

Manny steps to me. "Yeh, bud. My sister-in-law was doing just fine with me until she got that phone call." He's got the Indian pony tail thing and he rolls his neck muscles a lot, as if keeping a steroidal seizure at bay.

"Mommy." The dog's slathering Deena through her playful objections. "Can we keep Sasha?"

"Do *not* get *attached* to that dog!" Merci shouts and I really laugh, wanting to say "ker-plop" to her for her sudden non-grasping progress. Manny thinks I'm laughing in his face and stabs a finger unsoftened by dishwashing into my chest. "I am going to kick your ass. I'm going to do it now. And when an Indian makes up his mind—"

I'm not backing down, it's been that kind of day: "—he signs the next treaty," I say, banking on a quick mental image of my long-discarded wrestling trophies.

"Outside," Manny says.

"I'll just get out of these work clothes."

"Oh no," says Merci. "You put that macho crap to work and bend some ears on the phone."

Patti has put the leash on Sasha and holds it out to Manny as he puts on his jacket. He shoves her hand aside: "I am coming back for both you bitches."

Patti snickered. "Are you trying to make me jealous? It won't work; I know I'm your stand-up bitch."

He leaves the door open. I go to change into my sweats and sneakers and Merci confronts me. "I want that Buddha lump to go back,

I want that charge taken off, and I want my good name Merci L. Barcroft restored."

"And Mrs. Patti Barcroft Windeater. If need be," Patti adds. Then, "Oh I don't know anymore" and sits down to smoke. Merci sits next to her and they share drags.

I go out the open apartment door and start to feel foolish, school yard stuff. It's still pouring; the foyer window a flight down is in a car wash. The front door opens and I get a fear spike/ball tingle but a stroller noses in. I swallow and make a face. "Unused adrenaline," our wrestling coach told us, "is the worst taste in the world."

I go down the last flight, open the door and Manny is seated in a full lotus position on the walkway, smeared by rain, eyes fixed a few feet in front. His gaze doesn't shift when my sneakers enter his field of vision.

"I had no call," he says softly.

"What the hell—" I come up with.

"It's Choctaw storm sit. Go out in the worst night, blizzard, lightning, like that."

"Blizzard?"

"Raise your body heat with fire breath, that's not a problem. Worse is wolves. They don't see what I'm doing as strength."

I circle, unsure, then sit on my heels facing him. "You mind?"

"In our unique casino-slash-nature-based language," he says, "I'd say you bumped me from wolf mark to wolf shill."

I smile. "Casinos. Scalp us legally now, huh?"

The postman walks slowly around us into the lobby. Quicker going back. With the rain's clatter, it's hard to hear a common breath, but a seamlessness sets in.

"Is that your Zen?" Manny says after a while.

"Yeh. My roshi is now my koan. Never mind."

Our slowed breaths no longer vaporize and the rain seems less cold.

"I got a some frozen chicken pot pies in my trunk," he says. "I didn't think Patti would jump back so I planned to take a few days. Just a tarp, sleeping bag, stove. The pies'll keep in a mountain creek."

"What kind of chicken pot pies?" I say, remembering a bad experience with one brand.

"*Chicken* chicken."

"That's like when someone asks 'what denomination is that stone church over there?' and you answer 'stones.'"

"You mean the make? Swanson."

Cupped hands atop knees, clear ponds for "ker-plop" machine guns. Am I not at least one?

"Okay," I say, looking back at the window where neither twin is standing; no confusion there. "Couple nights."

"One thing up there. Don't try to convert me to your way of sitting. My elders got plenty of that whitewash crap from your pioneers. Sore point."

I rise and my joints are stiff. "I'll just grab a few things upstairs."

"Less grabbing the better."

"You're a quick study," I say, schoolmarmish finger wagging for effect.

Slight look, gauging, rain a sure bet down his face; he lets it all ride.

Einstein's Love Proof

There were only two men now working in the New Submissions section of the Patent Office in Bern. The other 11 had gradually been let go, as had the dozen or so in the two sections a floor below devoted to Trademark Filing and Design Registration. The austerity cutbacks were due to Switzerland's iconic neutrality which had finally pinched the revenue stream so hard that the Federal Assembly was in fact now considering a move to at least a "skirmish economy" if a profitable war with a neighbor was still out of the question.

The men, in their young 20's, though virtually alone on this floor and lacking all but cursory supervision from someone in the recently merged offices for Immigration and Chocolate Knickknack Export, still maintained proper business attire. The formality extended to their relationship not because of a reticence to be friends but, rather having one need to speak French deliberately, knowing no German, so the other, a German but knowing some French, could understand him.

Schupplater, a handsome man with a meticulously-kept mustache, got up from his desk and pulled a tome from the fusty shelves, suddenly freeing hundreds of floating motes backlit from the sun's reflection off a building on Speichgasse. They reminded him of the supernova of powdered sugar that burst in the air this morning from a dropped tray of profiteroles in the bakery; his stomach growled but he said to his associate "it's your day to take the early lunch."

The man at the adjoining desk was curiously sizing up a sheet of paper, almost as though he were testing his eyewear.

"Herr Einstein," he repeated, "it's your day for the early lunch. I'm from one to two and don't be late coming back, with that 'time is relative' manure. I have a boot maker appointment."

Not even a blink. "Do me the courtesy," Schupplater said, his voice rising, "of—"

Albert Einstein suddenly crumpled the paper forcefully into a ball and stuffed it into his mouth, chewing savagely with his mouth open and trying to gag it down. "H_2O," he managed.

Schupplater jumped up and reached into Einstein's mouth to pull out the near papier-mâché lump and toss it down. "You cannot let the work get to you so, Herr Einstein. What was it this time?"

Einstein took out a handkerchief and wiped the paper's ink stains from his tongue. "A muttonchops equalizer," he said.

"Really?" said Schupplater as he picked the soggy paper from the floor. "I am considering growing them—"

Einstein smacked it from his hands.

"I mean," Schupplater said, "there's no machine out there for that. Perhaps it's what the world needs."

"Yes," Einstein said rummaging folders on his desk, opening one. "And the Earth has been waiting five billion plus nineteen hundred and four years for this, a 'cigar pre-macerator which gives your cold, stiff new stogie a warm, chewed texture.' Or, or, here, we've been waiting also for a 'canine sandwich board so dog walks earn money from your quadruped billboard. Expandable to fit any size dog.' Oh, here, a 'gentleman's gimbaled bowler.' Aagh," he said and he crumpled the paper, stuffed it into his mouth, retching in his attempt to swallow it.

Schupplater removed this one also and read it as Einstein disheveled his hair further and sat heavily. "'Gimbaled bowler. No hand necessary to tip hat to ladies. A nod of the head will cause the hat to dip and level itself, accommodating required courtesy and saving social gaffes as all hat tips are 100% consistent.' But Herr Einstein, we get dozens of these kinds of patent requests every week. I have one on my desk for a perambulator with pontoon outriggers folded above the wheels in case of flash flood while taking in alpine air."

"Humanity is hopeless, Herr Schupplater. We are surely down to the last three or four generations. And if only I could split the atom, I could hasten that with a bomb big enough—"

Schupplater threw his hands in the air. "Oh Albert, you with your big bangs again to end the world, to start the world, to end the world, who can tell with you. So, now to end the world, which can mean only one thing—a female whose legs are not parallel." Einstein lamely objected. "It always is," Schupplater said. "Plus all this masticating at your desk."

"My hand," Einstein said indignantly, "never dallies below my drawers, I mean drawer. Desk drawer!"

Schupplater mimed chewing the paper he held. "*Masticating*," he said.

Einstein, embarrassed, said, "Ach, my French is not so good."

"Better than my German," Schupplater said. "By the way, why is it all you Jews chew with your mouth wide open? And that is not part of the anti-Semitic piffle going around."

Einstein said, "Why do you Protestants examine all your various mucouses like you pinned the world's last butterfly?" He blew his nose into the handkerchief, then examined it minutely. "Yes, your kerchiefs, fingertips, sleeves—"

"Even your morning cottage cheese makes noise."

"—phlegm, snot, sputa—"

"Oh now," Schupplater said, "'Sputa' is not a word for polite society. You must be quite upset to be that rude."

Einstein slumped. "Oh Josep, I am beside myself."

"Ha!" said Schupplater. "You admit it! 'Beside yourself,' just like a quark particle cannot be where you measure it."

"They are hypothetical," Einstein said, rising to the bait. "They would not only violate lepton number conservation but charge-parity-time reversal symmetry as well. No science can explain them, and God does not play dice with the universe!"

The two men burst into unbridled laughter.

"Here we are," Schupplater said, "two brilliant minds, evaluating whether to give the Swiss patent office stamp of approval to…," as he picked a random folder from his desk, "a 'Love Proof Machine.'"

"Bosh. That's quite redundant; a machine *is* love proof. That's why we trust the heart of it. Not subject to vagaries—yes don't shake your head—a perpetual motion machine would hum its loyal perfection light years beyond any so-called 'everlasting' love, with its jealousy, vicissitudes, vapidity, snideness. Ach."

Schupplater put his arm around Einstein. "You wish to talk about her?"

"Ah Josep, you are an astute observer of the psyche. It *is* a woman. How keen to see I am upset."

"Well, suicide by esophageal paper cuts is a red flag in any psychological text."

Einstein keened: "I am doomed. Emma and I are doomed!"

"Emma?" his associate said. "I don't know this—"

"Ja," Einstein wailed, "my dear Emma, with the legs that aren't parallel! Hmm, or are parallel in a non-Euclidean universe where they could still meet…."

"But who can this possibly be?" Josep said. "You have no luck with women. Even the haggish street lamplighter told you to stop looking at her smudged ankles when she got on tiptoes."

"It was when," Einstein said, "you were taking the waters at Baden-Baden-Baden—"

"They've shortened that," Schupplater said. "Modern times."

"—while you," Einstein continued, "were having your way 'masticating' with shaped hot towels in the steam room, I had a *real* woman."

"I should have never mentioned that to you. But tell me, you hound—oh if I could only get a woman—tell me every detail. Wait! Let me get a hot towel from the lavatory."

"Stop! I will tell you nothing of this."

"I must hear these things. How did you meet, at least?"

"Well, she was having difficulty holding and quaffing her yard-long glass of ale at the Kloetzlikeller and so I explained the principle of dynamic equilibrium."

Schupplater gave a nod of appreciation. "You smooth talker you. Continue."

"We then sat and I ordered some head cheese, blood sausage and pickled pig's ear. I'd been homesick for some German delicacies. As usual, I was nervous, so I started babbling about multiple—"

"Orgasms?! I've worked some calculus that gives them credence!"

"No, multiple *universes*. Emma asked me coyly if she had been naughty in another universe, could she be a virgin in this one?"

"Of course, of course! End of discussion."

"Yes of course, " Einstein said, hedging, "since *if* I were an *apprentice* in this universe—"

"Call it a 'virgin,' which you are."

"—I could still know what I was, um, supposed to do, uh, *during*, in another universe, for example."

Schupplater was impressed. "Irrefutable statistical confirmation of manly experience. With just two universes; very tidy equation."

"So I took her to my garret, sneaking past my landlady and her insomniac dog, click, click, click every night with his nails on my ceiling, click click click...."

"Don't be a quark particle conversationalist, Herr Einstein. Stay in place; one topic at a time!"

"Well as you prefer what you call 'polite society' I will have to stop."

"Damn 'polite society,'" Schupplater said, "what with *loinality* being broached."

"That is an idiom I am not familiar with."

"Not an idiom. *I* am just babbling. I have no words for my frustration. I need succor: just one thing, then, Albert."

"These are personal matters."

"Just *one* thing!"

"Go on."

"The *one* thing I need to know is *what every follicle of her thicket looked like!* I can plot on graph paper a woman's nether region's private matrices—at least a pygmy's from an anthropological drawing I found—to assist your memory."

"No. I will just segue to the next day's cruel light and...no Emma. Since then, nothing. Nothing, but these billet-doux." He took a beribboned packet from a pocket. "Every day a new letter, all with the same regrets. Quote, 'the morning light blinds me with the darkness of no love' unquote. That's all she writes each day."

Schupplater felt a bit of schadenfreude was well overdue and took this opportunity. "You must have ruined the night for her."

"Apparently I was very shvartze."

"That would ruin it," he said, beginning to gloat.

"No, it was meant as a compliment."

"What? She told you you were like a Negro? Down there? Are we talking x axis or y axis?"

"I think it was both," said Einstein, smiling. "It was very exciting; I thought she was in pain because she was out-howling the landlady's mutt and saying 'stop it some more'—you know how convoluted German can be. But then came the knocks on the ceiling and Emma fled half-dressed, saying I had impugned her honor."

"Well if she had left *fully* dressed, perhaps. You said she admitted she had been naughty in another universe."

"You're missing the point, Josep. She wants me to marry her. It's one of the conditions for seeing me again."

"*One* of them? *Marriage* isn't enough? Is this the kind of truculence I can look forward to from a woman? Maybe I should stick to hot towels."

Einstein winced. "Please, Herr Schupplater, your imagery. Ach, the sticky of you."

"No," Josep said laughing. "*That* one is an idiom. So, what other conditions?"

"Oh, it's not going to be easy. I have to prove my love for her. Yes, prove. As Emma was dressing to flee the landlady's imminent appearance at my door she said I had been very aloof, unfeeling, you know... during."

"You, unfeeling? You who once spent three hours working out the probability that falling snowflakes could completely cover the poor dead faun's face in my mother's shaken snow globe? How dare this Emma. On what basis?"

Einstein demurred. "I was excited, mind you."

"Perfectly understandable, considering the vectors: what gets pulled, what gets pushed."

"Apparently, I was ranting, uh, during, about that old parlor mathematical trick of proving two equals one."

"Perfectly à propos. Even poetic, considering the, let us say, imagery."

"I thought it poetic myself. But I also called out other names."

"Uh oh. Even I, an apprentice in love's orgasm union, know that is a mistake. Who?"

"Fermat and Poincaré."

"Ooh," winced Schupplater. "The exculpatory explication for those two mathematicians would not quickly roll off the tongue. Pythagoras, perhaps, with conjoined triangles...the imagery again."

"I was beyond that, I tell you! I was in Poincaric ecstasy, solving quadratic equations off the cuff."

"I've heard of opéra bouffe, but this is opéra 'woof.'" He began howling like a dog, moaning like a woman, thumping his foot on the floor and reciting "X squared times x minus 2 equals 4."

Einstein did not see the humor. "Yes and now I am doomed. By the way, x would equal minus 1.54 and plus 3.54 to two decimal places."

"Aah. Still in the afterglow."

Einstein picked the paper off the floor. "So what is this?"

"Oh, the love proof machine? It's for two people just getting to know each other to verify the level of their compatibility, you know, as a mate, new potential parent or such. They stick a moistened finger all the way into a chemically saturated potato, and if it sprouts an eye within a couple of minutes the couple should start fecund."

"*Fecund*? It suggests that?"

"Not what you think, Albert. It's your French."

"It's a hoax anyway. The eager wiggling fingers of the man will no doubt push an eye to breach the potato skin. Patent denied. Although...."

"You have that do-I-use-my-power-for-good-or-evil look in your eye, like the time you discovered the letters in the molecular formula for methyl ethyl ketone peroxide were a slang term in Russian for 'cocktail.'"

"I should have kept $C_8H_{18}O_6$ to myself," Einstein said. "It unfortunately set the four very drunk Russians at the party on a quest under the host's kitchen sink. Even when I said it was explosive that only encouraged their pursuit."

"Okay, my friend, so what is it this time."

"My Emma wants proof of my affections, mathematical ejaculations notwithstanding. This potato hoax you showed me has given me a legitimate idea. I will first pour her a glass of the finest Liebfraumilch I can afford—"

"Yes."

"Then I will interlock our arms as we sip in the Continental manner, eyes engaged—"

"Yes!"

"Then I will whisper in her ear—"

"Her combination lock is ready to be opened; just twirl your fingers!"

"I'll whisper a doubt-quashing equation of unimpeachable—"

"What?! Wait you're losing me—"

"—no, make it a syllogism of unimpeachable logic—"

"No Herr Einstein!"

"A white paper, a treatise," he said, pounding his fist.

"Absolutely not!"

"I will use the most alluring—"

"Yes, back to her thicket! I'm a-tingle."

"Persuasive—"

"Knee-buckling—"

"Blood rushing—"

"Shoe flinging—"

"Pulse pounding—"

"Brassiere wrenching—"

"Hormone surging—"

"Girdle strangling," said Josep, "or whatever they do to get it off!"

"Lips parting in acquiescence—"

"My god, man, you make me need a hot towel!"

"Yes, I will use—" one said breathlessly and the other, echoing him closely, said, "you will use—"

Their voices merged: Einstein said "a pie chart!" and Schupplater said "Spanish fly!"

"What?!" they both said.

Again their voices merged: one repeated "a pie chart" and the other said "you've synthesized cantharadin," adding hopefully, "enough for both of us?"

"No. A pie chart."

"Don't even *say* that. It sounds too much like 'cow flop.'"

"Is it my French?"

"No, but trust me, it will to her," Josep said.

"Bar graph, perhaps."

Josep shook his head. "You're going to swoop Emma off her feet with what, some squiggles on paper?" He took a sheet and started writing. "You're banking on something like: 'Herr Einstein,' let's make that 'E'…so 'if E would equal Emma,' then ipso facto—"

"No, it's not that simple; you can't just square us immediately like that," Albert countered, snapping his fingers and adding, "at the speed of light." He paused. "Wait a moment, 'E equals Emma squared'…." He grabbed the paper from Josep and started jotting numbers, symbols, and arrows manically, throttling his pen when the ink flow couldn't keep up with him.

Schupplater pulled his pocket watch out. "If you think acting important and scribbling like a demon is going to gain you more lunch time—"

"Of course!" said Einstein, looking up enraptured. "Of course it must!"

———

The Kloetzlikeller Pub was a place that had a tidal flow of regulars and after the business lunch crowd left, there was little for the wait-staff to do until happy hour from 4 to 6 began.

One customer had been by himself since noon and had been so absorbed that no one wanted to disturb his notations, although over the last hour they had become so slow as to barely deny rigor mortis had set in. And when a drop of blood grew glacially and eventually dropped from his nostril to the paper so slowly as to nearly defy gravity, a scared waitress who noticed tried to grab the manager's attention. But since the late afternoon rush had begun, she was shrugged off brusquely. Recognizing his friend Schupplater at a table near the street, she anxiously approached him and pointed out Einstein in the alcove.

As he neared, Schupplater thought he saw a nimbus surrounding Albert; he entered a cocoon of chill that made him shiver in the hot pub. He stepped back from it and watched, unsure if his friend was even alive but then grew more puzzled at the vaporous exhalation of each weak breath that seemed to go on forever.

He whispered his name a few times, afraid to jostle him from some trance, but thankfully Einstein ever so slowly—as if the Sphinx awoke—looked up from the pile of notes. His attempt at speech was an echoic rasp.

"What are you doing here?" Schupplater said. "You never came back from lunch. I thought you went home."

"Your...comment...about...lunch...time...helpful...the... faster...I...go...the...more...time...slows," Einstein managed.

"You're just drunk," his friend said. "Your words are slurred." He shook Albert and as he came out of his torpor, his scribbling suddenly went from nothing to frantic, tearing at the paper, before slowing to normal, then stopping. Some vitality came back to his Einstein's face, but Schupplater's relief was short-lived.

"You brought me back, damn you!" Einstein said. "I was outside our Milky Way, approaching light speed—2.997 times 10 to the fifth kilometers per second—astrally projecting myself to see what happens; the most complicated equations were falling into place!"

"You were in a bad way, but you look better so I'll just continue on to the lavatory. And not for a hot towel. Guess!"

Einstein was muttering: "Past R136a1 in the Large Magellanic Cloud, gravity was beginning to bend—"

"Hint: Her body is so perfect, if her corset were a logarithm, there would be no mantissa! You know, mantissa! The decimal spillover of a logarithm?"

"Everybody knows what a mantissa is. Quiet! Now, if gravity bends everything, an eclipse of the sun should show light rays curving—"

Josep poked Albert. "Pay attention. I'm talking about a corset, which holds a thicket."

"So it's a woman."

"A woman?! She is dream. You are genius."

"And I see you are drunk."

"Drunk enough to tell a large caddish oaf who inserted himself into our tête-à-tête over there that if he persisted, I would cuff him so soundly he would need revival with something stronger than water: 'H_3O!' Oh did we laugh in his face. Thank you, you genius you. Luckily you have no patent!"

"Patent?"

"This woman," continued Josep, unsteady on his feet as he pointed over his shoulder, "she pressed my hand. Her pools of eyes are limpid, her haughtiness blushes her blossoming cheeks—"

"'Pools of eyes'? Stop. You're babbling. So she pressed your hand."

"But my hand was in my pants pocket reaching for a pen! You're a genius. But no patent, so not so smart."

"Again with that. What is this 'patent'?"

"I used your gimmick. The pie chart." He pulled papers from his coat. "I drew these after our first beer together. Two circles. First pie, before I met her I said: The whole pie is 100% existential angst. Second pie, after knowing her for these few minutes: 53% existential angst, 17% localized tingling, 12% misery, and 12% misery."

"Makes no sense."

"Yes it does! I would be twice as miserable losing her after I met her…than before."

Einstein raised an eyebrow. "So she made you miserable before you met her? Romantic."

"It made more sense before she ordered us another yard of ale. The second one is harder to balance; I think I spilled some on my coat."

"Wait. This woman can drink a fathom of ale?"

Josep lolled some and reached for a chair. "When we work so hard on an equation and still end up with two halves that aren't balanced, what do we exasperatedly write between them instead of a spurious equal sign?"

"'Oops, insert a miracle.'"

"*Oops.* Yes, so handy. Oops, I forgot to mention that the woman of my miracle towels…it's your Emma. In my defense, at least I told you before you saw us together."

"Hello Emma," Einstein said to her as she stopped behind Josep and reached around him to put a pen in his front pocket and pat it.

Josep squirmed a bit, nervous and proud at the same time. "You didn't tell me she was so attentive. You made her sound prudish."

"No I did not. I said she out-howled the mutt."

Emma, whose face in the subdued lighting of the pub belied her worn middle age look well, adjusted her carriage to present herself more soberly. "How dare you discuss me in that manner. Impugn me once, shame on me; impugn me twice, shame on me!" She giggled. "Wait, I got that backwards. Anyway, Albert, I received *his* proof of love within minutes of knowing him. I waited a week for you and got nothing."

"You mean his pie chart with six percent missing?" Albert said.

Emma frowned at Josep, who did the math. "53, 70, 94...uh, yes. Well," he said, covering, "love has to have some mystery, no?"

"I hope I never forget how handsome you are right now," she said.

"Perhaps best then," said Josep coyly patting his pocket, "to write it down?"

"Don't push it, Schuppie," she said. "Seventeen percent localized tingling is plenty. Without marriage."

A look of discomfort washed over Schupplater's visage and Einstein laughed. "She talks 'caught' and it catches in your throat, eh, Josep? Emma, I have my own pie chart as love proof, the idea for which he stole from me—"

"No patent," Josep said.

Albert retrieved notes from his hanging coat and she read them aloud.

"'My years on earth to date equal 8916 days. Total days spent untying knotted shoe laces, one point two—'"

"Because," said Einstein, "I use double knots and the Möbius strip factor—"

She shushed him: "'—days tamping pipe tobacco, one point 7; days spent tuning violin, 3 point 5. Days spent waiting for mother to annoyingly count out backgammon moves instead of just intuiting where the counters should land—.' What does your mother have to do with me?"

"More 'astral projection' Albert," laughed Josep, "to distance yourself from that one?"

"But," Einstein said, "look at all these slivers of my life's minutiae. There's one slightly larger: days spent obsessing over Emma—seven!"

She shook the notes. "So I'm ahead of, let's see, 'checking for milk sourness' but behind 'tongue tooth probing.'"

"I have gaps," Einstein said, "and the food, even in my sleep it bothers me."

"His cottage cheese makes noise—"

"Shut up" and Albert pushed Josep back, grabbed Emma's shoulders. "The point is that seven days is 100% of the time since we met. Don't you see how relative it is?"

"This is all piffle!" she shouted. "I need a man of means."

"He and I make the same salary," Albert said angrily, and now the patrons were listening in. "Plus, I just now have deciphered the ultimate secret of the universe!"

Emma giggled. "And that makes money *how*? Join the thousands of Indian seers who say they're one with the mud they're sitting in. Josep is going to partner with the muttonchops equalizer inventor, and as I look around, if this scruffy bunch is any indicator, the market is very big."

"You cur," Albert spat out at Josep. "You Jezebel," he spat out to Emma. "I should have thrown you out the window like your Biblical namesake."

Now the pub was quiet.

"I will *not*," Emma said, hooking Josep's arm, "feel guilty for seeking someone to keep me in fine French perfumes."

Some in the pub voiced a collective wince in sympathy for Einstein and he felt his cheeks blush with embarrassment. He blurted out "the only thing you can put behind your ears to keep men interested is your knees!"

A raucous laugh rolled through the Kloetzlikeller. Now it was Emma turn to blush, and she shot back "You have no future!"

"You should try having no past," Albert said, "give your bed springs a rest!"

Some in the room cheered and clapped for more. "A star is born," they said. "Entertain us."

Einstein basked in this shift of momentum and wandered until he was under a spotlight of sorts. He started singing, badly, an improvisation: "Stars are born when gravity compresses enough space matter so tightly a thermonuclear reaction is ignited...sort of like Emma's thighs." The pub cheered wildly for more but then several added, "but no more singing."

"This afternoon, from that alcove," said Albert to the smiling faces at the bar, "I started traveling at 1/5th the speed of light—faster than Emma's knees buckle...thank you. I traveled for five minutes from the Kloetzlikeller at 5:55 and after five minutes, my watch, where I was, read 6 o'clock. But when I looked back across the distance to the pub's clock here, it was 5:59 to me because it takes a minute for the light to reach me. And if you look at *my* watch, it's going to read 5:59 since it's going to take a minute for the light to reach you, too. So it would seem to be a true miracle: Happy hour would never end!"

More applause and whistles, calls for Einstein for mayor. He held up his hands, working the whole pub now.

"But no," he said, "when you look at *your* clock in the pub it says 6 o'clock because five minutes *have* gone by for you."

The room went quiet. Then one spoke up for all: "So...happy hour does end?" There was grumbling.

Schupplater whispered to Einstein, "you're losing them. You better do something. Make some more jokes about Emma's honor."

She overheard this and slapped Josep hard. "How's that for localized tingling? *He* can impugn me, but you can't."

Josep tried to rub away the smartness as patrons relished the scene. "And to think I was going to corner the muttonchops equalizer market for you."

Emma slid her arm in Einstein's. "I'm going to be in show business...as manager of this man, the new Mark Twain, and he made *thousands* on his European tour." She dumped out a bread basket and went to the regulars and got an offering from all of them. She came back and shook out 25 francs on the table and told Albert, "give them something, fool, before they want this back. Or throw things; this is a beer-filled crowd that can turn."

He now looked less comfortable in the spotlight. He coughed, took a sip of water. "Um, did you ever wonder if we move ahead *into* time only because billions of years ago the Big Bang that started everything, *that* event carved out the time we can then slide into? Like, what, always walking in a canyon created by erosion eons ago? Otherwise, how does one moment become the next if it wasn't already there?" The unease of the room became palpable. "Or, or, this is funny, perhaps there's no continuum at all; nothing to guarantee we move forward from one moment to the next. It's all...kind of... uh, infinitesimally stitched...by each moment we...advance," he said, frustrated and feeling the foreign nature of this new role as entertainer. "Each step of ours creates a new iota of...time...extending the present into nothing that was there before. Perhaps?"

"Yes," Emma said to the crowd while she divided the money, "the Big Stitch! Imagine the infinitesimal fun!" She whispered to Albert "I'm taking my manager's half."

"*Half?*"

She ignored him: "Stitched, of course you clods! Because, look, here's a moment. Hey, here's another one. Or was that a continuum?"

she said, doubling over in mock laughter. A few boos were heard. She poked Albert hard in the chest several times: "Look, you frizzy-haired fop—." He had heard tell of blood boiling in anger; now he knew what they referred to. He was finished with all this; he wanted out of there at light speed. He slipped more easily into his earlier trance, speeding through the blackness of space, light from the stars he neared actually disappearing due to the Doppler effect shifting them out of the visible spectrum, Emma's shrill voice deepening to a rumble as her sound waves lengthened. "I'm *talking* to you. You're my dancing bear," she said, "so tell some jokes, shake a chained leg before they get dyspep-*tic*—"

Everything in the pub stopped: the clock's pendulum, the flow of beer into a stein, a pipe's curl of smoke, a sneeze. Everything, that is, except Einstein who took tentative steps in pleased disbelief into the tableau. He circled a few people in the pub as his projected self sped away; he fluttered his hands in front of their unblinking eyes. "It's a theory no more," he thought and took a satisfying breath and, knowing the outcome, off-handedly said "tock" and slowed his projection sharply. Molecules resumed motion and a chorus of concern rose. "What was that? What happened?" they said. Josep finished his sneeze and looked frightened.

"My theory is proven!" Einstein shouted. "By astrally projecting myself at the speed of light, I can slow time to a halt around me." He grabbed Schupplater by the lapels. "I have to expand on this. Yes, I can make a singularity...reverse time and collapse the universe and...."

Schupplater couldn't decide if Einstein, quivering, was now afraid or ecstatic. "A Big Bang?" Josep whispered in deference to the unimaginable. "You would attempt such a cataclysmic thing?!"

"Yes, re-create the universe in my image," Einstein said, lost now to himself until Emma waved the pie chart in front of him. "What about your love proof?" she said.

His laugh was hostile and his look through Emma gave her a child-like vulnerability. "What about us?" she said simply.

He swatted the paper away. "Bosh! I am beyond you, woman, beyond *all* you minions! I am God!"

"Why you cad," she said, set to slap him, "you despo-*tic*—"

As he now could switch himself quickly back and forth from light speed, all the room's molecules stopped including those in Emma's hand. Einstein leaned his head away, said "tock" and her slap struck only air. A burly patron hurled a full stein straight at him, yelling "luna-*tic*" and as the molecules stopped, Albert adjusted himself a centimeter out of the path. "Tock," Einstein said and the stein flew by and smashed against the wall. "I can stop cannonballs," he yelled, "mortar shells, charging cavalry. World leaders will vie for me; I'll start with Switzerland—they could win a war!"

As he turned to leave the Kloetzlikeller, wary patrons shunned him and then cowered en masse when he bumped full stride into an instantly materialized figure—himself.

"Oh no," he said, "it's my wormhole universe doppelgänger. You're only hypothe-*tic*—"

And Einstein and all else stopped, except his doppelgänger.

"Tock," the doppelgänger said after a satisfying survey of his power. Time, and a renewed wave of fear from the patrons, was restored.

"This can't be! You're only my doppelgänger."

"You're *my* doppelgänger," was the reply, and he removed Einstein's notes from his coat.

"No, I need those," Einstein said. "They're cri-*tic*—"

Molecules halted. The doppelgänger shifted Emma in front of Einstein and cocked her arm several times. "Tock," he said and her reflex slap caught the reviving Einstein flush.

The doppelgänger disappeared in the patrons' confused push for the doors and Einstein immediately rushed back to his alcove and began scribbling notes. Emma put her arm in Schupplater's; he shrugged and unpocketed her half of the 25 francs and gave them to the bartender who had lingered over concerns about his pub.

The three of them stood transfixed, watching Einstein's writing became more frantic, then a blur. Then he slowed to nearly a statue, a malevolent look on his face.

"Oh no," Schupplater said, "he's doing it; he's going to play God!" He started toward the alcove but the freezing cocoon stopped him short.

Einstein was oblivious to anything earthly, sweeping past disappearing stars again. But the three saw furrows slowly crease his brow because now he was tumbling in space out of control. The furrows began to resemble graph paper; then his forehead started to fold in on itself; Schupplater thought of the crumpled patents on the office floor.

In Einstein's gyrating glimpses he saw his doppelgänger tumbling right at him but no matter which way he projected himself, he couldn't avoid the crash. Within the silent obliteration of both entities and nearly lost to the few evanescing molecules he had left, an ethereal dictum washed through Einstein: "*Only* God plays dice out here."

—-—

Made in the USA
Columbia, SC
27 August 2017